THE KING OF PAIN

a novel with stories

Seth Kaufman

This is for Susan Pottinger.

In memory of Adam Kaufman, who told me about prison, and Michael Kaufman, who showed me the world.

Contents.

One	7
The Stocks	21
Two	39
The Daiquiri Case	47
Three	67
The Gift	80
Four	90
Great Escapes	103
Five	116
Pierre the War Criminal	130
Six	136
Baxter Blood	149
Seven	163
Longman	177
Eight	191
The Gizless Days of Thomas Binder	200
Nine	214
The Gizless Days of Thomas Binder (Continued)	221
Ten	240
Snow Island	254
Eleven	268
Twelve	280

ONE

When I come to, it's hard to nail down my primary source of anguish.

My throat is clogged with a vile substance that makes it difficult to breathe and hard to swallow.

I'm groggy. I'm flat on my back. My head is pounding. It's a 200-proof hangover throb mixed with an a-safe-has-been-dropped-on-your-head ache.

Also, I seem to be blind.

Which means it's no use jerking my head up to look at my right foot, which is numb, and at both my ankles, which have something cutting into them, and at my hips, which feel like they are gripped in a vise. But I do it anyway and am rewarded with pain so intense my body doesn't really know what to do with it. I open my mouth, offer a silent scream, then a gasp, then a shudder. When part of your body is under attack, you move it away from the source of discomfort. So I try to free my ankles, bring my legs up, and shift my hips, but I can't move a damn thing except my mouth, which opens again. This time, I let out an actual, audible scream.

As far as sounds go, it's pathetic. No volume, thanks to my gummy throat. It's sort of an agonized gargle. But at least now I'm really, truly awake. And I realize I can move my arms, too; they can slide under whatever is pinning me down. So I bring them up and rub my eyes, attacking the grime that has sealed my eyelids. The left opens first, after I pull it open carefully, like I'm peeling a piece of tape off a development money check. It's bright out, wherever the hell I am. I can see ceiling lights. They look familiar. I move my head to the right and discover that I am lying in my own living room.

"What the fuck?" I croak through the disgusting crust in my throat. There is a familiar taste to it. The rich, iron-and-salt zing of blood. I look at my fingertips. Dried blood. I wipe my nose: more of the same. I look to the left and back a little and I see a Bang & Olufsen speaker lying innocently on the floor, a mere three feet away. It must have clocked me.

So now I'm cooking with gasoline, piecing it all together. I work eye number two open so I can enjoy my surroundings in stereo. I bring my head forward again, slowly, and discover my incredible 25-foot-long, wall-lining home entertainment system, once the object of jealousy and derision throughout Hollywood, is no longer attached to the wall.

It is attached to me.

I hold my slightly vertical pose and study the landscape. I can see a panorama of wires and power cords, and the shiny black, silver, and chrome backsides of every high-tech gizmo known to geek-kind: Wii, PS3, Xbox, Bang & Olufsen, Harmon Karden, Blu-ray and DVD players, TiVo, and three flat screen TVs, including the 72-incher. Woofers, tweeters, subwoofers. Plus, the heavy blonde wood shelving unit. I knew I should have gone with the lighter metal.

As far as I can see, which is not very far, I am trapped beneath four shelves and the collective weight of this wall of gadgets. The edge of a shelf is digging into my shin, just above the ankle. There is no fat in that area, so it's cutting into the skin and bone. I have this feeling that blood is seeping down my leg. And if I could move just a little more I might actually see it, but I'm locked in. There's a second shelf—the shelf that housed my Oscar—digging into the middle of my right knee. For some reason my left knee is slightly bent and actually has a few inches of flexibility before straightening against the wood.

The third shelf is the one that served as the platform for all my favorite photos—my Oscar victory shot; me and my son Jared on safari; me and Jared by the dugout at Dodger Stadium; Jared getting a peck on the cheek by the over-enhanced Samantha Rexxx in Vegas on his 18th birthday. The pictures are gone, of course, strewn about me on the floor; so currently, this shelf's primary function is to hold my lower hips in place. And the top shelf of the unit, which served as more of a frame than a shelf, has landed on me mid-chest. It hurts like a motherfucker. Breathing is a struggle. And it doesn't help that there's this nasty burning sensation right around my heart, just below my left nipple. Fortunately, my chest has more girth than my arms, so I can slide my limbs out and put them to use. Thank fucking god.

The monstrous TV is just to my left. Life is clearly a game of inches: If it had landed a few inches the other way, I would have been pancaked. I shake my head at this lucky twist of fate, although, given my predicament, perhaps lucky is not the right word.

I'm famous and reviled for firing off more notes per second than pretty much any other producer in Hollywood. So here are the first ten to myself:

1. What was the name of the mountain climber who had his arm wedged behind a boulder and cut his arm off with a knife?
2. What day is it?
3. When is Marta coming?
4. What the hell happened?
5. Where did I leave off with the network?
6. Where's my cell phone?
7. Can I make it through this without my meds?
8. When is *The King of Pain* finale airing?
9. Or did they cancel the finale?
10. Was the CNN show last night?

Considering my addled state, I'm very proud of this list. All these questions make perfect sense, even if the order is slightly screwed up. I'm especially proud because #8 and #9 come so late. There are legions who would expect those questions—which are about my hit show—to be the first thing on my mind. But this time survival, not my career, comes first. Although in this town, some might say they are the same thing.

Those first six questions are dead serious. I don't need the climber's name, of course. I don't have the balls to cut my arm off with a chainsaw, much less a knife, even if one happened to be lying within reach. Still, he is an inspiring figure. The guy stood for days before slicing his way to freedom. Me, I'm lying down. Numbers 2 and 3 are related. If I can remember the day then I can figure out how long until Marta, my fabulous housekeeper, will show up. Or is supposed to show up—we had a little argument last week.

Given the carnage that surrounds me and the throbbing in my head, I suppose it is conceivable that I was knocked out for a full 24 hours and it's already Sunday. But that seems unlikely. I believe it is Saturday. So in the worst case, I've got to last about 48 hours tops until Marta arrives on Monday morning. That's assuming nobody else shows up before her.

Number 4 is such a big question, it would take a book to answer.

Number 5 is a doozy and sort of related to #8 and #9. What happened with the show? My memory's blurry. I remember network president and creative black hole Walter Fields calling a few times. And me trying to call Jay, my lawyer, who is out of the country. I also remember pouring myself a huge drink after the first call from Walter, who was upset about everything: my CNN appearance, the misinformation episode, and that prick Adonis Troy, as if I had any control over him. And then he threatened to take the show away, yammering on about Clause 18a.

And that's as far as I get.

The cell phone question is disturbing because if it was in one of my pockets, I'd be rescued faster than you can say St. Bernard. But it's not. Perhaps it's nearby; it's almost always within arm's reach. I turn to the left and see Blu-ray discs, CDs, and video games on the floor, and that damn murderous speaker. A little further away is what's left of a wooden chair from my kitchen. What the hell is it doing there? And what happened to it? Two legs are missing, so it sits like a listing ship, sinking into the floor. Christ, I've got no memory! To my right there is more of the same. No phone. But within my grasp is a book. Which is a bit weird, because I'm not a big book guy—mostly I wade through an endless ocean of scripts that flood my office. So this book catches my attention. I grab it. It's a thin hardback, used, but not very old. It's called *A History of Prisons*, by somebody named Seth Kaufman.

WTF? My memory is shot. I have no recollection of buying this book. But I sense that a book is a good thing to have in a jam like mine. The jacket says Kaufman writes short stories about, surprise, prisons. And there are quotes calling it "a gem," "a small miracle," "a moving blend of history and fable," and—god help me—"a mandatory sentence for all readers of good fiction."

I stick it under my head, like a pillow, and then it hits me that Amanda, my gorgeous, always thinking ex-associate producer, sent me the book right after she quit. Normally I would have insisted on assigning it to coverage for an evaluation, like any other self-respecting producer. But since it was a gift—and because I was touched that Amanda thought I still read—I put it on the shelf next to my giant TV to remind me to crack it open when I had time. But of course I never had time. I was busy producing the most infamous and wicked TV show in history.

My show. Created and produced by me, Rick "the Prick" Salter, former Tinseltown darling, now Tinseltown pariah. Or is it my ex-show? That is question number 11. Unfortunately with me here, pinned, tortured by crushing weight, I have no way of finding out. Last night remains a boozy, bruising blur.

My head hurts—not just from booze and that knock on the head, but from psychic pain, too. Will I be crippled for life? How long will my heart hold up? I can feel it pounding away. And it scares the hell out of me.

Breathe, I tell myself.

Just breathe, goddammit.

I'm calm for a minute. Then I wonder, how long can you last without food or water? A long time, I think. Weeks probably. Maybe even a month. I think of Bobby Sands, the Irish guy whose hunger strike lasted over 60 days back in the '70s. I remember hearing something about the body consuming muscle to keep going.

The heart is a muscle. And I have a bad heart. I am really going to need my pills.

I put my hand over my heart. I can feel it pulsing to the tempo of an inaudible speed-metal song. My head is throbbing. My legs are numb and aching at the same time.

Breathe, you moron, I tell myself. Stay calm. Think about something else.

Think about last night. Replace one pain with another. Try to remember.

Think about CNN.

This is what happened: Yesterday morning CNN called and offered me prime time to discuss *The King of Pain*. I thought it was going to be me and that red-hot redhead Kitty Andrapov with her faint but oh-so-sexy Russian accent. I wanted to win her over.

As even my ex-wives will attest, I have a gift few men possess: I can listen. In fact I can listen so hard it seems my eyes may pop out of my head and my ears are actually growing. That, ultimately, has been my biggest secret with women. Unfortunately, when you listen as well I can, it feels like a heinous crime when you stop listening. It's like a total slap in the face to a woman who has grown to expect your antennae to be pointed in her direction at all times. I was going to listen hard to Kitty Andrapov and charm both her and America in one go. With the finale of the show approaching, I thought, why not? Let's send the ratings into the stratosphere.

Instead, it turned out to be a perfectly orchestrated TV assassination. Kitty introduces me and sets up the story by playing all these great clips of the show. Then she plays a montage of naysayers railing against my show. Then we have some chitchat and just when I think, "This is easy," she turns to the camera and says, "We'll be back in a minute, joined by America's favorite doctor, Surgeon General Premshaw Choudry."

I should have pulled off my microphone right there and then and walked off stage. Instead I turn to Kitty.

"Choudry? Listen, if you wanted to screw me, all you had to do is ask."

"He was a last minute addition. Our producer did it after you agreed."

"I didn't agree to this." I fiddle with the microphone clip.

"Don't chicken out. You can take him."

"Are you kidding? He's like a good-looking Gandhi. Everyone loves him. I don't want to argue with him."

"I'll let you have the last word."

"Really?"

"Really. Also if you leave now, we will skewer your show every night for a week. There are a zillion academics and social critics ready to cut your balls off."

"I've got balls to spare," I say, but I settle back in my chair because I'm not sure Walter Fields, the network honcho, does. I figure he'll want me to defend the show, otherwise Choudry will slaughter us.

So I stay on, and together Kitty and Choudry drag me and *The King of Pain* into the history of torture, shackling me to Spanish Inquisitors, Mengele, Romans who watched lions eat Christians, Hannibal Lecter, Jeffrey Dahmer, and the Marquis de Sade, as if I'm a sadistic mass murderer, cannibal, and pervert. Talk about torture! I was getting drawn and quartered and then raked over the coals. Still, it would all have been fine—this is hardly the first time some bloviator professes moral outrage at my show—but then Choudry launches into an annoying monologue on the dangers of endurance, of pushing the body too hard, and suddenly I can't take it any more.

"Hey, Apu!" I cut in, letting my inner moron fly on national fucking television, "Where's the pioneer, can-do spirit? This is America. We have a history of starving and enduring. The Pilgrims, the Donner Party, Guadalcanal, one war after the other, the Great Depression, girls in college. And anyway, this show isn't causing a health crisis. Fast food and greed and poverty and poor education are doing that. *The King of Pain* is creating a moral crisis, and that is the problem for everyone. Americans watch other people suffer and die all the time on the news and in movies. Only we've turned it into pure spectacle, without pretending it ever was anything else. And certain people can't deal with that. Meanwhile the media stokes up the outrage, because outrage is what sells. You want outrage? How about you show up for a solo interview and people—like the beautiful Kitty Andrapov—ambush you with a Surgeon General who looks like he just stepped off the lot at *General Hospital*?

You want morality? That's bait and switch. And frankly, I'm disgusted."

"You accuse us of ambushing you," says Kitty. "But isn't that what you do to your contestants? Hit them with life or death choices?"

"That's not an ambush. They signed up for anything, any test of will or endurance. That was the deal. How tough are you? Me? I'm a wimp. I just agreed to an interview with a beautiful, intelligent woman. Not a three-way with Dr. Trauma Drama over here."

"But I speak the truth, sir," insists Choudry.

"A truth," I say. "Maybe."

"Your show is completely dangerous. It is a cancer for our youth. It perpetuates our culture of abuse."

"Isn't it time for a commercial break?" I say, pulling off my mic clip and walking off the set.

Outside, against my better judgment, I dial my once and hopefully future pal Amanda. She picks up on the first ring.

"Apu? Are you fucking insane?" she says.

"I know, but other than that?"

"You were golden. Justifying the unjustifiable. Debate teams will study this for years to learn what not to do."

"Yeah," I slump into the driver's seat, double over like I have 300 pounds of donuts and depression in my gut, and pound my head against the steering wheel.

"I guess getting indignant and pointing out the ambush might work on some people," Amanda says, and I'm touched that after everything that's happened she's actually trying to make me feel better. "You had some smooth moments."

"You think so?"

"In a clever, bad boy way. Some women love bad boys, and you are the worst."

"Evil is wasted on the young," I say, turning on the ignition. "Can I come over?" I'm trying hard not to beg.

"No."

"How about dinner somewhere?"

"No."

"Brunch?"

'No."

"That hurts," I say.

"Hurts? Who are you kidding? You could have won your own damn show."

She hangs up. She has an infallible sense of the dramatic.

I drive home and start drinking.

I shake my head at this memory and am rewarded with the sensation that my lobes have somehow split apart and are now merrily banging against each other like a pair of castanets.

I try to shift my hips, and searing jolts of pain travel in both directions. My body wants to jackknife in sympathy, but the wall unit stops me, and that burning zone in my chest starts to sizzle.

"Fuck!" I yell.

Marta is going to have to save me. Thing is, she was yelling at me last week. She asked to have her hours cut, since I'm so busy with the show and nobody is around. She wanted to go hang out at her son's restaurant. But I told her no way. "Take a day or two, but I need you here."

"But Mr. Rick, it's boring! And there's nothing to do."

"Hang by the pool. Watch *Oprah* or *Ellen*."

"I do. But it's boring."

"Boring?" I say. "It's the American dream!"

Even now, I shake my head in disbelief.

Who else but Marta comes to the house? The pool guy. He's my best hope, whatever his name is. Actually, I think there might be different pool guys. Whatever. Whoever he is, I think he comes at the beginning of the week. I can't remember. Marta will know. Jesus, I hope she comes. She was giving me the silent treatment on Friday morning. Then there are the landscaping guys, but unless they deal with the plants near the pool deck, they probably won't come near enough to hear me. And they never come on weekends, per my orders. I hate having people around working when I'm here. My son, Jared, sometimes stays here when he's home from college. But his trips back to the West Coast have grown rarer and shorter with each semester. Then there's UPS and other delivery guys. They might show up, too.

So as I've said, I'm looking at 48 hours. No food, no water, no medicine.

Where's a Jehovah's Witness when you need one?

I close my eyes and try to meditate, something I've never done for more than 15 seconds in my entire life. "Clear your mind, Rick," I tell myself. "Breathe."

I make it to 20 seconds and then the image of network scumbag Walter Fields pops into my mind. I'm gonna kill that guy. Murder by lawsuit.

I can feel my heart pounding again. This is not good.

I pull the book from under my head and open it up. On the first page is an inscription.

Dear Rick,
Read this book. The stories are meant for you.
And at the end you'll really be...you know!
Thanks for everything,
xoxo Amanda

What the fuck am I supposed to make of this? There's a lot to ruminate on here. Naturally I try to gauge the meaning of *xoxo Amanda*. Is that a fond but tragically chaste xoxo? A meaningless air kiss of an xoxo? Or an "I want to do a lot more than play tic-tac-toe with you, baby" xoxo? I think the big tipoff on interpreting the salutation is what comes just before it: Thanks for everything. That is so damn perfunctory. It's a far, far cry from "you've changed my life and shown me silver linings I never knew were there and given me a reason to live. Plus, you light a fire in my loins that burns like California in the summer time." In other words it totally negates any hint of heat behind the *xoxo Amanda*. She's just being appreciative and affectionate. Not amorous.

So that solves that. I had my moment with Amanda. Actually, it was more like 20 minutes. Now she's sending me puzzles. I understand *Dear Rick*. I get *Read this book*. I think I understand *The stories are meant for you*. She's speaking metaphorically—I don't even know this author Kaufman—so there's no way they could be literally meant for me. But to Amanda's mind, they apply to me in some way. Or to my show. I'm going to have to stay with that one. At least for now. I have not one fucking clue what *At the end you'll really be...you know!* means. I stare at her perfect handwriting— that amazingly round and perky script that must be embedded in XX chromosomes. It's so clear. How come I can read a woman's writing so easily and never fucking understand what's actually being said? I try to recall a conversation with Amanda about the future. Any conversation about what I may have hoped to become. But I doubt such a conversation ever happened.

"At the end," I croak to myself, trying to guess how she'd want me to complete the sentence, "I'll really be…alive?"

I force myself to smile. I start to read.

THE STOCKS

If Leader hates you, he will throw you to the crocodiles. If he really hates you, he will put you in the stocks and then he will throw you to the crocodiles.

My pastor says I am absolved. That these are extraordinary times. That Jesus would urge me to comfort the condemned men whenever possible. This is the exact opposite of what Leader wants, which is for the men to suffer as much as possible. Sometimes he comes to inspect the suffering. He has had me cut down the trees that are near the stocks. He will say: "These stocks are in the shade. I want this zombie burning in the sun." I will apologize and say that the sun moves and the trees grow.

"I know," fumes Leader. "You think because I only finished Standard 6 that I am an idiot?" When he says this I must bow and shake my head frantically: "Not at all, Leader. I was just trying to explain that the shade is a new development."

Luckily, the prisoners fill him with such hatred that he quickly forgets about me. Often he will attack them, smack them, kick them in the behind, laughing all the while.

At night in our home, when the children are asleep in their corner of the room, I whisper to my wife that I want to kill Leader. I want to tell this to our pastor, but I know I can trust no one beside my wife.

Miriam, which is the name of my wife, tells me I am a good man. She, too, would like to kill Leader. "Maybe the Christian Militia will come and remove him," she says.

I do not like this thought. For one thing, the Christian Militia is not very Christian. To many of us, it seems like a name that was taken for devious purposes, to help them get to power. They are killing many Muslims in the north, and raping girls, and hijacking food and oil. The other problem about the militia is that if they come, there will be civil war again. And if they succeed in winning this war, there is a good chance I will be killed for being one of Leader's jailers, which would not be good. My wife and daughters—God only knows what would happen to them.

When I look at things in this way, I feel that I, too, have been put in stocks of some kind. It is impossible to move. There is no other work in the country. Industry has stopped. No foreigner would be stupid enough to invest here. The border has been sealed, and even if we did cross it, who knows what lies on the other side? A refugee camp? Starvation? On our radio I listen to the news from the BBC, to reports on the crisis, to the calls for relief and food and medical aid. Crossing the border does not seem to be the answer for us.

Six days a week I tend to the stocks, to the prisoners at the edge of the Palace grounds, a few minutes from the notorious Falls and the crocs. I bring the prisoners food, I dump buckets of water upon them on hot days, I bring blankets on cold ones. I release them temporarily so they can eat and do their business. When I lift up the bar, there is always a grateful moan as they unfurl themselves, as the muscles, which become locked in a cramp, try to uncoil. The men are mostly docile. They have had their souls beaten out of their bodies. Why the stocks? Leader saw a picture in a book and ordered four to be built. "This is what they used in America when it was a young country. And we are a young country, too," he once said in a press conference announcing this "penal innovation." Shortly afterwards, I was appointed Palace Guard Stocks Jailer No. 1.

In the early days Leader would make the rounds, inspecting the torture devices. "How you doing, stretch?" he would say. Then he would throw his head back and roar, his big teeth flashing. The jokes would continue: "You, rafikki! You don't seem yourself today. Try to loosen up!" More laughter. During these visits, I tried to keep my distance, cleaning buckets, polishing latches. I did not want to taunt the prisoners. I have to work with them. Sometimes, if I am feeling generous, if it is dark outside, and if I am certain that Leader is away, I will scratch a prisoner's back with a branch. But I do it quickly and rarely.

The palace grounds are very beautiful. And even the stocks section is very appealing. We have jacaranda trees, banana plants, huge sisal bushes. I admire them as I approach the stocks, thinking that God is truly mysterious to make so much beauty and so much horror. And then, one day, as if God himself has heard my thoughts and wants to prove me right, I walk into work and see that Nelson Makere—Major Nelson Makere, the man who hired and promoted me, the man who put so many men in the stocks, who rubber-stamped Leader's penal whims and wishes—is locked before me.

"Ai, what is this?" I ask my nightshift companion, Francis Nguffi.

"He came late last night. Palace guard brought him. No trial."

"I'm screwed, Victor," says Major Nelson, looking up at me. "Be careful, both of you, with that madman. He has syphilis, like Caligula."

I do not know who this Caligula is. Perhaps Miriam, who finished secondary school, will.

"Major," I say. "I am very distressed just now to see you here. What has happened?"

"I have been wondering the same thing," the Major says. "I have been beating my brains on this matter."

"And?"

"I believe that it is because my brother's wife's brother is married to the cousin of Leader's third wife. This scoundrel has left her for another woman."

"That is bad, "I say.

"Yes, but it is nothing Leader has not done himself."

"That is true."

"But Leader's cousin has a sickness. And she has two small children. Leader told me to have a talk with the bastard, but the man says his wife is impossible."

"Why did Leader not just kill this man?"

"I ask myself the same question. Why? This is crazy justice. Even for him."

"Leader's scales of justice have been broken for years. Perhaps Leader is hoping to use you as an example to this man."

"Please, Victor," Major Nelson says, "can you pull my shirt down and my collar up? I can feel the sun pounding me and it is not yet noon."

"Major Nelson, I will do better than that," I say, unhitching the stocks. "Let us go to the infirmary. I believe you were unconscious when I arrived this morning. Is that not true?"

"Oh, yes," laughs Major Nelson. "And I have a very serious heart condition. I need to be fit if I'm to be fed to the crocs."

❧

That night at home I read from the Bible to the girls. About the Jews wandering in the desert. I sometimes think that the Jews must have been Africans, as their story is the story of so many of us. We are here, some of us nomads, some of us in one place, but all of us wandering. Looking. Searching. Surviving. It's one bad thing after another, but we try to endure and prosper and change what feels like fate.

When the girls are asleep, Miriam and I begin our whispering. But the volume rises as soon as I tell her the news.

"Major Nelson! Oh my goodness!" cries Miriam. "He has been so good to us. Without him..." She looks around and makes a sweeping gesture as if to indicate that the Major was in some way responsible for all our worldly possessions.

"That is true," I say. "And now he has been marked for death."

"No!"

"Everyone who is put in the stocks has been marked. You know that."

"Oh my goodness."

"I will take him every day to the infirmary. And read to him from the Bible."

"That is good."

"But I told him no funny business. Any attempt to escape and I will show no mercy. He was my mentor. But for each one of us that he has favored, there are ten others he has condemned or robbed or abused. I will not join those men."

"I know you will do the righteous thing, Victor."

The next day I have to work a double shift, noon to dawn. In the morning, I walk the girls to primary school. As I am holding their hands, I feel proud and happy. My youngest, Sarah, says, "I wish you had your uniform on, Daddy."

"Why is that?"

"Because then you look like a soldier and I feel safe."

"Do you feel in danger now?"

"Oh, yes," says her older sister, Catherine. "There are many bad men. Sugar daddies, panga gangs, tricksters."

"Who is telling you this?" I am shocked.

"Sister Genesis."

I think for a minute. If the Sister is telling them this, perhaps she is trying to keep them safe through knowledge. "It is true," I finally say. "There are many bad men. But there are also many good ones." Then I think about how I must stay alive to protect my daughters.

⌘

At noon, when I arrive for work, Major Nelson tells me he is ready for the crocodiles.

"Not yet," I say, lifting the headpiece.

He straightens up very slowly.

"I'm serious. I am 50 years old. I have kids and grandkids. I have been to Europe. I've seen snow! I've seen sex shows in Bangkok. I've helped people and I've hurt people. I'm ready for the crocodiles."

"Major Nelson, let us not talk of such a thing."

The Major is rolling his thick neck, stretching his arms overhead, shaking out his legs. "You are right. The madman has changed his mind before," he says, extending his arms straight out so I can handcuff his wrists.

As we walk, Tobias John sees us and calls out from stocks #3: "Victor, I need release! Please, sir. I beg you."

I do not like to handle two prisoners by myself. But I hear desperation in Tobias John's voice and remember my pastor's instructions about performing acts of kindness whenever possible. I take both men to the infirmary, but before I cuff Tobias I say: "If either of you tries any funny business, I will beat you both to death."

⌘

The funny business comes later, when both men are back in the stocks. It is after dinner, and the prisoners, much like the dogs of rich people, have been walked to use the latrine. It is a long way to go until dawn. The other guard on duty, William Ordunga, is a member of my church. When we complete our rounds, we play checkers and listen to the Voice of America and the BBC and discuss what it would be like to have a President like Jimmy Carter leading the country. When we are tired of the news, we listen to local radio, which rarely tells the truth, but plays very good music.

The sound of a blaring car horn interrupts the happy sounds of Orchestra Mambo Jazz. Cars at night mean one of three things: New prisoners or Leader or both. William is losing at checkers and he rises to see who is coming down the road.

"It's Leader," he calls from the guardhouse door. "He's driving himself."

I put on my cap, tuck in my shirt, attach handcuffs to my belt, and grab my nightstick. I am at attention at the doorway in time to see Leader get out of his Mercedes.

"Inspection, hut!" he bellows. Leader is always loud.

I fall in next to William. This is not a good situation. I have seen Leader before at night. He only comes here when he's been drinking.

"At ease, my friends, at ease. I don't come to inspect you. I want to visit your tenants!"

Tenants. That is a step up from crocmeat, zombies, living dead, and other descriptions used by Leader.

"Where is Major Nelson?"

William, who knows I am not happy about Major Nelson's imprisonment, steps up. "This way, sir," he says.

They go together. I salute Leader and return to the guardhouse. Inside, I kneel and pray. I ask the Lord to help me. To grant peace between Major Nelson and Leader. "O Lord," I say. "Please remove me from the stocks." And then I pray for forgiveness for imagining that the Lord would even bother to pay attention to me when there are so many bigger things in the world. The pastor says that miracles are proof of God's existence, but that his teachings are his real gift. To expect miracles is not what Jesus taught. So although I pray, I do not expect divine intervention. I grab my nightstick and go outside.

Leader is bending down to be face to face with Major Nelson. From afar it looks almost intimate. But I can hear that it is not. Leader is screaming: "I have been your champion! Your benefactor! Without me, you would be lucky to be a parking boy, you piece of shit! How much have I done for you? Big house? Cars? I ask you a simple task and you are not man enough to carry it out? Suddenly you forget who your real family is?"

This tirade goes on for some time—cursing, insults, accusations of ingratitude. Major Nelson remains stone-faced throughout. Leader straightens up and starts pacing. He is sweating and shaking with rage.

"What do you have to say for yourself?"

Major Nelson says nothing. William and I exchange glances.

"WHAT DO YOU HAVE TO SAY?" screams Leader.

"What can I say? I'm bound here, tortured, humiliated by a man with a little dick."

I close my eyes for a second, as if that will erase what Major has just said. When I open them I see Leader rush up to Major Nelson, his arm swinging forward.

Thwack!

"Little dick!" Leader throws his head back. "That is good, crocmeat, because soon you will have NO DICK!"

Thwack!

Leader lowers his face close to Major Nelson. "How do you like that, Dickless?"

Thup—a gob of spit and blood splatters Leader's face. As Leader recoils, William rushes in and smacks his nightstick against the stocks, just above Major's head. "You bastard," he screams. Then he grabs Leader's arm. I am amazed at his quick thinking. "Please, Leader, let us take care of him. Go wash off."

"Get away from me!" Leader says, wiping a sleeve across his eyes. He backs up a few steps. "You like a little football? A little soccer?"

In the stocks, a man's head has nowhere to go. His body can't really move to absorb the blow. The stocks act as a vise. A kick can break a man's neck.

Leader steps forward, building momentum for his blast. His foot sweeps forward but before it connects, my nightstick comes crashing down on Leader's skull.

He goes down instantly. There's a big groan and I hit him again, even harder this time.

"Victor!" William cries, "What have you done? We will all die now, you fool!" He rushes to check on Leader.

I just stand there, completely numb. I am asking myself the same question. What have I done? But I also know in my heart that I have done the right thing. I have stopped the wicked.

"He is very injured," says William.

"Good!" says Major Nelson.

That gets my attention. Suddenly I have a plan. I unlock the stocks.

"Let's go," I say. "Help me get Leader in the car."

"No," says William, assuming a fighting crouch with his nightstick at the ready. "You are under arrest."

"William," I say. "Leader is dead, or going to die. I cracked his skull. His brain is bleeding. I will crack yours, too, if you don't help me. I have a plan, but let's go before his guards come looking. Help us, or Major and I will blame you."

"Is it a good plan?" William asks.

"Yes. There is no time." I get into Leader's Mercedes and pull the car closer. We put him in the backseat, face up in case we are stopped. I hope he will look like he is sleeping.

"We must go to the crocs," I say. "This is our only hope. William, you stay here. Our story is that Leader demanded to take Major to the river. At the river, both men fought and fell into the water."

"What about the other prisoners?"

I look back. The stocks are lined up, one behind the other. There are only two other prisoners beside Major Nelson. And only Tobias Johns of the People's Marxist Movement could have seen anything. And even then, he could not have seen me strike Leader.

"Ask Tobias what he thinks he heard. Then explain to him what he actually heard."

Then Major Nelson and I get into the car and drive toward the falls.

"Thank you," says Major Nelson.

"Why did you not do this, all these years?"

Major Nelson opens his mouth, but remains silent.

"Major," I say. "That man was not a man. He was a monster, an evil spirit. The devil. You and I have been working for the devil. If we survive this we must do better."

"Victor, you are a hero."

"Or a dead man."

I cut the headlights and reduce our speed. Just before the parking area by the river, I pull off the road.

"Wait here."

I get out and head toward the Falls. There are no cars. Good. I walk to the observation deck. It is a dark night, which is also good. I listen, but all I hear is the Falls.

Back at the car, I lift up Leader and haul him over my shoulders. He is huge, but I am big, too, and nothing builds strength like desperation. "Come on," I gasp to Major Nelson.

At the edge of the Killing Pools, I drop Leader.

"Push him in," I say.

"But..." Major Nelson looks horrified.

"Push him in. Be a hero."

"Yes, yes. Of course."

He gets to his knees and starts to roll Leader off the cliff and into the water.

"Wait," I say. "Get his necklace. If his necklace is discovered, it will be proof he is dead."

After some effort, Major tosses me Leader's necklace. It is a heavy gold chain with a large diamond affixed to it. Then he rolls Leader off the cliff and into the water.

"Now what?" asks Major Nelson.

There is a short path to the river. It is not a very popular

spot, as the crocs are also there. But I have no choice. I take
the necklace, which is probably worth more money than exists
in all the shantytowns of our nation, walk toward the water,
and throw it down river. It lands, as I hoped, just at the river's
edge. Then I run back to the Major.

"You must disappear. Follow the river. At the edge of the
Palace grounds, there is a fence. Climb it, dig under it, or
go into the river and swim around it. Then get out of the
country."

We go over our story again and I give him 20 shillings.
Then we shake hands and say goodbye.

～♒～

For a while, it looks as if our story is going to work. When I
get back to the guardhouse, I call the Palace Guard and tell
them about Leader, Major Nelson, and the Killing Pools. They
come and pick me up and then rush to the river. Immediately they begin shooting at crocs in order to safely search for
Leader. But then someone decides that this might put Leader
at more risk, so the shooting stops, and a group goes back to
the palace for spotlights and a generator. By the time we can
see properly, Leader is nowhere in sight.

In the morning, the next shift of stocks guards arrive. And
just before we are taken for questioning by the Palace Guard,
William tells me he forgives me. "Leader was an evil man.
I just hope his replacement does not continue his work." I
thank William for his support, and as Church brothers and
longtime friends, we pledge to take care of each other's family
if either of us survives.

At first the guards question us together, which of course
is very stupid. But I don't blame them; we are palace guards,

too—all dedicated to protecting Leader. At any rate, this allows us to rehearse our story. And when they finally separate us, I feel we are unbreakable.

For the next hour, things are going as you might expect. I know the guards who shuttle in asking questions. I don't feel like a man presumed guilty. But when General Stanley Errol, who was merely a Lieutenant until Leader tapped him to replace Major Nelson, attends the questioning, this changes. Errol seems more concerned about Major Nelson, though. Where is he? Did he fall into the waters, too? Was there any chance of his escaping? What kind of shape was he in? Was he in handcuffs? They haven't found any cuffs, but they did find Leader's necklace, he tells me.

Then another guard comes in and pulls the interrogators out of the room. Fifteen minutes later they come back with anger in their eyes.

"Why," asks General Errol, "is there blood in the backseat of Leader's car?"

"That is Major Nelson's blood," I say, but my heart is sinking, and I curse myself for my stupid mistake. I can only hope that William will back me up. "Leader kicked him in the head while he was in the stocks."

"Why?"

"Major Nelson spit in his face. I told you."

Smack. General Errol slaps me with the back of his hand.

"What else have you forgotten?"

"Nothing."

"We will check the blood. If that is Leader's blood…Take him to the stocks so he can think about it."

❧

I have been mistaken about the stocks. Or rather, when I spoke previously about feeling as if I, too, was in the stocks— thinking that Africa is trapped in stocks of poverty, greed and illness—I was not giving the horror of the actual stocks enough credit. People always have options. The options may not be very good: starve here or go to a refugee camp and starve there; spend your last money on medicine or just try and beat malaria on your own; steal from someone weaker than you or pray for a miracle. Still, at least you have options. In the stocks, there are no options. This is torture. I beg forgiveness from God and from all the men I have placed in here. I think about the men who stayed bent and broken for a week, even two. I pray to Jesus for forgiveness. And to my wife and daughters, for leaving them alone. I have been up for 36 hours now and although the pain and fatigue and fear should be driving me mad, I have a skill that saves me: I fall asleep.

❧

I wake to gunfire. To a machine gun raking in the distance. I strain my neck, trying to raise my head, but it bumps against the wood. More bullets. Is it celebration or devastation? Is it target practice or more murder? I have to urinate. I call to my former coworkers. "Guard!"

"What is it, Victor?"

"Jackson!" I say. "Good to see you."

"I cannot say the same, Victor."

"Yes, I understand. What is that gunfire?"

"I do not know. No one is answering the radio."

"I need to pee. Let me out."

"No funny stuff."

"Believe me, I have no interest in dirtying the name of the stocks guards. Where is William?"

"In No. 4. We were told to keep you apart."

I turn and see William's head hanging like a broken doll. It is a familiar sight to me, but this time I see it differently. My heart breaks.

Jackson cuffs me and walks me to the latrine. "Is it on the radio?" I ask.

"No. Lieutenant—I mean, General Errol has ordered a lockdown of the Palace and the grounds."

"But surely there are telephones."

"I've heard nothing. And nothing on the BBC. I myself am wondering why he does not make an announcement."

"Perhaps he needs allies to make such an announcement," I say.

"I am thinking you are right. No doubt there are many men who would like to rule the country now that Leader is dead."

We are back at the stocks. "Jackson," I say. "I know you're only one man, but if there is anything you can do to protect William... I was with Leader and Major Nelson, but he was not even there at the Falls. He is truly innocent in this matter."

Jackson draws the stocks up and looks me in the eyes. I am not sure if he is studying my soul or just thinking that I must be an idiot. Then he says, "Okay, my friend," and locks me in.

❧

At dusk, the end—whatever it will be—sounds near. There is more gunfire, but now the sounds are bigger than guns. Mortars. Bombs. Tanks rumbling. One of our few MIG jet fighters flies overhead. I hear an explosion in the direction of the Palace.

After another latrine run, Jackson brings out a transistor radio. We listen to the news. There is an Organization of African Unity meeting in Addis Ababa. There are riots in South Africa. The dam project by the lake has fallen behind schedule due to lack of concrete. There is no mention of Leader.

"Jackson," I say. "I am thinking that the silence is a good thing. The news would cause chaos."

"Yes, Victor. Perhaps you are right. Oh, my goodness! Smoke from the Palace!"

Of course, I cannot see.

Then the metallic voice of a loudspeaker fills the air. We cannot make out the words at first. But gradually we hear "surrender" and "Lt. Errol." It gets louder and clearer, or our ears grow familiar to the distortions, just as eyes grow used to the dark. The military tribunal is united, says the voice. The Palace Guards do not have the firepower: Surrender.

I can hear a vehicle rumble in our direction. I look up from my view of the ground and see a tank approaching. It smashes through the wire fence that marks off the stocks and rolls toward us. Jackson blows his whistle. A whistle versus a tank! At this moment I am praying for my daughters, I am sending my heart to my wife. I am asking God to protect them and to stop the Christian Militia from bringing another madman to this place. And then the grinding metal wheels of the tank stop.

A metallic voice calls from the tank: "Is Victor Mbeki here?"

The blood tests. They know. Will they shoot me or try me or feed me to the crocs? No, they will beat me now until they are sure I have told them the truth.

"God be with you," murmurs Jackson. Then he calls out: "Yes. He is here."

"By executive order of Major Nelson, leader of the interim Tribunal, Victor Mbeki is to be released and brought to Parliament immediately."

Jackson frees me from the stocks and I demand he release William and the others. We are stretching our limbs and grinning. A military jeep races toward us, a soldier with a machine gun at the front. An officer gets out of the back.

Major Nelson.

William, Jackson, and I salute our former boss. "You have been busy, Major," I say.

"Yes, and I am still busy. We must go to Parliament to tell our story."

On the ride to Parliament, he will tell me how he made it off the Palace grounds, located the road, flagged down a midnight matatu and offered the driver my 20 shillings plus a future 100 dollars for a ride to Fort Kezenga, our biggest military base, where he woke the Fort Commander, who summoned the Air Force Commander. And how they called the Palace Guards and learned that Lt. Errol was making noises about seizing power, so they decided to eliminate Lt. Errol and ensure that all our forces would be united to prevent the Christian Militia from attacking.

But that comes later. Now, I just say: "Major, I beg your indulgence. May I have five minutes before we depart?"

I hobble to the guardhouse—I am still stiff—and try the phone. It is dead. I had been hoping to call our neighborhood shop, which has a phone, and transmit a message to my wife. But that will have to wait. I go back outside and grab a jerrycan from the back of the guardhouse. I lug it back to the stocks. Then I lift it over my shoulder and tilt it so the top of Stocks No. 1 is soaked in petrol. I repeat this for all the stocks until the can is empty.

William, who smokes, hands me a box of matches and I strike one. I drop it on the top of Stocks No. 1 and then quickly jerk my hand away. Flames shoot up and engulf the contraption, and I watch for a moment as the fire dances. Then I flip the matchbox back to William and turn to Major Nelson.

"Let us be going," I say.

TWO

Well, that story hits a little close to home, doesn't it? I gotta hand it to Amanda. It almost makes me wonder if where I am now has anything to do with this book. As if that's why she wrote that this book was meant for me. But that's crazy. It's just a coincidence. Either way, I take the fact that there's a happy ending of sorts as a good omen. I need one of those myself.

Meanwhile, I also gotta hand it to this author, Kaufman. He got the pain thing exactly right. I mean, I don't know what it's going to be like to be able to move again, but the not moving is killing me. My body is just begging to move, bend, twist. Thank god I can at least move my hands and arms and head. Jesus, imagine a rack: you can't move a damn thing. I hope that's not in any of these stories. I wonder if what I've just read is actually based on a true story; it might be something that nut job in Uganda, Idi something-or-other, would have done. But, man, what a story to read right now. I'm in the freakin' stocks. And I can't wait to burn this goddamn wall unit down.

Strange to think about how being a torturer can be a privilege in some places, although that protagonist was also an angel of mercy. And isn't it amazing how Victor gets his job by knowing Major Nelson? Hollywood works exactly the same way: Most people who come here know someone in the biz. Or go to work in the mailroom. Or they apprentice with a union. Me, I drove and dealt my way in.

It was 1969. I arrived in Hollywood fresh out of college and filled with dreams and ambition but without much of a plan. If that sounds like a fucking cliché, let me assure you that I was. Within a couple of months I had spent my meager savings and was desperate for cash, so I got a job as a parking valet. As I've said, it was the late '60s, and getting high had become pretty standard. Turns out there are always connections on the set. A lot of extras are dealers. A lot of the low-level grunts—hospitality, catering, security—make good money on the side. But I had the novel idea of providing party favors as people drove up to a party, or headed home. I began with pot. But as demand grew, so did my menu. I got hold of speed, coke, mushrooms. It was dangerous, but I had zero connections in the industry, and I needed to make money if I was going to write and produce my own stuff. Fortunately, valet parking opened doors very quickly.

Picture the scene: It's Thursday, October 16, 1969, and I'm feeling miserable because back in New York, the Mets have won the World Series—not that I'm a super big sports guy, just that the city must be in a great mood while I'm getting nowhere in L.A. Today, I'm somehow trying to conquer Hollywood by working a bash in the Hills. A 40-something guy with a red Karmann Ghia pulls up alone. I take his keys and make my pitch: "If I can get you any recreational additives, please don't hesitate to ask, sir."

"Recreational additives?" he repeats. "Very catchy. I'll think about it."

An hour later he comes out of the party with two champagne flutes and hands me one. "What have you got?"

"Just party staples: weed and speed."

"Do you know who I am?"

"No sir, but my name is Rick."

"I'm Lance Barton, I run marketing at Visionary. And you, buddy, you are a true innovator."

At this time I am not too clear on what marketing is. I can tell you the difference between key grips and best boys, but marketing, that's a little blurry. Still, I have a sense an opportunity is right in front of me. "You know how it is, Mr. Barton," I say. "Sometimes you have to bring the party to the party."

My stoner wisdom hits home. He laughs and says I have marketing in my bones. "Sometimes you have to bring the party to the party!" he repeats. "There's a tag line!" He buys an ounce and gives me his card. And a week later I get my first studio job: Promotions department gofer and dealer.

The poolsides of Tinseltown are riddled with undeserving auteurs and opportunists. There are former call girls and boys. Trainers. Casting couch starlets, procurers, godsons of powerful men, dealers, domineering shrinks. And, yes, as a valet I suppose I am no better. But I have been studying all my life, pestering camera store sales clerks to show me 16mm hardware—Bolexes, Victors, Bell & Howells, Keystones, and my favorite, for its stupid name: Filmos—going to double features, reading the trades in the public library. Taking notes for films I would make. Scrawling endless lists: Best movies, comedies, bit players, sequences, and scores. Books that should be made into movies. Bad movies that could have been good. Good movies that could have been great.

Ah, shit. Why am I going over this? This is the cliché, right? Take stock of your life while standing—or in my case, lying—at death's door. But it's not just that. The infuriating thing about being stuck here is that out there the world is going nuts over my show, no doubt exhuming my tainted past, transforming me into a bad guy, an immoral ratings shill. And I can't fucking respond.

I deserved my foot in the door as much as the next guy. And when I got in, I was ready. What made Ricky run? Movies. I wanted to make movies. That's why I was here. That's why I didn't go back east for three years. I worked hard at whatever they gave me. Posters, billboards, trailers, gossip sheet PR, radio buys. And when I wasn't working, I still worked: I read *Variety*, *Hollywood Reporter*, *TV Guide*. I studied the landscape. These were the days of yore: drive-ins still existed, and so did independent theaters. There was a slew of distribution chains, not just a few giants. Lance Barton promoted me. He dubbed me Captain Buzz—his little joke about my side business and my day job. He introduced me to clients. And just before he took a job at Arrow Entertainment, two years later, his last act was to make me a Vice President.

Now I had access. VPs of marketing work closely with development and stop selling pot. And that's exactly what I did. I hung out during filming. I watched. I learned. I met other producers. I met Nelson Twillinger, an agent at Morris. I learned about funding. I waited.

At the end of 1973, I took my bonus and commissioned my first script. *Donny Cycle*, a comedy based on *Don Quixote* about a doofus who fancies himself to be a biker. Naturally he gets his ass kicked in scene after scene, and gets in the way of an undercover drug bust, but proves to be surprisingly tough and helps do good in the end. Nelson Twillinger found me a sugar daddy—an automotive parts manufacturer from Ohio—and we made the movie. It got decent notices and made $14 million, which made us profitable, believe it or not. So boom! I'm a little player. I even started dating one of the actresses in the film, Rachel Wares.

Then I co-wrote another comedy-thriller called *Break a Leg*, about an unemployed actor with a loud, obnoxious neighbor. One night he steals his neighbor's business cards and starts handing them out at a bar and acting like a rainmaker, promising people drug deals, kinky sex, whatever—just to screw with his neighbor. When the neighbor is murdered, cops find all these bizarre messages on the dead man's answering machine. The actor becomes suspect number one and has to assume all kinds of different roles to solve the murder and prove himself innocent. *Break a Leg* was cheaper to make than *Donny Cycle* and did better. Now I had some money, and I hired a different writer for *Evergreen*, developed it, scored great backing and–

Ah, shit. My house phone is ringing. I reach for my cell—it's a reflex—but of course it's not there. I go through my pockets one more time. Nothing. No keys. No coins. Not even a pack of matches to set off my smoke detectors and alert the fire department. Of course, with a messed-up back and my legs in horrible shape, fire is not such a great option right now. The phone stops ringing, and I try to fall back on movie wisdom: What would Indiana Jones do? Or Super-man? Or Mister Fantastic, Reed Richards? I notice a beam of light coming in through the window. I grab a DVD—one of those For-Your-Consideration Oscar freebies—and pull out the shiny disc. I hold it up to the light and angle the reflection back out the window.

Dot, dot, dot. Dash, dash, dash. Dot, dot, dot. I send the beam back up, catching the light quickly and then pulling away and repeating.

I do this for god knows how long. Quick, slow, quick—sort of like Marta trying to teach me salsa dancing. No, that was slow, slow, quick-quick, slow. Cha, cha, cha-cha, cha, right? What the hell, I try that too. But I have this feeling that my SOS/salsa message is futile. Who will see it? That window looks out to the front of the house, so maybe—*maybe*—the clowns with the Hummer across the street will notice it. But they live almost a quarter mile away.

I look at the murderous Bang & Olufsen speaker. It's wireless. Maybe there's some kind of mobile bullshit in-side it that I can use. I stretch to reach the elegant cube. It's too far away. But with the help of a DVD case, I nudge the speaker's far end, angling it closer and closer until I can ac-tually lift it—it's dense, but not that heavy—above my head.

One look at the solid rectangle and I have to laugh. If I were Bruce Banner, the scientist who becomes the Hulk, or Tony Stark, who becomes Iron Man, or even frigging Tintin, I could probably rejigger the thing. But I'm Rick Salter, city boy. I can barely change a disposable razor blade without cutting myself.

I give the speaker a frustrated and pathetically frail heave and gasp as a searing pain radiates from my lower back, spreading to my hips and then lower. When it subsides, a big imaginary billboard pops into my head: It's an ad for my show featuring yours truly trapped and broken beneath a massive heap of domestic crap. The image makes me squeak out a laugh—not too big or it will hurt. It's obvious, right? I'm stuck in a situation worthy of my own merciless TV show. Jesus, the town is going to have a field day with this. Thing is, when I get out of here—if I get out of here—I should declare myself a winner. I mean, nobody broke a bone on my show. Sure, there might have been a muscle tear here, a herniated disc there, but that can happen to anybody. And OK, there was some hypothermia and a case of pneumonia, but nothing on the show was actually life-threatening. Me, I have medicine I'm supposed to take. Glycerin for the old ticker. My HPB doses. Plus, I'm majorly stressed out after the fucking bloodsucking network trolls knocked me around last night. Walter Fields threatened me. The last thing I remember, he was talking about taking away the show. I squeeze my eyes together as if that will help me recall the exchange, but everything is blurry: I'm drinking; I'm on the BlackBerry; I'm throwing shit around the house; I'm ranting about network scavengers feeding off everyone else's ideas. But I have no memory of anything to do with my goddamned entertainment system.

Amanda was right. I should have hosted the show myself on the Internet. Such a girl. What would Amanda do in my situation? First of all, she would have her cell phone, fully charged, in a tiny designer handbag that she purchased on sale at 50% off, as well as breath mints, and whatever anti-depressants she currently favors. She is so sensible and tenacious; she would try and crawl out. But how? I look around, hoping for inspiration. And then it comes to me: I need a crowbar! Yes, that is the way to lift this thing off me. Leverage.

Which also is the key to negotiations and deals—that's why the network is out to screw me. Those pricks. I'm going to take my show back even if I have to put my house in hock. I can feel my heart race at just the thought. Marta would tell me to do "joga." I can hear her: "Just breathe, Mr. Rick," she would say after listening to me rant about—oh, choose anything: the weather screwing our production, the division of standards screwing our production, the long-legged blonde extra screwing the assistant director instead of me. You name it, I complained about it. "Do your joga. Take a class."

So now I try to breathe. It seems to work a little because I realize that the room is filled with potential levers: there's a sculpture by Phillip La Forge that I bought at an auction fundraiser for—I swear to god—Bram Zenith's Cattle Flatulence Reduction Fund. The piece is four feet away and weighs a ton. Toppling it in my direction would do the trick as long as it landed near me, not on me. It's a long strip of metal, maybe even steel, with small bulbous knobs jutting out. It's called "Amputated Tree." But when I "won" the piece, a woman at the next table with a teardrop tattoo dripping from her eye said it should be called "scary vibrator." Amazing what you remember, flat on your back, trying not to think about dying.

THE DAIQUIRI CASE

Salim Azziz was found naked, hanging from a light fixture. He was attached to the fixture by his own pants. One pant leg had been tied around it; the other was knotted around his neck.

Pvt. James C. Cruz discovered the suspended body at 10 p.m. during his rounds of the cell block. Following protocol, Pvt. Cruz checked the prisoner for signs of life. Finding none, he cut Azziz down, called for help, and began to administer CPR.

At 10:10 p.m. an army medic pronounced Salim Azziz dead.

Ten minutes later, Major Samuel Shane, senior investigator for the military police at Guantánamo Bay, arrived at the scene. Shane was a good soldier and a good cop and so he was instantly pissed off; not only had the body been moved, but there was a good chance that the movement had resulted in post-mortem head trauma and bruising. That meant more work for the medical examiner, and potentially murky autopsy findings.

Shane introduced himself to Pvt. Cruz, who looked stunned, and the block Sergeant, a huge guy named Mackelson, who didn't.

"You cut him down alone?"

"Yes, sir," said Cruz.

Shane nodded. "Don't you guys have video cams on these guys?"

"We've had a snafu with our cameras," said Sgt. Mackelson. "Just recently."

Shane nodded. Imagine that.

"I can't believe he did this," said Cruz.

"What happened to you?" asked Shane, pointing at Cruz's bandaged knuckles.

Cruz looked down at his hands. "Oh, this. I hit the heavy bags. No gloves, no wrap."

"When?"

"Yesterday morning. Early."

While a photographer took pictures and video footage, Shane started inspecting the scene. Lt. Green, also of the MP, showed up a few minutes later. Shane liked having another pair of eyes. Together they looked down at Azziz, a small man getting smaller by the minute. They looked up at the light bulb fixture, noted the four small screws that held it in place and the flimsy prison-issued pant leg still attached to it. They looked at the toilet to Azziz's right, which might have been the way for a man to boost himself up to hang the noose, if that man were 6' 5" or taller. Azziz was nowhere near that height. Finally, they looked around the cell, and Shane realized that it was completely empty except for a Koran lying on the bed. It was stamped "Property of the U.S. Army."

The medical examiner arrived as Shane and Green headed out. "Looks more like murder than suicide to me," Shane told the doctor in a quiet voice. "Let me know your thoughts."

❦

They had Pvt. Cruz brought in.

"Thanks for coming," Shane said. "What did you think of Mr. Azziz?"

"He was a good guy. He never railed at us like some of the other prisoners. And he sang us gazals."

"Gazals?"

"Love songs from Pakistan. We got to like 'em. Pretty cool stuff."

"We?"

"Me and some of the other guards. You can ask them."

"So what did you think of the setup?"

"What do you mean?"

"The suicide." The alleged suicide, Shane thought.

"Oh, like what happened to Salim?"

"Bingo."

"I don't know. I guess it's hard to know how Salim got the noose up there."

Shane nodded.

"And I can't believe those pants didn't rip. Although he wasn't the biggest guy in the world. Guy was a featherweight, if that."

"Anything else?"

"No."

"Did you happen to notice if he had an erection when you found him?"

"Permission to speak frankly, Major?"

"Granted and encouraged."

"What the fuck are you suggesting?"

"Pvt. Cruz, it is a physiological fact that men have erections when they die by hanging."

"Really? I didn't know that. I thought maybe you were suggesting I'm..."

"I wasn't. Did he have one?"

"I don't remember. What happens to women when they are hanged?"

Maj. Shane allowed himself a smile. "I have no idea. That's an interesting question that's never surfaced. But think. He was naked."

Cruz frowned. "I would have remembered an erection, I guess."

"Were you surprised to find Mr. Salim Azziz dead?"

"He was depressed."

"And how, exactly, Pvt. Cruz, was his depression different from everybody else's on this base?"

"Salim wanted to get home to his family."

Green broke in: "So what do you think happened?"

"I have no idea."

"Who did you relieve in the rotation? And at what time?"

"Corporal Margolies. At 8 p.m."

"And did he say anything?"

"No sir. He seemed the same as always: Happy to get off duty."

"Thanks," said Shane, without really meaning it.

⁓

Shane placed a call to Operations to ask about garbage pickup and confirmed that on the weekends they let most of it sit. Then he left a message at the gym. Then he sent Green out with two MPs to drive pickups around the cell block and the guards' quarters. "You are looking for anything strange: booze bottles, squeegee bottles, blindfolds. Any interesting items, tag them."

Then one by one, Shane called in the cell block guards. He got nothing but blank stares, head shakes, and professions of admiration for Salim Azziz. According to them, Cruz had indeed been the friendliest with Salim Azziz, but everyone got along with the dead man. Shane thought the autopsy was going to shake things up, but he wanted to wait for it. If he pressed these guys and his hunch was wrong, he'd look like an asshole.

When the preliminary medical report came in, Shane read it and went to the infirmary to go over it again with the doctor.

"Tell me about the alcohol?"

"Yes. A helluva lot. .28 percent. You could lose your license in many states with those levels. He was drunk as a skunk."

"Too drunk to make a noose?"

"Too drunk to pour himself another drink. He must have been blotto. I mean he barely weighed 100 pounds."

"Have you gotten to cause of death? I'd bet the house it wasn't the hanging."

"You would have won, Major. He had major head trauma, but that could have happened when he was cut down. More importantly, he has two kinds of stress marks on his neck. One high up where the noose strung him up. The other was much lower, with evenly spaced bruises."

"Choked, huh?"

"Crushed windpipe."

"Thank you, Doctor. Anything I should be looking for?"

"A man with strong hands. And a motive."

Shane was actually looking for two men with strong hands, minimum. He doubted one guy could have attached the pants to the light and then propped up Salim Azziz and tied a noose around him. This was a pretty obvious case of misdirection: Someone with access to the cell had gotten him drunk, killed him and staged the hanging. Shane wondered if the booze was part of the plan, if it was supposed to provide the motive for the hanging, as if Azziz felt guilty about drinking.

It was hot and humid. Shane hated this weather. He was pale. He was from Seattle, where the sun was a theoretical construct. When he retired, which he was planning to do soon, he thought he'd go back there. His mother and brother were still there. And it was cool there most of the time. Gitmo weather was brutal. But today he hoped it would get hotter. He knew he was about to hammer at the camouflaged wall of silence that had gone up the minute alcohol touched Salim's lips, if not earlier. The heat was an ally; it put everyone on edge. He needed an edge.

He called in for the service records of all the guards with access to Salim. There was an eight-man rotation for the cell block. Usually two men were on at a time. Cruz had been working solo because Saturday night was Saturday night even at Guantánamo Bay, and a bunch of guards had taken off.

Shane also asked for Salim Azziz's records, even though his gut told him that nothing in the prisoner's background was going to matter in this case. He could have been a pious holy man or Osama bin Laden's chief strategist, and it wouldn't have made a difference.

He read about the eight guards. They were mostly clean and mostly young. Two of them, Cruz and Foley, had criminal records prior to enlistment. Drinking and driving charges for both of them. And Foley had a possession charge for pot. Shane needed to find the weakest link. He was on his way to visit Foley when Green returned, clear plastic bags in his hand. He held them up.

"Cups and a funnel," he said. "We found these in the garbage outside the block."

"Knuckleheads," Shane sighed.

"I'll see if we can get some prints."

"I'll see what Foley has to say."

⚜

Foley was on his bed, playing a video game when Shane knocked. "Come in," he said.

He saw Shane and flew off his bed. "Sir?" he saluted.

"At ease, Private. Just a little drop-in visit."

"Yes, Major." Shane noticed Foley's eyes flicker to the bathroom door.

"I hope I'm not interrupting anything."

"No, sir. Just playing *Call of Duty*."

"Where's your roommate?"

"Creager? He's at the gym, I think."

"Do you know anything about drinking in the cell block?"

His eyes lowered away from Shane. "Drinking? The guards?"

"Yeah, booze. Guards or prisoners."

"No, sir."

"Nothing? No fun with the prisoners? Muslims love to booze it up, don't they?"

"No, sir. We are trained not to offend the detainees."

"So you know nothing about any drinking the night Salim Azziz shuffled off this mortal coil?"

"Sir?"

"I mean the night he died."

"No, sir. Nothing."

"You mind if I use the head?"

"Ah, it's a little nasty in there, sir."

"Come on, Private. We're in the army." Shane opened the

bathroom door and closed it behind him. It wasn't too bad if you liked pharmacies. He inspected the bottles lining the sink. Unprescribed pills, all nicely labeled—Dexedrine, Codeine, Mandrax, which Shane knew was a British version of Quaaludes. He flushed the toilet and ran the faucet, just to mess with Foley a bit. He put two bottles in an evidence bag. He couldn't believe the drugs were just lying out here: either Foley had absolutely nothing to do with Salim Azziz's death or he was a fucking moron. The odds were on moron.

"Pvt. Foley, let's take a walk to my office and you can think about the booze. And I'll think about all the pills in there."

"Pills? They aren't mine."

"I might be inclined to believe you if I didn't already think you just lied to me about the booze. Let's go."

"We don't have to go. I'll talk."

"Let's go enjoy the mid-day sun," insisted Shane.

They walked back to Shane's office to get the interview on tape. Green joined them, handing Foley a can of coke. Shane pressed record.

"Tell me about booze in your cell block."

"Two weeks ago Cruz lost a massive hand in a poker game, like a whole paycheck. Sarge offered him a deal: Get to Daiquiri and bring us back the real thing and the debt would be forgiven."

Daiquiri was the closest town to Gitmo: 30 miles or so. But it was off limits. Every inch of Cuba was off limits to the army.

"Why? What was the point of that?"

"The guys had been talking shit. Margolies, who wants to open a bar one day, says the drink was invented there. But

Sarge says it's up for debate. They had an argument about it at the table. Something about an American coming to Daiquiri and then actually inventing it in Havana."

"Did Cruz go?"

"Ask Salim Azziz."

"Booze could come from anywhere."

"Ask Cruz."

"Who else knew about the Daiquiri bet?" Green asked.

"Everyone at the table: Cruz, Sarge, Margolies, me, Stuttlefeld, Creager."

"Come on. Stop bullshitting me. What happened on Saturday evening? Salim Azziz had as much chance of hanging himself as you do of getting into Mecca."

"I don't know. I had popped some Mandrax when Cruz showed up with the booze. Booze and 'drax is quite a combo. I was out of it and crashed in my room."

"Anyone can vouch for you?" Shane said.

"Creager. He did 'em, too."

"Where the hell are you guys getting Mandrax anyway?"

"I was stationed at the London embassy for a while. Great city."

Shane studied Foley. The pasty-faced private was making eye contact. He was leveling now. Or he was getting to be a better liar. Shane opted for the former.

"You can go. If you say anything to anyone about this conversation, I will find out and you will go to prison." He held up an evidence bag with pills. "This bottle has your prints on it, doesn't it? If I don't like what you are telling me, or what happens, you are going down for a long time. You understand me?"

"Yes, sir."

⚭

Shane ordered a sweep of the perimeter. Two hours later, Green phoned in. The breach had been located. There was freshly turned earth under a barbed wire fence at the north-west perimeter. Shane ordered them to dig through and follow it out.

Green called back. A second breach, this time at the electric fence, had been discovered.

Shane called Intelligence and asked the Pentagon to arrange for an operative to make inquiries. He informed the base commander that there had been a breach, that it appeared at least one soldier had escaped into Cuba and returned. The Commander claimed this had never happened before, which gave Shane a sense of grudging respect for Cruz. On these boiling sweaty days Shane wanted to see Daiquiri, too. He imagined a sleepy river town, rundown and beautiful, fighting back the jungle. And tired, handsome women running sleepy cafés with limes piled high on ancient wooden counters.

The phone rang. It was Watson, who ran the gym. Cruz hadn't been seen in the gym all week. And his name wasn't on any sign-in sheet. Shane left a message for Cruz to come in first thing the next day.

❧

Shane and Green made Cruz wait for the interview. The longer Cruz had to sit and stew the better. Plus, the delay gave Shane time to check with Intelligence on any news from Daiquiri. An operative had confirmed that a man matching Cruz's build, with a weird Spanish accent, had been seen at the Hotel Nacional. He had taken a room for an hour with a young lady.

Shane asked Cruz about his trip.

"Who gave that up?" said Cruz. "I'm not saying anything."

"Why not?"

"Fuck those guys. Who gave me up?"

"We found the spot you went out."

"Okay, but if this is about Salim, you are barking up the wrong tree."

"What about Daiquiri?"

"Nah, that's right. I did that. But I didn't kill Salim. No way. And I didn't give him any booze."

"So tell me what you did do."

"I brought back a friggin' jerrycan of daiquiris. First I did a little tour, though: I went to the Hotel Nacional and met a girl at the bar, got a room. Two hours later I put down $40 and got a huge batch of Daiquiris, no ice, and hauled it back to base."

"That's it? What happened then?"

"Isn't that enough? I'm in deep shit already, no? But as for Salim, if that's what you're asking, I swear I don't know. I didn't see him until I cut him down. I was tired when I got back. You try dragging a jerrycan around for miles. I gave Mackelson his booze and I crashed."

"Do you want to revise your story about the injury to your hand?"

"Oh sure. Those are fucking blisters from all the digging and carrying the can. Nothing to do with the heavy bag. Sorry."

"How'd you get to Daiquiri and back? It's far."

"I jogged for an hour or so when I got out. It was dark. Then I hitched a ride. On the way back, I hired a car."

"What did you talk about with Mr. Azziz? Were there things he would say that might have rubbed the other guards the wrong way?"

"Salim? I doubt it. We talked about politics a little. But mostly about family and how life is back home. He was interested in America. You know the thing I feel really bad about? When we first got him, he came in with a bag over his head, and we had instructions to keep him inside. And when he came in, me and Walls spun him around and took off the bag. He begged us to point him toward Mecca, but we just pointed him south. After a couple of days, I had a change of heart. So I told him I'd made a mistake, and I pointed him in the right direction."

"Anyone in Daiquiri make you for an American G.I.?"

"Maybe, but not from the base. I wore civilian clothes as soon as I got outside."

"You think a guy walks out of the jungle with a funny accent and a crew cut and everyone in Daiquiri assumes he's just blown in from Havana? Jesus, you are lucky you are not rotting in a Cuban jail right now, explaining an international incident. You better be telling me the truth about Azziz, Cruz, because you are in deep, deep shit."

"I was in deep shit the moment I got assigned here, sir."

Shane dismissed Cruz, disgusted with the entire case, disgusted with the whole Gitmo operation. The army was disgraceful. First Abu Ghraib, now this place.

A report came in. Salim's wife had burned to death. An investigation in Pakistan was pending. Shane had worked in Islamabad years ago, so he had a pretty clear idea about the investigation, and it wasn't one that made him happy. Investigators, their palms greased, would rule that Ms. Azziz's sari or shawl had accidentally caught fire in the kitchen, or that the grieving widow had set fire to herself. That was pretty much always the determination. It had nothing to do with her husband's family not wanting to keep her around. Strange how this flammability problem only seemed to afflict South Asian women.

Shane looked out his window. The sun was bright, the white-washed concrete seemed to bounce the light right at him. Shane thought about the case: a lot was already in—the autopsy, a reliable confession from Cruz, a semi-reliable one from Foley. And Creager was supposedly doped up, too. That left five out of eight guards to crack.

There was nothing to do but press on.

Shane called the Tech Division. "Who handles our video surveillance?"

He got Harlow. Shane knew him as a firing range regular. He was one of those soldiers who had nothing to do with combat hardware, but couldn't get enough heavy metal. Or even light metal. Shane, on the other hand, practiced at the range because his life, theoretically, depended on it.

"Harlow, it's Shane here. I need a favor. When did the guards at cell block A-6 report their video cam outage? And what was the problem?"

"Sure thing, Major. Gimme a sec."

Shane looked out the window again, searching the sky. Gitmo in the summer—every cloud was a silver lining.

"Got it," Harlow came back on the line. "The report came in Friday evening, too late to get anything done. I sent somebody over on Sunday after they found that guy swinging. The system looks like it was vandalized, like they went to the back of the deck and took a hammer to the cables and inputs. Now nothing fits. I had to order a new one. "

"I'll get someone to come over and collect it."

"Is it evidence?"

"Yeah, probably. One more thing: was this deck just for one cell?"

"No. This is a big piece of hardware. It holds memory for a ton of adjacent cells."

"Is the memory on it okay?"

"Sure. Assuming you love jigsaw puzzles."

❧

Shane read through the guard files again. He examined the roster for the last two months. Every single guard had gone on leave during that period. The most recent was Sgt. Mackelson, three weeks ago. Shane was convinced that Mackelson was the key. It was his team. It was his poker game. It was his booze. So he had him brought in.

Mackelson was huge. His voice was rough, with a rasp that made his words sound thick, as if they lasted longer than they were supposed to. His smile was a daunting affair of thick lips unfurling to reveal enormous teeth.

"Good mood today, Sgt.?" asked Shane.

"Not bad." The smile widened.

"No smiles for Azziz. Or his wife. She burned to death yesterday."

"No! Shit. What happened?"

"Officially? It was an accident."

"Jesus."

"We know about the daiquiris."

"What daiquiris?"

"Mackelson, you get a Z minus for the cover-up. We know about Cruz. We know about your bet. We know about the booze. So how about you fill in the rest?"

"No idea what you are talking about."

"I'm talking about locking you up right now. Let's go. Connect the dots."

"Cruz is a liar."

"Cruz? He didn't give you up. He's tough, just not very smart. We got a match on his boots with the dirt by the fences. But that's a slip-up anyone could make. So far none of you guys is getting into Mensa."

"That your best material?"

"Never mind. You got the rum, what then?"

Mackelson shook his big head.

"When did you decide to rip up the video unit? That was your idea, wasn't it?"

"You terrorizing me over fucking terrorists? I'm saying nothing."

"You think Salim Azziz was a terrorist?"

"He was here."

"Not anymore. You got a problem with prisoners?"

"These fucking guys?" Mackelson stopped, with his mouth open as if he were going to say something, but thought the better of it. "Listen, I'm just here doing my rotation, marking time. There are better gigs."

"Salim Azziz was drunk as a skunk the night he died. And you had just gotten a delivery of booze, hours before. And you're telling me there is no connection there?"

Mackelson shook his head.

"I'm going let you think about this. We'll talk tomorrow. You make this easy, maybe there's some hope. Some leniency."

"The guy's a fucking terrorist. What do you care?"

"You can think about that, too."

～∽～

Shane called in the grunts two at a time. He worked on Stubbs and left Walls out in the waiting area with nothing but quality prison literature: *Thugz* and *Hoodz* magazines. He shook Stubbs' hand and decided to open with his version of Simon Says—pile on the truth, insert one lie, see what happens.

"You want to tell me about the booze?"

Stubbs shook his head.

"Look, I know about the daiquiris and Cruz going AWOL and the bet and Foley's drugs and the funnel with your fingerprints on it."

"I didn't touch that fucking funnel."

Bingo. Shane amped it up. "Prints don't lie, Private."

"It was all Mackelson and Walls. If I touched that thing, it was by accident."

"Okay. I believe you," said Shane. "Why don't you tell me about Saturday night?"

Stubbs shared his version and when he was done, Shane was in a blind rage. Then Green walked in and said:

"The cell block is empty now. Pending the new video set-up."

Shane nodded.

They called Walls in, and he confirmed Stubbs' version, including Mackelson's drunken threats against his own men. Then they called Margolies in and got the story in triplicate. It was 9 o'clock in the evening.

"You think they are lying?" Shane asked Green.

"All three?"

"Maybe. Just asking."

"Hard to pull off. And why? To make Mackelson the fall guy?"

"They are still accessories."

"But with cause. They could claim they were forced by chain of command."

Shane sighed. "To quote my old boot camp sergeant, that excuse won't hold water in a storm. Let's go kick this around."

"I'm hungry."

"Okay," said Shane.

❦

Just before midnight Shane and Green went to look for Mackelson. They kicked his door in for a little effect, and because the story of Salim Azziz's final hours made them so angry. They were in the mood to fuck with Mackelson. Give him some terror of his own.

But he wasn't there. He wasn't in the Block Lounge, or the gym, or anywhere.

"Think he got lucky?"

"I sure hope not."

The two men checked the beach and the pool. No one had seen Mackelson. It was Tuesday night. Not a big night on Gitmo. Then Green remembered one more place.

❦

Major Shane had been to Afghanistan. He had been in Iraq for Abu Ghraib. He had seen overdoses, suicides, helicopter crashes with no survivors. But few things in his career had ever shocked him like the sight of Sgt. Mackelson, his neck broken, his tongue askew, choked by his own belt, his face purple, his huge body impossibly stretched, pale and dead.

Shane gagged. He fought off the urge to puke.

He thought about Stubbs in the room when Green said the place had been cleared out, inadvertently letting Mackelson's men know they had a space. He and Green had wanted to do the same thing—put Mackelson in a cell, scare the shit out of him—they had even talked about it over dinner. But this was rough justice. This was too rough. This was what you got for forcing a man to drink, humiliating him, killing him. Time for a drink, Salim. Time to get happy. And some of the men had said no, this is too much. Even though they were already drunk. Stubbs, Margolies, and Walls had watched Salim refuse, watched him flail at Mackelson, heard him cry for help. Mackelson had just laughed. Then he threatened to write his men up and beat the shit out of them. He was a terrible drunk, Walls had said.

The men had seen the headlock and the nose pinch and heard the order to get the funnel and jam it in Salim's mouth. And when they were too slow, Mackelson did it himself. Just thinking about it made Shane close his eyes and turn his head, as if that would stop the image. They had been there when Salim puked and Mackelson forced him to sit back up, tied his own belt around the prisoner to keep him up, and poured more daiquiris into the man.

They had seen Salim slide in slo-mo down the bars as Mackelson undid the belt. They had heard Salim's head thump on the concrete floor, the back of his head taking the impact. And then he was out. And Mackelson got scared. Salim wouldn't wake up. Mackelson was bombed. He was furious at the fucking Paki terrorist. He shook him, he choked him. Stubbs tried pulling the massive man off, but it was too late. And then the plan. And the cover-up. Mackelson himself destroyed the video system. Then they wiped every inch of the cell and the guards left. Mackelson did the string-up himself. He was big enough.

⌒∞⌒

What started as a suspected suicide was. now two murders, an AWOL, and a drug possession charge. Mackelson's death probably involved kidnapping, but big deal. Shane hated everything about the case. What he hated most was that he sympathized with the grunts. They couldn't help it if their boss was a douchebag. And now they were going down. Or some of them were. You can't murder a commanding officer and expect to walk. Cruz had to serve time, which was too bad, thought Shane He was a good soldier. Foley was a dirtbag. The sooner the army chucked him, the better. As for the murder of Mackelson, he didn't think any of them would break or go for a deal.

The M.E.'s report came in. Shane read it and called Smith of the Criminal Investigation Command. He would present him two privates, Cruz and Foley, and evidence against them. Maybe between Smith and a reasonable JAG, he could get Cruz off easy. Mitigating circumstances. Plus he cooperated fully. Or almost fully. Let's face it, he liked Cruz and kind of admired his journey to Daiquiri. The U.S. had been in Gitmo how many years? And this was the first time he'd heard of a breach. Shit, Cruz deserved a citation.

Shane looked up retirement forms. You could do the whole thing online now, but he wanted to read through it first. He hit "print" and got up.

"I'm going for a walk," he told Green.

He walked to the beach. He passed the empty cages that held so many Haitians back in the day. He tried to imagine

it, a friggin' so-called humanitarian human zoo. Camp Delta
was slicker, sparsely populated but much the same. He had
started off a soldier and a cop. Now he was an officer and a
zoo keeper.

The Medical Examiner had found a ton of Mandrax in
Mackelson's blood stream. Death was probably by asphyxia-
tion but the victim suffered massive head trauma as well. Considering how drugged he was, he probably didn't suffer too
much. Too fucking bad, thought Shane.

He was at the water now. He bent down, unlaced his
boots, and hopping on one leg at a time like a spastic pelican,
he pulled them off. He dug his toes into the sand, then hiked
up his trousers and waded out a little. The ocean felt great.
He thought about the retirement papers back in the office.
It was a done deal. He looked out at the empty horizon, and
then back at his boots and the black socks lying on the sand.
This was the image he wanted to lock in. Not the images of
a broken Salim Azziz or Mackelson. No, a still-life of Gitmo:
his old boots, his stinking socks lying in the sand, the surf
edging closer.

THREE

Hey, that was some sort of hard-boiled, modern pulp, wasn't it? A noir showdown at the Gitmo Corral with a sheriff named Shane. I love noir—John Huston, Raymond Chandler, Edger Ulmer, Sam Fuller—but man, that story was not your typical noir. Dark stuff in the bright Caribbean sunlight. And it worked even though it broke a major, major rule: there was no femme fatale. I kept waiting for G.I. Jane to show up. But I guess booze was the closest thing to a Veronica Lake stand-in. The sexy old daiquiri. Speaking of G.I. Jane, I don't get how Amanda thinks this particular story could be meant for me. I mean, I liked it. But it's not even good for *The King of Pain*. It's not like we're gonna hang anyone. And Shane is hardly a role model for our show; he's had enough of the whole damn thing: prison, isolation, incarceration. He's retiring. I'm not retiring. No way, although crazily enough I have this vague memory of Walter Fucking Fields, that network numbskull, talking to me about "calling it a day." Did that happen or did I dream it? Any way, screw him. That's ridiculous. *The King of Pain* has inspired me, not dragged me down like Shane.

What's inspiring me right now is curiosity—how much fucking damage have I done to myself? My legs—what the hell is going to happen to them? And I can't really feel my feet any longer. There's just a light tingling, as if they've fallen asleep. When I try to flex my toes, I'm not sure if I am.

My right knee throbs like there's a heart in there. I can feel it pulsing. And Jesus is my chest sore. The burn is turning into an itch as well.

I have visions of the future: me in traction like you see in the cartoons, all mummified in a body cast; me in a wheelchair, trying to push myself out onto my bed and sliding down to the floor; me as a wizened old geezer with a cane and a heavy limp. None of them is particularly appealing.

I can't help wondering what I'll need: surgery, physical therapy, hip and knee replacements, live-in nurses? Fuck! This wall unit was a bad, bad idea. But I can't even play the blame game, because it was my idea—I've got a busy mind, it bounces around, so I thought three TVs would be fun. I thought video games would be cool. My son Jared could play them. But whoever my decorator Sophie Van der Voom (whose looks match her name, just in case you were wondering) hired to attach the damn thing must've used scotch tape. Not that I'm blaming Sophie; she's always done a great job—plus, she redid the house for me for free. Or not exactly free, but as an extension of a movie project I hired her to do. She was so excited to be working with me that she threw my house in for free. That's what I call dedication. Or a kickback. And now, if I snuff it, Sophie's freebie is going to mark her career. Bad for her, but worse for me, because while plenty of other notable people have died under embarrassing circumstances—auto-erotic asphyxiations, drug binges, alcohol poisoning, night swimming, electrocution by vibrator in the bathtub (or is that last one just an urban legend?)—nobody that I'm aware of has been crushed and starved to death by his own home entertainment system. If

I really go out this way, Leno, Letterman, O'Brien and every other stand-up in the nation will turn Rick Salter into a punch line and make my name immortal for all the wrong reasons.

But my name deserves better. I deserve better. I made *Evergreen*, for Christ's sake. You remember: "The breathtaking collision of Vietnam and Americana right on Main Street." "A cinematic eruption, an historic distillation: Norman Rockwell meets rock 'n' roll." Actually, you know what it was? An update on the ultimate American play: *Our Town*, circa 1970, that's all. The kid who grows up to be the mayor? He's the stage manager. Sure, there are some jump cuts to flashbacks in the jungle. There's a Mai Lai-like massacre; some wife-swapping. And instead of Emily dying of childbirth, George returns in time to learn that one of his buddies didn't make it back. I wanted to show Grover's Corners rocked out of isolation, exiled from Main Street, and it worked: my movie made a cool $160 million. Richard Halloway, Ray Loomis, and Fiona Ransom all became major stars. My cameraman Nestor Di Franco made the jump to director. My director Luke Peterson got to produce. Oh yeah, and I won Best Picture. It was a great time; I did a lot of boozing and floozying.

Unfortunately, in Hollywood, you're only as good as your last notices and receipts. *Goldengrove*, my epic, or epic failure—also known as *Goldengrave* and *Barrengrove*—turned my name from an aphrodisiac into a prophylactic. It was a misfire of Iraq-like proportions. It was the first time I directed and produced. Bad move. During production I was drunker than all of Poland on a Saturday night, and higher than Jupiter when I wasn't drinking. A total 24/7 mess. I was so out of control that Sally Fine, my associate producer, who managed everything on my first four movies, who did everything but change my underwear, quit three months in, after I refused to dry out. I was on my post-Oscar, Hollywood high, and every studio snake and producer and production company honcho was an enabler, stroking my ego, promising funding for whatever I wanted to do next. So it's no wonder *Goldengrove*—and yes, I stole the title from my high school English teacher's favorite Manley Hopkins poem: "Margaret are you grieving / Over Goldengrove unleaving"—crashed with a seismic boom. Never mind that the story was fucking genius: it was Genesis in reverse, an epic journey from the American heartland to a new Eden. Our young, innocent couple, Aden and Ella, journey across the country—after Aden's father dances naked, Noah-like, in front of Ella—looking for a perfect world, a world without sin and booze, for themselves and their children. And when after many trials and tribulations they finally arrive at the most luscious spot on earth, they are naked, worn and heartbroken, their kids dead or missing. They are filthy and starving, and an apple falls to the ground. And Ella, famished, picks it up, bites into it, and starts jumping up and down in sudden elation, as if she's just tasted the most marvelous fruit. How Aden must try it! Must taste it. It's a sudden high. Then she's choking, and Aden rushes to her, but there is nothing he can do. She is gone.

Sounds pretty depressing, huh? But I loved this story. I loved the crew. I loved the two leads. Is it my fault that they fell in love? They might as well put that in the contract, Rider 10a, to wit: "Male and female leads will engage in intimate relations within the first seven days of shooting, or shall receive a $7,500 payment in lieu of consummation." And is it my fault that, six months into the shoot, Missy Atkins, our gorgeous star, announces she's 12 weeks pregnant and is going to keep the divine gift? I should have folded the film right then, but instead I cracked open another bottle of bourbon and said, okay, we can change the shooting schedule, maybe do the finale sooner rather than later. But then at five months she has to go on bed rest and we are shooting on the other side of the world in Australia and both my principals are locked up listening to the steady pings of a fetal monitor. And still I didn't cut the cord. No, I was in too deep now. And I figured I had plenty of filming to do with the brothers—Charles and Arthur, my Cain and Abel knock-offs. Insurance covered some to the delays, but once the eight-month policy ran out, the studio had to back me or shut me down. We were already $100 million in. Too much to write off, so they backed me.

For the finale of *Goldengrove*, we are on location in paradise: in the Seychelles, surrounded by coco du mer trees and their fruit, which is basically a brown coconut shaped like a woman's hips, pudenda and all, the sexiest fruit in the world. Missy Atkins is back with us, as are three imported nannies that I'm paying for, and we are almost done. There are just two weeks of shooting left when then the most ass-kicking tropical storm—a biblical storm, really—hits. And when it's over, the island is devastated. Dozens are dead, houses are gone, the power is out, scores of the marvelous trees are down.

At this point, I finally sobered up and flew a skeleton crew to Hawaii, which was, according to Missy Atkins, "just like the Seychelles, but with drugstores and hospitals around." But those hospitals didn't help much when a helicopter doing aerial shots crashed and we lost the pilot and the cameraman. The film got two wrongful death suits. But at least we were done with the shooting.

I went into the editing room with four other editors. Editing is so easy now, there's no threading, no rewinding, no splicing, no fuss; digitization lets you move the pieces around at the click of a mouse. Back then it was a Herculean task. We were yoked to those massive Steenbeck editing machines for six long months. I had ordered multiple takes, I had asked for improvisation and changes to the script. It all makes sense to me now, in the crystal-clear Technicolor glory of 20-20 hindsight: I was a crappy nervous director, enveloped in a cloud of alcohol fumes, consumed by the pressure of proving that *Evergreen* and my Oscar were no flukes. What drove me killed me.

Now what still gets me about *Goldengrove* is not that excess destroyed it. I knew what I wanted to do. I had a great story. But because it was long and grandiose and a downer without a chance at redemption—the movie ends with Aden weeping alone in his Eden over the lifeless body of his beautiful wife, and heaven is turned to hell as man learns there's no going back to the garden—all the good stuff is ignored, and all anyone remembers is that the movie is too long, too bleak, and took down a studio. Sure it's long, but so is *Gone with the Wind*. So is *Lawrence of Arabia*. Those are considered classics, but my film is called pretentious and bloated. Give me a break.

I'm sure this sounds like a mound of the sourest poisoned grapes imaginable. It sure as hell is. And it's what's motivated me ever since.

I refused to die after *Goldengrove*. I retreated. I downsized. I got divorced. I reversed.

I went back to what I knew I knew best: low-budget comedy. That's what I had done before. But finding backing for adult comedy was pretty damn rough. I was damaged goods. Finally, an acquaintance threw me a bone and let me handle a straight to cable and video skateboarder movie, *Xtreme Dream*. Sort of *Breakfast Club*-meets-*Meatballs*-meets-*X-Games* with tons of product placement deals for energy drinks, clothes, and skateboard gear, and a TV premiere on ESPN.

It was horrible, but it paid the bills, and more importantly, it was instructive. It reminded me to focus on teen-targeted, family-friendly movies. Children are this magical crop. Every year a new slew comes in. The annual mutation of 10 million toddlers into kids, and 12-year-olds into teenagers: Pure magic. And that's just in the U.S.

I ordered up another movie for the junior league: a rip-off of "The Ransom of Red Chief" called *Lil' Kobi's Ransom*. It opened against an action-hero blockbuster, *The Mutationists*, and managed to pull in $70 million during the summer of 2006. I didn't pocket much of that change, unfortunately. I was still a marked man, so I'd had to take a tiny percentage on the deal.

But then, thinking globally and acting locally, I dreamed up a demographically perfect comedy, *The Diplo Dynamite*

Six. Six kids—an American boy, a German girl, an Indian boy, a South African girl, a Chinese boy, and a Brazilian girl—get chosen for diplomatic camp at the U.N. They fight, have crushes, insult each other, and are taken hostage. They annoy their captors with incessant complaining and teenage behavior, but they learn to work together to escape and foil a terrorist plot to blow up the U.N.

This cheapo film rocked the box office. It took in $180 million worldwide, and I made some coinage this time, although not nearly as much as a creator, co-writer, and packager should have.

I didn't care; what really mattered was that Mr. Damaged Goods had miraculously become Hollywood's preferred family entertainment guy. When the networks started calling, trolling for pilots—they wanted to turn *The Diplo Dynamite Six* into a series—I listened politely. I had no interest in TV, really; I'd come to Hollywood to make movies. The problem was that whenever I mentioned movies for grownups, my suitors would smile benignly and start telling me how much they loved my kid stuff. It pissed me off, and that's when this strange idea hit me.

When people ask me about the genesis of *The King of Pain*, I usually say it is a product of the times. And that is true. But I really owe the idea to my two bowling buddies, Lars Gooding and Frank Bellamy, who are also among my oldest friends. I know them from my days of "bringing the party to the party."

Lars, who teaches poetry at L.A. Community College, is a bowling devotee who extols the spirituality of the sport.

He's not some Lebowski clone; he is the original. "Bowling is a meditative quest. It is the search for perfection. You do is the same thing over and over again in search of the perfect result. It's Zen."

Frank also has nothing to do with Tinseltown. He is a headhunter. When Lars starts rambling about the quest for perfection, Frank just shrugs. "I'm shallow," he says. "I just like it: the sound of the ball hitting the pins, the beer, the clown shoes."

Lars was the one who, after a horrible game filled with unmakeable 4-9 splits, missed pairs, and teetering pins that would not fall, says, "This game was the perfect manifestation of the zeitgeist."

"English, please," says Frank.

"That game was torturous! And torture is everywhere in the U.S.A."

"No torture for me," says Frank, who has bowled a 187. "I was knockin' 'em down, and my bonus came in this week."

"Come on, Frank," I say. "It's everywhere but your friggin' bank account. You must have seen those prison shots—what were those guards thinking?"

"Abu Ghraib, Bush, Cheney, CIA, torture memos, TV shows," Lars rambles on as if he's at a fucking poetry slam.

"TV shows?"

"Reality TV is about torture," says Lars.

"I thought it was about singing," says Frank.

"That's *American Idol*," I say.

"All those other shows—*Survivor, The Great Race, Fear Factor, Biggest Loser*—they're all about suffering, sadism, and voyeurism," adds Lars.

"Oh, come on, Lars," says Frank. "You're over-thinking this a little, egghead."

"I'm not. This is sanitized spectator sport. Don't forget, death and torture were family entertainment in the Middle Ages, and the Colosseum used to be filled with people coming to see the lions eat Christians and gladiators hacking each others' limbs off."

"Interesting," I say. "Marta loves those shows. We should all watch."

"Really?" says Frank. "In Saltervision?"

"You bet." I used to love it when my friends got excited about my home entertainment system. How ironic is that?

So they came over for dinner. And so did Marta's pal Ines, a zaftig housekeeper from the neighborhood. We ordered in and watched *Castaways, Season 2*.

Not only can Marta throw a party for 100 people with three hours' notice and get red wine stains out of my Brooks Brothers dress shirts, she's also a reality show expert. Not that the rules are very complicated: challenges, judges, councils, text votes, participant votes. She and Ines had their own scoring method. They gave points for looks and teamwork. If you helped others and were well groomed in the face of adversity, you earned their respect, admiration, and cheers. Contestants who were cutthroat, had poor hygiene or no sense of style were not worthy of their support. Of course, for two women who were castaways themselves—smuggled into the country, let loose in the sprawling jungle of L.A. without papers, a car, or cash—all of this makes sense. They have style, these women. It might not be Martha Stewart-approved, but the clothes are neat, the makeup is perfect in its way. They take pride in the things they can control.

Their take on reality TV comes as a shock to Lars.

"So you watch to cheer the people you like?" he says. "You're looking for heroes?"

"Yes," says Ines.

"What about the suffering?"

"What do you mean?"

"Don't you like watching to see how hard it is? How much they hurt?"

"I guess a little. But we just like it."

"That's en-ter-tain-ment!" croons Frank.

Lars mutters something about torture operating on a subliminal level.

We are watching a fast-talking, chiseled contractor on *Heartland Heroes* now. You can tell he is going to win this thing, even if he has to caulk his rivals' eyes closed, but Marta despises him. "He is no caballero."

"Marta," I say, "Who is your caballero? Where is he? What are you doing with us old guys?"

"Mister Rick, you know the story. I only think I meet a gentleman. I haven't seen him never for 20 years."

"And the boys?"

"The same."

Lars says: "How about you, Ines?"

"Men? Don't get me started."

"At least she don't have kids," says Marta.

"I still got kids. Your kids, my sister's kids."

"We should do a single moms reality show."

"No, Mr. Rick." Marta smiles: "Single dads. Like you, remember?"

I slap my head and laugh. "Marta was part of my divorce agreement. She had to be working in order for Jared to come stay with me. I was a disaster."

"It's okay. You were doing big things," says Marta.

"What's bigger than raising a kid?" asks Frank.

"Ouch," I say. "I was not to be trusted. The brief that was filed said that even if a kid came with a user's manual, I still wouldn't know what to do."

"Naturally, you had no defense."

"Nolo contendere."

Ines turns to Marta: "They funny."

I went to work thinking about reality shows. Over the next couple of weeks, I watched every single one I could find: *Fear Factor, 1882, Desert Dwellers, Homesteaders, The Bachelor, The Bachelorette, Love Quest*. When we bowled the next time, Frank said, "Lars, torture was in the zeitgeist again today. Waterboarding. You were right. It's everywhere."

"Yeah, it's mind-numbing, isn't it?"

"You mean the debate about whether or not strapping a man to a board and submerging him under water so he feels like he's drowning is torture?"

"Yeah, where's the debate in that? Of course it's torture."

"I don't want to be cynical, guys," I said, "But I bet we could float a show on this."

"Waterboarding?"

"No, not exactly. Torture. Endurance. Pain."

"Isn't that *Survivor*?"

"Nah. Not exactly. I'm thinking something a little more individualistic. There's a group dynamic at play in *Survivor*.

And there's this political factor to it with all these alliances. I'm thinking that—oh, never mind. Let's bowl."

But I could not stop thinking about it. And the next morning I set up a meeting with Walter Fields to pitch *The King of Pain*, the greatest reality TV show of all time.

I knew it was going to be big, the hit I needed to make people forget about *Goldengrove* and rekindle my career so I could get the movies I wanted to make off the ground.

I just never expected the damn show to put me flat on my back and kill me.

I'm no hero. The thought of death frightens me. I pick up the book again. I need to distract myself, and I need to figure out what the hell Amanda thinks is in here for me.

THE GIFT

When Yi Huiqing arrived at the prison, she smiled and bowed to her new cellmates—a dirty, skinny, forlorn bunch—took in the dark, horrible, concrete room that was to be her new home for the next two years, noted the small piles of clothes under the room's three bunk beds and the wrinkled magazine pages that had been stuck to the wall, and remembered her father's words: In prison, you must lose the desire to desire. Unfulfilled desire only causes more pain.

It sounded like one of the Noble Truths. But she was not familiar enough with Buddhism to be certain. Perhaps it was just her father being her father.

She learned the pecking order of the cell quickly. Wu Sui was the undisputed queen. Her husband worked a good job nearby on the outside. Consequently, he brought her money, so she had the means to make trades with the guards. She had the top bunk by the window in the summer, and the top bunk by the western wall in the winter. She was serving four years for vehicular homicide.

The rest of the cell was made up of four women, three of whom were old enough to be Huiqing's mother. A woman with long hair and a very creased face, Wang Ma, had broken the single-child rule three times. Sun Li, who sold medicine and charms, had accidentally poisoned a couple that was try-ing to get pregnant. The woman died. Zhou Fan was in for thievery. She had robbed a number of restaurants. And finally the bottom of the rung was a mute young woman they called Wuming, or Noname, who smiled a lot.

"She is a street girl," explained Sui. "She steals food, clothes, everything. She steals to live."

"How did you find out if she can't speak?"

"A guard brought me her file."

"Oh!"

"But I prefer not to pay for information about my cellmates."

It took a moment for Huiqing to realize that Sui was fishing for her story. Then she said: "Me? I'm here for crimes against the interest of the state."

"You a spy?"

"I wrote an essay that was posted on the Internet. Someone complained."

"So you are a writer!"

"Oh, no. A teacher."

The prison was a work camp, although camp is not really the right word. Work factory was more like it. Hundreds of women sat in a huge tin-roofed bunker attaching things. It was simple, unskilled, mind-numbing labor. Heels to shoes, labels to cans, lids to boxes. Whatever the guards brought, they attached. They used tape, and paste that they would nibble on, and glue that they sniffed. They folded papers, they stuffed boxes. It was boring work. For no pay. I am worse than a prisoner, thought Huiqing. I'm a slave.

At times she would think about her father and his advice about trying not to desire anything. It was futile. Huiqing desired simple things: A cup of tea. Sunshine. A walk, seeing children, sleeping late. An extra blanket. But she did not expect them. Desire was not the problem. It was a question of degrees, of intensity. It was the needing and the yearning that hurt.

One day, after she had been in prison for six months, a big package arrived. A guard brought it to her cell. "We X-rayed it," said the guard with a laugh. "No guns, sorry."

Huiqing studied the package. It was addressed to Yi, Lonjian Work Prison, Shaan Province 122598. She did not recognize the handwriting or the return address, which had no name attached. It was postmarked from Xianpan, and she did not know a single person from that part of the country.

"Ooh, a gift. Open it," said Ma. "What are you waiting for?"

"I am…shy," Huiqing said. But in reality she was unsure whether she should open it.

"We all use the same night pail, Huiqing. No secrets here!" laughed Li.

"Who is it from?" asked Ma.

"I don't know. I don't recognize the return address."

"Open it!" commanded Sui.

Huiqing knelt down and began to undo the twine. With her thumbnail she cracked the tape that held the newspaper wrapping together. She unwrapped the newspaper carefully so she would have something to read later. Then she opened the flap of the cardboard box.

"I hope they sent food."

"Probably books for the teacher," said Sui.

The first thing out of the box was white cotton fabric.

"Oh my," Huiqing said.

It was a shirt.

A man's shirt.

A huge man's shirt.

"Did you lose weight?" cackled Ma.

Wuming came over and rubbed a sleeve against her face.

Huiqing folded it up and looked back in the box. She lifted out a bottle. There was English writing on the label, a single word on the label: "HIM!"

"This is not my package," said Huiqing. "There must be a mistake."

"What is in the bottle?"

"Cologne," said Huiqing. "Perfume for men."

Everyone laughed. Next, Huiqing pulled out a ball of white cotton. As she smoothed out the ball, her face turned red.

"Three pairs of underwear!"

Sui grabbed a pair. "Let me see."

She held it to her nose, closed her eyes and inhaled as if the underwear was a drug.

"Sui is dreaming!" laughed Ma.

The younger woman opened her eyes. She threw the underwear at Ma. "At least I'm young enough to dream!"

"Ooh! Food," said Li, watching the next offering from the box.

"Bean cakes!"

Wuming grabbed at the tin. Huiqing slapped her hand away.

"Is there a men's prison here?" asked Huiqing.

"Yes," said Li. "Beyond Eastern House. I know a doctor there who sold opium."

"There must be a man there with my last name, Yi. This is his package."

"Too bad for him. This is a gift!"

"What will I do with this stuff? With cologne?"

"Trade it with the guards! Tell them it is sexy sauce. Don't be stupid."

And that is what she did. They all ate the bean cakes and a package of dried dates. Huiqing traded the underwear, cologne, and a pair of enormous slippers for a notebook and two pens. The large shirt was cut into strips for the women to use each month. They gave their worn, faded red rags to the women in the next cell.

When work was over, Huiqing would sit in the yard to catch the fading light and write to her father or her friends. She wrote about feeling like a drone. About how she repeated her father's advice as if it were a prayer. But still it felt wrong to her, like the opposite of life. She was not a greedy person; she did not want to live like an emperor or a billionaire. What was the harm in thinking about food, warmth, or movies? Desires like these were at the heart of survival.

One evening, an older woman interrupted her writing. "Excuse me, young daughter. Would you write a letter for me?"

The woman had grey streaks in her hair. But her eyes looked young to Huiqing. Or if not young, then at least lively. Huiqing thought it might be interesting to write a letter for someone else and said, "Of course. I will be happy to meet you here tomorrow after work."

The woman's name was Changchang. And the first letter was not all that interesting. Huiqing hoped to learn about the woman and about her family. But firm information was slow in coming. Grand Uncle was coming for a visit and Changchang wanted to tell her daughter that Grand Uncle's favorite food was snake soup. The letter was mostly a recipe, but it contained a question about someone named Mielu: when was her school graduation? Who was Mielu, Huiqing wondered. A granddaughter? And what was she graduating from? But by the time Huiqing finished writing—ending with a very formal "From Your Mother"—these questions were not answered.

Changchang, who could not read, was very pleased with the look of the letter and asked if it would not be too much trouble for Huiqing to write for her once a week. Huiqing said she would look forward to it. And it was true, each letter revealed more and more about Changchang. About her daughter, about her stepson who only talked to his stepsister (her daughter), because he felt Changchang, like a storybook stepmother, had brought disgrace on him. Huiqing got the sense that Changchang missed this boy very much, as if he were her own son.

It was like a great, unfolding mystery. And even though Sui called her a fool for not charging money, Huiqing liked writing the letters.

❧

Three months after the gift had been mistakenly delivered, the guard who brought it to the cell stopped by.

"Huiqing, do you remember the package I delivered some months ago? Was it meant for you?"

Huiqing was instantly nervous. She felt fear and desire creeping up her chest, entwined the way ivy vines climb a wall. The desire was to be able to go back in time. To not write on the Internet. To never open a package that wasn't hers. To not be worried or fear being punished.

"It had my name on it," Huiqing said.

"Yes, but only your last name."

"Yes. That is true."

"I am told it was meant for a male prisoner."

"Oh, my goodness. I am so embarrassed."

"You must have known. He is a very fat man, this prisoner."

"I thought maybe someone was playing a cruel joke on me. Maybe teaching me a lesson."

"What kind of lesson?"

"Not to expect anything. No miracles."

"Well this could turn into a difficult lesson, too."

"What do you mean? What will happen? I thought this was a practical joke from my cousin."

The guard sighed. "I don't know. Maybe I will get a mark on my review. I hope that is all."

◈

But that was wishful thinking. A few days later, Huiqing was informed of a hearing. Now the gift had turned into a curse. She had tried to follow her father's advice. She should have trusted her instincts to return the package. But her cellmates… It had been too hard.

Huiqing fell into despair. She had one more year on her sentence to serve and she did not want anything to prolong it. There was that word again: Want. Desire. Well, it was true. She had desire because she could not tell herself that one place is no different from another. One moment is the same as the next. It wasn't true.

"Will you tell them that we urged you to keep it?" Sui asked.

"No. I will tell them it was a mistake. An honest mistake."

"But there were men's clothes."

"I thought my frugal father was sending me fabric," Huiqing practiced her lie.

"But the perfume…"

"He has no taste."

"They will never believe you."

That evening after her shift, Huiqing started to write to her father about "The Gift," about the investigation and the hearing. "My brain is smaller than the gnats that follow me," she wrote.

As she finished, Changchang approached. "I'm sorry I'm late," she said.

Huiqing looked at the sky to judge the time. "Quickly," she said, going to a fresh page in her notebook.

A guard by the door called out to the yard stragglers: "Five minutes!"

They started on the letter. Changchang reminded her daughter that it was the anniversary of her father's death, the event that in many ways had led to Changchang's imprisonment. And just when Huiqing thought she would learn some crucial information, the two women were interrupted by a low rumble, and the stone they were sitting on began to move from side to side, as if a wild animal had just woken up inside it. The wall at their back began to shake. They stood up quickly and stepped on the rock, trying to stop its spasms.

"Earthquake!" shouted Changchang.

The rumble turned into a loud crash punctuated by screams and shouts as the prison—all three stories of it—collapsed. For Huiqing, the collapse occurred in a sort of slow motion, a sensation that comes when you witness an action that you can do nothing about. She saw it all: The walls caving in, the roof folding into the third floor, crashing through the second, then pancaking the first, and settling into a huge, dusty mass of broken cinderblock, beds, bars, and bodies.

There were screams. Huiqing and Changchang added to them. Within seconds, flames rose out of the rubble. The tin roof of the work camp factory came clanging down.

Then, as suddenly as it started, the earth stopped moving. The screams and cries for help continued, but the feeling of insanity and powerlessness that comes with an earthquake was over. Although everything was still, Huiqing's mind was racing. Before her, part of the stone prison wall was broken and crumbling. There was a gap offering a way out, an escape. Behind her were death and chaos. If she stayed here, prisoners would be the last to get help, food, and water. If she fled, what would she do? Where would she go? And if she were caught, how much time would be added to her sentence?

She sat down on the rock and buried her head in her hands. She could hear screams, yelling, calls for help, ambulance and fire engine sirens, car alarms throbbing. It was pandemonium, the sounds of hell.

"Here," said Changchang, ripping her letter out of Huiqing's notebook. "I don't need this now."

She stroked Huiqing's hair. "My daughter lives not too far from here. Maybe 30 miles. Let us go. If her house is there, we can stay with her. If not, we will be like everyone else: people who have lost their lives. We will get new ones."

Huiqing remembered the gift and the upcoming hearing. Would that even happen now? It was impossible to know. She wondered about taking other people's advice. But this was different.

"Yes, Changchang, that is very kind of you. But—" she looked back at the prison.

"They will think we are dead," Changchang said. "Isn't that funny? We will be more alive than ever!"

Huiqing rose up. Surrounded by rubble, noise, and uncertainty, she felt completely overwhelmed. Then she thought of her father's words—unfulfilled desire only causes more pain—and she knew what to do.

"Yes," she said, answering Changchang. "It is funny. Although I'm not sure funny is the right word."

Then she took the older woman's arm and together they stepped over the rubble and into a wail of sirens.

FOUR

Holy hand of god! That just swooped in there, didn't it? Although in China—if that's where this story takes place—they do seem to manufacture earthquakes with the same efficiency that they crank out electronics components.

Come to think of it, that story reminds me of a Bible outtake. I can't remember which Testament—probably the New—but I could swear there was a tale about God rumbling a tectonic plate and destroying the prison and unshackling the inmates. Not that I can bust anyone for stealing a story. Shakespeare did it, and so did yours truly. Half of my movies were inspired by books or plays or other movies. So I can't blame this guy for lifting from the Bible. Besides, everybody knows that writers and storytellers are liars and thieves. Or should I say embellishers, elucidators, and rebuilders?

I sure could do with a hand of God right now to get me out of here before I go nuts or die or both. I guess this book is a gift of sorts—not just a gift from Amanda—but a true godsend for a guy who literally can't move a fucking centimeter: a distraction and a reminder that things could be worse. A lot worse. Is that what Amanda was saying? By the end, I'll be.... Thankful? Like, thankful that I'm not in some godforsaken prison? Okay, I'm thankful, because Christ, I don't want to be in a third world prison. God help me. Not a first world prison, either, come to think of it. Although

I imagine some European prisons might be civilized. A Swedish prison, say. I bet it's all done up in blonde furniture with cell designs named KORNNASKE or GRUUDEN. In Swedish prisons I have this vision of a lovely blonde nurse knocking on the doors with a tray of Viagra exactly one hour before a conjugal visit commences. Now, how's that for a prison story?

Anyway, a lot to think about here—although I'm still not getting how this book is going to transform me at the end, if that's what Amanda meant. It's not like it's the Bible. I'm not getting the Word here. At least not yet.

In TV, you actually do need writers, but you also need a couple of other things to succeed: An idea, some pretty and charismatic people, luck, and a huge amount of marketing power behind you. You also need a good first show, although continuous marketing can obviate that need. But I am a believer in a strong pilot, not a "we'll work it out as we go" strategy. That said, I'm the first guy to tell the network that they can't all be masterpieces, because they just can't. Even the Beatles wrote some lousy tunes, and if you don't believe me, listen to the *White Album.*

With *The King of Pain*, things go extremely well from the very beginning. The pitch meeting with Walter Fields takes 20 minutes. Boom, we have a deal for 12 episodes. Not that it was all cake.

"Tell me the name again?" Walter asks for the third time.

"*The King of Pain.*"

"Does *King of Pain* exclude women?" he wants to know again.

"Nah. We write the rules."

"So a woman can be the king?"

"Sure. I told you, it's our show. We can do whatever we want."

"Hmm."

"Walter, this is going to be huge. The 18-35 market is going to go nuts for this."

"Will you be able to find women contestants?"

"Walter, it's the 21st century. Come on."

"Really? Women? For this kind of show?"

"Walter, you jerkoff, women have a good chance of winning this thing. They give birth, they bleed every frickin' month. They starve themselves."

"I mean this is tougher than *Survivor*."

"Walter, my first wife, Laila, used to throw around a quote. I don't know who said it first, but it went something like, 'If men menstruated, there would floating federal holidays for them."

"No way. I don't see it."

When Amanda comes up with holding auditions at boot camp, I know we're in the zone. We assemble our team of judges: a hot, hunky English psychiatrist named Dr. Burns ("My name is Burns, James Burns," he quips for the camera), a boffo ex-marine turned trainer named Mayhew, and the editrix of *Fetish World*, a leggy leather-clad Asian babe, Ms. Mary Lamb, who purrs about being "as pure as Beijing air."

As a team of sadistic superheroes, they are perfect: they're funny, acerbic, damning, telegenic, and charming.

Months later, one critic will describe them as playing bad cop, worse cop, worst cop during the weekly contestant evaluations.

Thousands of applicants line up outside our barbed wire fence, most clutching portfolios with DVDs, head-shots, resumes. We need these along with their applications because it's not like we are going to put them on a rack and see how much torque they can take. The casting call is for future contestants to show up with head-shots, a resume of past pain exposure and endurance, and videos of themselves at their toughest. So we see guys doing 100 fingertip push-ups, running marathons, spending an hour in the sauna while lifting weights. That's the G-rated stuff. Then there are the freaks getting whipped, tied up, humiliated. One guy has his johnson tattooed. Every inch of it. In front of a running camera.

The network standards VP is getting just a little bit worried. Photographers snap pictures of this freak parade—the hopefuls wrapped in chains, inching their way up the line because that is the tiny distance their imprisoned feet can move. There are the human billboards with face piercings—I'm talking wall-to-wall tattoos plus the metal: ears, nose, lip, tongue, cheek, chin. Yikes. Pain I can understand, but self-mutilation I don't get. "Amanda," I say, "Let's remember not to give the face piercers too much air time."

"Really? But I think people will get that kind of pain."

"It's disgusting."

"Rick, did you think this through at all? It's going to get a lot more disgusting than this. And we have to communicate that to the viewers."

"Good point," I admit, and then change the subject. "That reminds me, let's work on the most over-the-top viewer discretion warning ever and see how it tests for 18-35."

"Will do."

The first day ends with about 20 West Coast hopefuls. We meet with the screening team to discuss issues and swap stories.

"I should have listened to my mother," mocks one application processor. "She always told me to become a tattoo artist."

"There's gold in that ink," says his friend.

"I had a nun who wanted to audition. Can you believe that?" says a voice in the crowd.

"STOP!" I yell. The room goes quiet. "Who had the nun?"

"Me, sir." It's a young, preppy kid, a little on the short side. I've never seen him before.

"You had a nun apply? Where is she?"

"I don't know."

"You don't know?"

"She didn't have a video. She didn't have any pain expertise or history, except fasting."

"Are you kidding me? You had a nun and you didn't pass her forward?"

"She said her main qualification was love."

"And what is your main qualification?"

"Rick," Amanda cuts in.

"This kid just passed on the Beatles, Seinfeld, Johnny Depp, and Mother Theresa rolled into one."

"Go get your applications," she says to the kid. "Let's find her."

"Wait!" I say. "Tell me, was she young or old?"

"Youngish. Maybe 30."

"Oh my god. Any mustache?"

"No."

"You're sure she was the real deal?"

"Rick," says Amanda. "Would you please remember your New Year's resolution?"

Which is easy because it's been the same for the last 15 years: be a nicer person. And you know what? Every year I am a little bit nicer. I haven't screamed in this kid's face. Or fired him on the spot. Or insulted his mother. Or faked a heart attack to make him feel bad. Still, Amanda's reminder comes just in time.

"You're right," I say. "Kid, what's done is done. And maybe we weren't clear on what we were looking for. I mean, I'm sure nobody said, 'If you see a nun, notify the Treasury to print more dollars because we're going to make a fucking mint,' but when someone unique comes by, someone who might be a great story, ask a second opinion. Okay? In Hollywood, no one breathes without a second opinion unless they have tons of money or true vision or are totally fucking delusional. Got it?"

"Yes, sir."

"Now go find Sister Goldmine's application and Amanda will track her down." I turn to everyone else. "Any other good stories I should know about?"

"A Mexican Ultimate Fighter who walked across the desert. He's the only one who survived."

"A gay marathoner."

"Former terrorist. Says he was in Guantánamo, but I think he was nuts."

"Okay, that sounds good. Let's do one more round tomorrow and start on callbacks."

Later that night, Amanda calls. They've found the nun's application.

"What's her number? I'll call her myself and apologize."

"She didn't leave a number. I'm not sure nuns have cell phones."

"Jesus."

"That's not going to win her over. Look, she left an address. At a convent. I'll go tomorrow."

"Bring a camera crew."

"You know something, Rick?"

"What?"

"Jesus." Then she hangs up.

True to form, Amanda finds the nun, Sister Rosemarie, and we bring her in for an interview. She is perfect, a dream underdog. A look that is somewhere between pretty and plain—black hair, brown eyes, and a prominent nose that leaps out just a little too much. The judges give her a hard time for her lack of experience, and she tells them she is entering to demonstrate the power of God and the strength and power of faith. Watching the tape, I find myself rooting for her, and I'm practically a heretic. We also tape the ultimate fighter, an S&M call-boy—just because that's what everyone is going to expect—a couple of endurance guys and two surfers with awesome tans and frightening wipe-out footage, plus a free-style rock climber with before and after clips from a near fatal slip in Yosemite. And finally a French kid who's a *domestique* on the Tour de France and sounds like Inspector Clouseau's cousin, which could make for some light-hearted moments.

Before we close up shop to repeat the drill in Nashville and New York, I call in the young kid who almost missed the nun. "Kid," I say. "I apologize for my behavior yesterday."

"No problem, sir. It was a learning experience."

"That's a great attitude," I say, making sure Amanda can hear me. "Listen, if you hadn't said anything yesterday, we would have lost her forever."

"I guess so."

"You're damn right you guess so. How'd you like to come with us on the other stops?"

"Are you kidding, sir?"

"I'm serious as five points on the front end. Amanda, sign him up. What's your name?"

"Rick, sir. Rick Perez."

"Really? That's great. Except I'm Rick."

He looks at me to see if I'm kidding, but I'm not.

"You are now Little Ricky."

When it comes to making the final selections, I work a lot with our judges, but even more with Amanda. She is a great student of reality TV and knew instantly that when it comes to voyeur vision, *The King of Pain* was going to be the ultimate, especially in the key demographics—which is basically everyone from 18-35, plus 25-49. How can you have two overlapping segments? I'm not smart enough to understand. She also pushed for a great DVD deal, downplaying the advance in favor of the back end. With so many comical and nauseating outtakes from the auditions—guys burning themselves, girls cutting themselves, bondage, studs, spikes, dungeons, chains, vises, cages, ropes, ships, cat-o'-nine-tails—she knew the sales would be there. Anyway, whittling down the list of possible contestants was a tough call, but here, as you know, is who we end up with:

1. Sgt. Lenny St. James. If I have to pick a favorite to win, it's this lean, not-so-mean fighting machine from Special Forces. Born in Detroit. Father dead, mother in prison, raised by granny. Served in Iraq and Afghanistan. We have a lot of applicants from the armed forces, but Sgt. Lenny is the best-looking. Think Harry Bellafonte meets Shaq. A total beast.

2. Annabel Castro, the polar opposite of Sgt. St. James. Fans dub her the Castrator, a lesbian, tattooed former drug dealer and prostitute with mug shots to prove it. She gets her life on track when she replaces one addiction with another and pledges her heart to fitness. With two third-place fin-ishes in Iron Man competitions, she's hardcore.

3. Jeremiah Lovell. God, I hate this guy at first. I admit it: I think he's too old and too ugly. Who wants to watch a skinny 50-year-old hippie who drinks his own urine and runs 100-mile ultra-marathons while chanting prayers and koans? But Amanda is right, his holier-than-thou anti-pop culture attitude makes for great TV. He can't stand the other contestants, and they can't stand him.

4. Darcy Minett. When we cast Darcy, I turn to Aman-da and say: "If we can get her in a room with Jeremiah and Castro, they will kill each other." Darcy is a former prima

ballerina. She is rail thin, girly, rich, and spoiled. Everything Annabel Castro isn't. And everything Jeremiah isn't.

5. Derek Snead. Former offensive lineman of the Green Bay Packers by way of Nebraska by way of a farm in god-knows-where. Another potential fan favorite. Sure, he's huge, but when it comes to pain—two-a-day drills, farming, playing in minus zero degrees—he's a natural. These football guys have to play hurt all the time or risk being replaced. Plus, his family died in a tornado, and he's trying to come back from a torn ACL. I hope he goes a long way into the season.

6. Sister Rosemarie Aria. You already know about her. If I was a betting man, I would make her the fan favorite. Sure, she'll turn some people off with her lines to the judges about how the pain we might feel in competition is nothing compared to the pain Christ felt on the Cross. But she's the ultimate underdog. She may be a dynamo in the competition. Or she may crumble. Either way, I feel blessed to have her on board.

7. Adonis Troy. I know. He deserves to lose for his name alone. It sounds like a porn star wrestler, doesn't it? And of all the wackos, he is the one who deserves the freakazoid crown. He's our professional masochist. My first impression is that he's something of a ringer in this competition. I mean the guy sells videos of himself getting whipped. What a frigging nut job. But we discuss this internally and decide that while being whipped or having melted wax poured onto your nipples is torture, it's not what we're going to do on *The King of Pain*. And anyway, he's such a friggin' diva, I don't think he'll last.

8. Sanchez. Because every reality show needs a guy with a single name, like Prince, or Madonna. Sanchez fits the bill and more. He's the Mexican kid who walked across the desert with 10 teenaged compadres and the only one to make it through alive. He joins a gang, then gets saved by a minister/manager who channels his massive violent streak into focused acts of aggression against willing but foolish partners that propel him to a national ranking in some Ultimate Fighting division. My question during the vetting: Is he legal? I'm the producer, I don't want my star deported mid-season. Thankfully his handlers got him a visa. Anyway, after Rosemarie the Nun, Sanchez is my favorite. Pain? It isn't just taking a punch—this kid left his mami y papi to join his pals in a death march across the desert. "We buried the first two, but after that we were too tired. We left them to the vultures and buzzards, God forgive me." We use his quote in the pilot, and I swear you could hear the sound of 30 million girls texting each other about how Sanchez is muy hot.

So we have a nun, a military man, a Mexican hunk, a Cuban dyke, a ballerina Jap, a swami, an S&M deviant, and a football player. Eight people. But we have a guarantee of 12 shows with an option for three more. So we need 10 contestants, minimum. I ask Amanda what demo we are missing in our little circus of freaks.

"Me," she says.

I look at her as if she's lost her mind.

"I mean someone normal. An office worker. The guy in the next cubicle. A white-collar guy. Someone who isn't into pain but knows a different kind of pain."

"Like in a waitress?"

"Exactly."

"Or an administrative assistant?"

"See? Me."

"Amanda," I sigh, "you are a lot more than an admin. You are my soul by proxy."

"Thanks. I think."

But I digress:

9. Kaylene Aplee. 26, waitress, single mother of two. Lots of pain there, living in a trailer with her mom. Husband in jail for murdering his mistress. I know you think I'm making this up. But we actually recruited her. Amanda had a friend in Nashville at *The Tennessean*, and we asked him to keep an eye out for an attractive struggling young woman, and he sent us Kaylene. She was a no-brainer. Plus, she's blonde. She may not win, but she's the most likely to get a new career.

Number 10? I wanted a stockbroker or a retailer, but Amanda, my resident genius (if only she were 10 years older), found us a real white-collar sufferer: A call center customer service manager. Good God! It never occurred to me how much these people suffer. All they do is turn the other cheek, accommodate, and take abuse. Half their day is filled with ranting customers, pissed-off customers, and conniving customers looking to get something for nothing. And your CSR—that's customer service representative—has to be the public face of the company, working politely to smooth things over. Can we give all CSRs a prize, please? They do this with the cloud of cheap foreign labor looming over their head. So when Amanda found David Marks, night CS manager for a major online auto supply company, I was blown away. He wore a tie, he was balding, he was divorced. He biked and played bingo to relieve stress. He was Everyviewer. Or their dad or uncle. He was perfect. And we were ready to roll.

GREAT ESCAPES

The first day the Translator went on strike, he received three death threats while standing in line for dinner.

"Sweetheart, if I don't get my stories this week, I will kill you dead. I will claw your eyeballs out with my fingernails," warned one jailhouse queen, Phoenecia, holding up the stilettos sprouting from his fingertips.

"You want a porcelain suicide, Translator?" asked a hirsute gentleman known as the Wrestler, alluding to the occasional discovery of prisoners found drowned in the toilet.

The third threat was unspoken. But it came through loud and clear, courtesy of Anthony "Little Giant" Tomaso. He simply held his forefinger to his throat and quickly pulled it across his windpipe.

The Translator didn't give a damn. Nobody else in the entire prison could understand crazy Ari the Greek. He knew they needed him to translate the stories. Without the Translator, the Greek's tales were worthless gibberish.

The thing was, their relationship needed to change. The Translator was tired of cleaning up after the Greek, translating his madness, reminding him of the different story lines, handling the continuity, reshaping Ari's lousy vocabulary and adding extra color and detail. It was just as bad translating for his goddamn fans. They constantly approached the Translator and asked him to relay requests and suggestions for life on the wonderful and terrible island of Azbos. Or they wanted to discuss whether it was wrong of Sylvia to cheat on her husband, Ari, with his own brother, Khristos, while Ari was away in America. Or whether the Cretan hunk who lived down the road was gay. Or whether Sylvia's son, who did sums at the speed of light or maybe faster, was really a genius.

And then the worst: Watching Ari get showered with gifts—cigarettes, candy, magazines, even booze—while The Translator was lucky to get a stale cookie mailed by somebody's mom.

It was so much bullshit.

"Hey, Translator," called a crank dubbed the Professor. "They say they are going to carpe your diem, if you don't show up today. Must've been some cliffhanger."

"Oh yeah. The Turk was banging Sylvia right by the outhouse when his wife—"

"Fatima the beauty?"

"Exactly. She just got her period and was rushing to the john."

"Jeez, her brother Nico will kill the Turk, if she catches him. They've always hated each other."

"Yeah, but Khristos will want to kill the Turk too. For screwing his mistress."

"He's got to kill him. She's not just his mistress, she's his brother's wife."

The two men laughed, shook their heads, and said goodbye.

"Gregory!" It was Ari. The Translator rolled his eyes as Ari grabbed his arm and poured out in Greek, "Come, we have to get ready. I feel the story coming."

"Not today." The Translator shook his head. "Tell it yourself. I need a break."

Ari the Greek dropped the Translator's arm. "But my English stinks," he said, looking hurt.

"Then here is the deal," said the Translator. "You want to tell stories, fine, go ahead. But if you want me to translate, from now on we are going to work together. I'm tired of all this domestic b.s. with the same eight characters."

"But I never plan anything," Ari said. "The stories just rush out of me."

This might have been the case once, thought the Translator. In fact, the Greek had begun his tale out of sadness and despair. Alone, a stowaway who was arrested, jailed, and convicted of shoplifting within his first month on U.S. soil, the Greek had no one to talk to, and, being illiterate, no hope of letting his beloved wife, Sylvia, and their son, Domi, know about his predicament. He began to envision their life without him. He went over hundreds of permutations—whom they might have seen each morning, or in the evening, what they might have said, what they ate, how they slept and on and on. Gradually these micro-scenes expanded to vignettes and eventually to elaborate, impassioned performance pieces with different voices, gestures, and impersonations. He imagined his son battling pneumonia and embodied the awful shivers and coughs, lying prostrate and then pounding his chest as he described the nuns beating on his son's back to loosen the phlegm in the boy's lungs. He would sashay like the easiest floozy in the land as he enacted his wife's flirtatious Friday night promenade across the town square. Inmates began to notice this strange behavior and asked the Translator to explain. At first he would paraphrase, because translation is not an easy task. But he got better and faster and after a while his name was subsumed by his role, and Gregory became the

Translator. He had a feeling that at this point only a few inmates remembered his real name.

So when the Greek tried to insist that his performance was a spontaneous eruption, the Translator just laughed. "Bullshit, Ari."

The Greek looked hurt. "Okay, I think about some of it beforehand."

"You think it all out," said the Translator. "I've seen you working up stuff. I've watched you recite things in your cell."

"So what? They love it."

The Translator nodded. "Ari, are these people even real? Are you sure you are even married? Do you have a son?"

"Write to them for me, please. Again, I beg you! And, please, write to the President, too!"

"Okay, I'll write another set of letters tomorrow. As long as you want." He had done this months ago, wondering if a response from Sylvia and little Domi would put a damper on things, or inspire better stories. As it was, there had been no word from Azbos.

"No hugs!" He pushed the Greek away. "But I want to discuss the story lines with you after I write the letters. We need more action. Less shopping for eggplants. That crap slows down the story. I get all kinds of complaints and we really need some new girls. The men are tired of your wife, no offense. Plus, it's not a great message to all the guys here. Some of them don't want to think about their wives screwing around."

The Greek made a face. "But it's my story."

"It's our story now. Or no letters."

"Okay."

"I have some great ideas."

The Greek did not look convinced. "Tomorrow you write the letter."

∼∼∼

The next six weeks were the happiest time of the Translator's life since his days in high school. He had the Greek introduce a war with a neighboring village over a romance between the town dwarf and a young maiden from the next fishing town over. The prisoners lapped it up.

"Just wait until Valentine's Day," he would tell them. "Big changes are coming."

He wasn't exaggerating, either. For the Valentine's Day installment, he and the Greek had come up with a fantastic story line: The island of Azbos is covered in fog. Offshore, a ship carrying novices from Rome crashes into a ship of West African smugglers. The villagers rush out their long boats and save 15 novices—girls, 17 years old and each more beautiful and nubile than the next—and 8 smugglers. The Translator knew that the sorrow of the tragedy and the joy of survival, together with the discovery of this beautiful island and the Greek's depraved sexual imagination would offer incalculable pornographic permutations. And the Greek did not disappoint. For the first time in the history of his island hi-jinks, lesbianism was introduced, sending the inmates and guards protesting when the Greek tried to switch subjects. There was a ménage-à-trois that grew into an à-cinq. There was the redheaded novice who renounced her vows at the sight of a handsome, massive African, and the Greek's description of the dark-skinned man pistoning into the pale beauty—a bar of dark chocolate splashing into milk—drew hoots and hollers from some delighted inmates and boos from older prisoners. Not wanting to initiate a race riot—indeed previous coupling on Ari's island had been limited to men and women, men and men, and shepherds and goats—the Translator interrupted the gyrating Greek as he was describing the build-up to a nearly heart-stopping orgasm and instructed him to cut to the sexual awakening of the Mother Superior who, celebrating her immediate salvation, surveyed the manhood of a Turk, a Greek, and the Senegalese ship captain on the moonlit beach. When all were satisfied, the Translator barked: "End it nicely."

Not content to leave this garden of erotic delights quietly, the Greek tried to end the scene with another round of men approaching. But the Translator ignored him. "The men began to return her favors," he said, "Caressing her, stroking her, kissing her neck and ears. She shuddered, her body locked and recoiled and locked again. 'Stop, please,' she said, and they did. 'Hold me,' she said, and they did. She sat up. 'Pray with me,' she said, grasping the Turk and the Captain. 'O Lord, thank you for delivering us from a cold and torturous death to this land of love.' "

She remained there, the Translator continued, her grip tightening on the hands of her companions. Her body began to tremble. Tears streamed down her face. "O Lord, I have forsaken thee!" She rose up, her hands covering her breasts and pubic hair, rushed to her habit, which was lying on the ground, and ran off the beach, pulling it over her head, running into the darkness of the island with two of her most loyal novices trailing in her wake, calling, "Mother! Wait for us!"

The rec room was silent. The Translator realized that the Greek hadn't spoken for a while, and that in fact Ari was looking at him and sent a slight nod of approval in his direction.

That evening fans approached the Translator with a steady stream of reviews:

"Amazing. Thanks for the new blood. I was getting tired of that bitch Sylvia always getting it on with the Turk."

"The ending? Oh, my lord! My mascara ran a mile when that nun was praying. Please! And all the nice girls love a sailor!"

"It was good, but come on! I never saw a nun younger than 65 my whole life."

The next morning a guard approached the Translator at the cafeteria. "The warden has heard about your stories," he said. "Would you do a special performance for him—you and the Greek?"

"What? With all the dirty bits?"

"Clean it up a little. But not too much."

"No problem. We would be honored."

"Wow," said the Professor, who was also at the table, "You are on the warden's radar. Maybe you can get a cushy gig or early release."

Word travels fast in prison, which is why Anthony "Little Giant" Tomaso heard about the command performance and caught up with the Translator in the yard later that day.

"Translator," said Little Giant, who was built like a mailbox only with shorter legs. "I heard about your performance for the warden. Congratulations. Is it a private show, or can we all go?"

"Private, I think. For the warden and some guards."

"But you're still going to do a show for us that day, right? It's not going to interrupt your normal schedule?"

"No, I don't think so. The warden show is around dinner.

So we should still be able to do the regular show. Don't tell anyone, but a storm is going to hit and flood the village."

"What a fucking great idea. Do me a favor. Kill that hairy Turk. I hate that guy. You know how he's so proud of his son going to Mecca? Have him die right before his son returns."

"We'll think about it. He's a pretty important character."

"I'm not kidding. Do it." Little Giant was in for life thanks to a series of gangland murders. He was infamous for his disposal methods, which included a saw and sledgehammer. His opinion was always worthy of consideration among the inmates.

"Okay, I'll discuss it with the Greek."

Little Giant smiled. "So when is it? The warden's?"

"Tomorrow. Around six."

As it turned out, the following day's regular show for the inmates was canceled by the Day Sergeant, who had told the warden their act was "like if John Steinbeck wrote really dirty stories" and wanted to be sure they lived up to their billing.

The warden's meeting room was decked out with food on a grand table and booze on a side table. Most of the men were senior officers and guards.

The warden offered them a drink, but only the Greek accepted. The Translator, aware there was a chance the crazy Greek would spend the next hour musing on his elementary school teacher's mountainous breasts, wanted to keep a clear head. But the Greek was good that day and stuck to the outline. He talked about the shipwrecked Africans who were homesick for their multiple wives and children, and explained that even this beautiful island with endless fishing and fruit and nubile women was still something of a prison to them.

And despite the fallen novices, who pleasured them daily, they dreamed of leaving, because love and family are the strongest chains of all. So in between working and fucking they repaired the boat.

Every day the young boy Domi, whose father had gone to America and was staying in an iron bar hotel thanks to a travesty of justice (the Translator omitted this last detail), came to watch the boat repairs. He would help carry planks. He wanted to go with the Africans and search for his father.

"Stay here, your mother needs you," the crew chief admonished him again and again. But the boy insisted he was leaving and went around the village saying his goodbyes.

When he bid his Uncle Khristos adieu, the uncle smiled, marched him to his small barn, and tied him to a post. "Your mother has lost her husband. I will not let her lose you."

The Africans left, and the islanders watched them disappear on the horizon. Sylvia wondered how many pregnant novices were left in their wake. But there was very little time to ruminate on this matter, because that afternoon, after Khristos came to fill the void of his brother's absence, the wind came up, the temperatures dropped, and huge raindrops started hammering against the roof. Khristos looked out the window and saw the white foam of crashing surf. The sea had risen over the pier. "Flood!" he shouted. And then he remembered the boy tethered in the barn.

At this point, the outline for the story had Khristos and Sylvia go to the barn and discover the tethers unbound. Sylvia would unleash a heart-wrenching scream, thinking about her son dying at sea in this horrible storm. But that tragic image would turn into a fantasy one second later when they would turn and discover the boy sodomizing a goat, which would lead to a new round of screaming. Khristos would defend the boy from his mother's blows, claiming this was just an innocent rite of passage, which would disgust Sylvia so thoroughly that she would declare she never wanted to see Khristos again, and then promptly vanish into the storm. But the warden and his guards never heard that part of the story because just as Khristos remembered the boy, the prison break alarm went off.

Seconds later, a guard burst into the room. "Breakout!" He said. "Some scumbag in the infirmary. Myers was shivved."

"Who did it?" the warden barked.

"Don't know. We're looking."

"How's Myers?"

"Dead."

"Lock everyone down. Take a roster to see who's missing."

"What are you smiling about?" snarled a screw at the Translator.

"Nothing, sir. Just... This is crazy."

The Greek asked what was happening.

"Some men are escaping."

"English!" commanded the screw.

"Sorry, sir. He doesn't speak English."

The Translator and the Greek were hustled down to their cells.

That fucking Little Giant, thought the Translator. The goombah had screwed up his big moment with the warden. The Translator had had this idea that maybe, if the warden liked him, he might be rewarded with a good job, like in the commissary where he could steal, or in an office with a phone to the outside world. Or get a choice cell: a high floor with some sun. But there was no chance now. He would be associated with the escape forever. With Myers getting shivved. Still, there was something flattering about the breakout. It was a compliment. Little Giant knew the warden's office would be packed and the security would be lax. He had staked his life on the performance. Like every prisoner in the house, the Translator was rooting for Little Giant to get away.

⌒⌒⌒

That night the screws went nuts. They brought in dogs and hauled in prisoners for questioning. Intermittent gunfire exploded in the distance as sentries shot at shadows, birds, and fear. With each echoing shot, the prisoners offered silent prayers.

The Translator woke in terror, a screw's nightstick prodding him. He was dragged in for interrogation. Some bastard had ratted on his exchange with Little Giant in the yard. Apparently Little Giant had been looking all over for the Translator.

"What did he want?"

"Just to discuss the Greek's stories."

"Bullshit."

"He was a fan. He threatened to kill me once, when I went on strike."

"What'd he say about the stories?"

"He hated the Turk—one of characters. He wanted me to kill the Turk."

"That it? He asked three different people where you were to tell you that?"

"He wanted the Turk to die just as his son was coming home from Mecca."

"That's all?"

The Translator shrugged. "He really hated the Turk."

"You're going in the hole. Let us know if you remember what Little Giant told you about his plan."

"Why would he tell me his plan? Do you tell your wife when you're going to a hooker?"

That line of reasoning was rewarded with a slap in the face and an angry snarl: "Get him the fuck out of here."

~~~

The tough things about a stint in the hole are: no sense of time, of day or night, which leads to dislocation, hunger, then loss of appetite, fatigue and sleeplessness, anxiety, apathy, catatonia. There are no good things about the hole, unless you are getting raped or beaten by prisoners when you are in the general population.

The Translator, however, was undaunted.

He meditated. He imagined Little Giant's escape, although he never thought that Little Giant would store himself in the disgusting infirmary laundry pile for three days, shave his head to look like Dr. Moltz, tie Dr. Moltz up in the same disgusting laundry pile and then walk out of jail, catch a bus to Boston and vanish, which is exactly what happened. The Translator exercised daily—1,000 push-ups and sit-ups—and he imagined the island. He saw the destruction and despair that nearly consumed the island and all its inhabitants. But he also saw its glorious future.

When he returned from the hole after one month, he discovered the Greek had been released. The island flashed before him. He imagined Sylvia's husband finally returning home, and a joyful but tension-filled celebration. Soon after, developers would start visiting. There would be talk of a luxury hotel and even a casino. There was a plan to pave the roads. Two of the novices would give birth to beautiful brown children with long, elegant noses. The Translator combed his hair and changed his shirt. He had a show to do, and life on the island was wide open.

FIVE

Who the fuck is Seth Kaufman?

Because that was hilarious, although it hurts to laugh. With the wall unit pressing on my lower rib cage, each chuckle spawns a micro-bruise and chafes whatever the hell is festering on my chest. And any subsequent counter-grimaces send tremors through my lower back. They stop there because my legs—at least my lower legs—are pretty numb. But what a great idea: like *Kiss of the Spider Woman*, only funnier and crazier. And I loved the stories within the story. I'm not too clear on when, exactly, it's supposed to take place; I guess before TV, when storytelling was the best you could do. We didn't have a TV until I was a teenager, but by then I was already hooked on the movies, thanks to my mother. Television was okay, but movies on that big screen—I just loved 'em. Frankly, it's a little ironic that I have a TV hit at all; I came to the field of schemes that is L.A. hell-bent on making movies; TV was nothing to me. What really blows me away about the Translator, though, is that he didn't even need a screen. Just the stories and a voice. And he escaped, and took his audience with him. I wonder how much my movies set people free? I guess my best stuff was good for 90 minutes of distraction. The serial story, though, that's the long-term escape. And I gotta say, that's what TV does now pretty damn well.

I wonder where Kaufman got this story from. Hell, where

did he get all these stories from? The "About the Author" note tells me nothing. Apparently, Kaufman lives in Brooklyn. Big deal: so do two million other people. The acknowledgments are paltry—some readers, an agent, his friends and family. And the dedication, well, that's a little more interesting. After the shout-out to "Susan," his wife, probably, he writes "In memory of Adam Kaufman, who told me about prison, and Michael Kaufman, who showed me the world." Well that explains something, although I don't know what. If I ever get out of here, I will track him down. Get some answers. He would have been a good guy to have on staff, this Kaufman, although that reminds me of my favorite writers joke: "No writers?" says a producer, hearing about a writers' strike. "Great. Now we don't have to fix anything."

On the first movie I ever made, the biker comedy *Donny Cycle,* the writer was a fellow valet named Max. I sold him pot, he told me jokes. I made the guy. I gave him the title, the rip-off *Don Quixote* story arc, and some money to write a screenplay. Then I rewrote it with him and got the friggin' film made. Presto! Low budget hit. Now, years later, Max Winter gets a million just to rewrite a few scenes, while I still have to work hard to make and lose my millions. Anyway, whenever I see him around town, I always make sure to ask about his latest project.

"Max," I'll say, "I missed the opening. How was it?"

"It's not the movie I wrote."

He says this every time! Every single time, with a sigh of resigned frustration. Like a parrot: Not the movie I wrote!

Audience testing, focus groups, investors, investor groups, the director, the editor, the producers—hell, the damn focus puller can have more effect on a movie than the writer. I know everybody talks about the script, the script, the script. But if the script was so damn good, why did the movie bomb? Think about it. The writer delivers a fleshed-out idea, which helps put the whole thing in motion, but that idea can immediately get lost in the momentum it has created; the script gets consumed by the process.

"Of course it's not, Max!" I roar at him. "If you want control, write a novel, not a screenplay!" I mean, really, there are so many rewrites of the average movie that half the time these screenwriters go to arbitration—which is like surrogate parenting—to decide who gets the friggin' screen credit. I've had movies delayed over that kind of bullshit.

But not Seth Kaufman. His only delays are writer's block and the slow-as-molasses world of publishing. Whatever he is: fraud, conjurer, liar, dreamer, egotist, he owns what he's written. Although I am wondering if he stole these stories from the "Adam" in the dedication.

"Amanda!" I yell. "What is the fucking deal with this book?"

I'm a double moron: not only am I still alone, but Amanda is long gone. But I'm getting ahead of myself.

After the selection of our contestants, we set up base in a condemned reformatory camp. It had been shuttered a couple of years back because a new facility had been built in another county, but the place still worked. There was running water. A mess hall that needed fumigation. Some of the windows were still intact.

Our director, Casey Rittenhouse, looks the place over and proclaims it "in total violation of the Geneva Convention." We all laugh our own sinister laughs, and Casey says, "Maybe we should work that into the show."

One day later Amanda is in my office handing me a printout. "Look at this," she says. "The Geneva Convention. The third version, written in 1949. Let me read it to you:

"'Article 13. Prisoners of war must at all times be humanely treated.' Are we doing that here?"

"Well—"

"'Article 22. Prisoners of war may be interned only in premises located on land and affording every guarantee of hygiene and healthfulness. Except in particular cases which are justified by the interest of the prisoners themselves, they shall not be interned in penitentiaries.'"

"Hey, Rittenhouse was right. This was a penitentiary!"

"'Article 25. Prisoners of war shall be quartered under conditions as favorable as those for the forces of the Detaining Power who are billeted in the same area. The said conditions shall make allowance for the habits and customs of the prisoners and shall in no case be prejudicial to their health.'"

"What the hell does that mean?"

"It means that we should be staying here, too. Or they should be back at the hotel with us."

"Ha!"

"Do you think this is funny?"

"They signed up for it, honey."

"Don't 'honey' me."

"Sorry, Amanda. Just a term of endearment. But I don't

get you. These guys all signed their agreements and waived pretty much every single basic human right. This is part of the competition, part of the drama."

"But it's wrong."

"90% of reality TV is wrong. 90% of it is staged or engineered. And so is our show. But let's talk about this. Let's see if we can build this into the story line."

Amanda stares at me. I'm smiling. This is great.

"Don't look at me like I'm some kind of Mengele war criminal."

She just shakes her head.

"Amanda, if we can get Senator Tom O'Brien here, that would be something, right? Tortured at the Hanoi Hilton for seven years."

"Rick..."

"He's the living poster boy of torture. Get him and I'll double your salary."

"That's not the point."

"Get the new kid on it. Little Ricky. Maybe he'll tape a message or come for a visit. Who else can we get? These shows love special guests and surprises."

"Is Evel Knievel still alive?"

"No, but that is pretty good."

Just then Little Ricky shows up.

"Nunboy," I say, "we're thinking of guests who would be good on the show, like Senator Tom O'Brien. Any ideas?"

Little Ricky thinks for a little while and then says, "There must be other former hostages. Like Terry Waite or Patty Hearst."

"Not bad. I'm impressed. But we need better name recognition. Somebody more contemporary. Terry Waite sounds like some Norwegian long distance runner. Let's get someone who survived a beat-down in Guantánamo or Abu Ghraib!"

"Rick, have you lost your mind?" asks Amanda.

"Never saner. We could cloak them, keep them anonymous, alter their voices. That would be totally dramatic." I turn to the kid. "Little Ricky, go find me some torture victims. Start with Senator O'Brien."

I was right. There are always doubters—networks, money guys, associate producers, *Variety* reporters, bloggers (a new and particularly irritating species of doubter)—but once again, Rick "the Prick" Salter was right. O'Brien refused at first, pretending to take the moral high ground.

Then the ratings came in.

The first two shows, as I think I've said, featured auditions; they were freak shows, filled with deluded wannabes. But we also used them to establish our characters and introduce Dr. Burns, serving as the handsome, witty M.C., Mary Lamb looking like the dominatrix you'd want next door, and Mayhew, their drill sergeant sidekick.

"Please," says Mary Lamb, watching a time-lapse clip of some submissive screwball sitting bound and gagged in a giant birdcage contraption. "Did you get this notarized? How do we know you spent 48 hours like this? Do you have all 48 hours on tape?"

"No, ma'am," trembles the young hopeful, who's come all the way from Seattle. "I'll try to do better next time. I swear."

"Is this turning you on?"

"Being told off by a beautiful woman? Of course."

"Ugh. Gross. Listen, next time you do the birdcage thing, line it with newspaper. It'll be more realistic. Now get out of here."

"Oh, yes, ma'am!"

"See you next year!" calls Mayhew, shaking his head.

Then there's the whipping boy.

"You like being whipped, do you?" asks Dr. Burns

"Yes I do."

"Why?"

"It hurts."

"So why do it?"

"Because it feels good."

"I'm confused."

"The pain feels good."

"Let me ask you something, do you like opera?"

"No. I hate it."

"So opera is your favorite music, is it?"

"No. I just told you."

"He only likes some pain, Doctor!" laughs Mary Lamb. "Whipping is his kink. Not opera."

"Pity. Maybe you should try opera and whipping together."

When the judges meet Sgt. St. James, Mayhew barks "Drop and give me twenty!" To which Sgt. St. James hits the floor and knocks out a score of textbook push-ups. One-handed.

"I'll take him!" sings Mary Lamb.

The judges are less taken with Jeremiah Lovell.

"I don't mean to be rude," says Dr. Burns, being totally snarky, "but I want to pose a sticky question. Which do you think is harder—you running 100 miles or someone actually watching you run 100 miles?"

"Probably watching. Can't be too exciting."

"You get points for honesty."

See? Funny, nasty, entertaining. The only one they couldn't mess with? Sister Rosemarie.

"Why are you here?"

"To celebrate the power and the glory of God."

"Well, that's the first time we've heard that in these interviews! Sister Rosemarie, I'm sure you are no stranger to sacrifice, but can you tell us what qualifies you for this competition beside the big man looking over your shoulder?"

"I have fasted every Friday for two years. I spent four years working in an orphanage in Sudan with crippled children."

"Wow," says Mary Lamb. "That must have been filled with heartbreak."

"Yes. And love."

"I'm not sure that love is going to be a big part of this competition," says Dr. Burns.

"It's everywhere, Dr. Burns. You only have to stop and feel it. Of course that might be quite hard for you."

"Zing!" shouts Mayhew.

"Ouch!" cheers Mary Lamb.

Dr. Burns can't hold back a smile.

"Oh that's something else I've done," continues Sister Rosemarie. "Silent retreat. No talking for ten days."

"That settles it!" raves Dr. Burns. "Running 100 miles, I can imagine. Shutting up for ten days? Impossible. You've got my vote. But God forgive me."

Those two introductory episodes—powered by critical buzz and interstitial promos with over-the-top viewer-discretion warnings—landed us in the top 10 during opening week. Then we had two shows built around endurance tests.

The first was an obstacle-athon. It was, as the contestants all agreed, "Brutal."

"The worst day since I crossed the desert," says a zombie-fied Sanchez.

"I'm out there, and I'm fantasizing about two-a-day drills at football camp," says Derek Snead.

We start everyone off with boot camp drills cribbed from the instruction manuals at West Point. You know the stuff: tire footwork, going hand over hand on monkey bars (or "horizontal bar navigation," as Judge Mayhew called it), crossing a balance beam, climbing a wall, scaling a 20ft horizontal ladder, crossing a 32ft vertical rope, and a sprint (carrying a 6lb medicine ball for the first 120m). But that is just the warm-up. For the next day's episode we follow the contestants as they repel down a rockface cliff, hop on a bike and go thirty miles to an ice rink, skate 20 laps, run 5 miles to a pool, swim a mile, and then rollerblade 30 miles back.

I even arrange for some finish line drama. As Sanchez and Sgt. St. James battle for the lead, I radio ahead to have a production assistant leave only one bottle of water in the middle of the road. As Sgt. St. James slows down to pick it up, Sanchez rushes past him and sweeps it up. Then, to rub it in, he takes just one sip and then tosses the bottle into the shrubbery before skating to first place.

"He dissed me, and I'll remember that," vows Sgt. St. James. "How do you say, 'What goes around comes around?' in Spanish?"

Two weeks in, and we're the top-rated show in the country.

I'll be honest: The competition we aired in week three had me a little worried. We split the contestants into two teams and gave them 16 hours to move two families into each other's respective mansions. Pretty benign stuff, you might think, but it turns out it was a great competition.

Because what sucks more than moving?

Moving in a rainstorm with incompetent teammates.

I admit it: when we made the teams for this one, we thought they were evenly matched. But it turns out moving is as much a strategic art form as it is a brute-force skill.

So, with Sgt. St James turning out to be a master of deployment and action, with Sister Rosemarie revving up managerial skills she learned in Sudan, with Darcy channeling a control freak's need for order, and Jeremiah and service rep David Marks doing steady grunt work, the Green Team completely outperforms their brethren.

And no wonder: Sanchez and Kaylene of the purple team can't stop staring and fondling all the pricey stuff on hand. Adonis Troy and Annabel are great at hauling things to and fro, and so is Derek Snead, but his knees slow him down on the stairs. And there are a lot of stairs.

And then there comes the rain, as if we had ordered it. And the purple team discovers that their truck wasn't packed efficiently. Annabel Castro and Sanchez start getting into it. In Spanish. And then Annabel turns to Derek Snead and says: "You're friggin useless with your knees. You know what? You're too fat, you're hurting yourself."

"I'm a football player, you b-BEEP-tch! Size is the name of the game. Anyway, I'll happily load–I mean, reload–the truck and you can do the stairs."

Ah, there's nothing like a real reality TV spat to keep

things lively and goose those ratings. When they came in, it was clear: America was now officially in love with us. And so was Senator O'Brien. He called back Little Ricky and said he had reconsidered. He wanted to send a video greeting, but I told Little Ricky that wasn't good enough. "We want him to be a guest judge."

After more haggling—the only people with as many handlers as actors and pop stars are politicians—he agrees.

We leap into action, flooding the network with promo clips for a "shocking guest," the "original King of Pain," and a "true American hero." For the show we order up a mini-doc about "a great patriot, a naval pilot who was shot down, booked into the Hanoi Hilton and subject to relentless torture as the ideal prisoner, given that he was the son of a U.S. four-star general." We use some early war footage along with grainy clips from a French interview with O'Brien when he was in a POW camp.

Once that was over, we brought the Senator out to a rousing ovation. We had a quick Q&A, and then he was allowed to schmooze with the contestants, telling them they would all make great soldiers on day.

"I already am," laughed Sgt. St James.

Mayhew and Mary Lamb fed O'Brien some softball post-election questions, and even asked him what was tougher: a failed presidential campaign with a good-looking airhead Governor as your running mate or doing seven years in Hanoi.

"Apples and oranges," he said with a big grin.

Sister Rosemarie thanked the Senator for his stance on waterboarding and torture. At this point I had Dr. Burns step in and deliver a message:

"Ladies and Gentlemen," he says archly, "I'd like to take this opportunity to remind everyone that there is no water-boarding on this program."

"Nor any other form of torture," adds Mayhew. "All our contestants want to be here."

"That's right," says the lovely Ms. Lamb. "This is a show that, at its heart, is about endurance and strength in the face of adversity."

Our timing was perfect: the next week we ran the Hunger episodes right at December sweeps, and interest in the show went into the stratosphere. Walter from the network was ecstatic.

"Rick," he calls me the moment the Hunger episode overnights come in, "I want to thank you. You have made my year and possibly my career."

"My pleasure," I lie.

"I mean it."

"Me, too," I say.

Once you pull off a great buzz-worthy gimmick, there can be a tendency to think you are done. It's only natural. So I push Amanda and Little Ricky to see what else we can do. We are brainstorming and getting nowhere when Amanda says, "Why don't we ask the contestants?"

"Genius," I say, because I am totally stumped for a better idea. "Film it when you ask them. There might be a great moment."

The next morning Amanda and her sidekick rush in. Little Ricky hooks some kind of computer stick into my computer.

"You won't believe this," Amanda gushes.

Rosemarie the Nun's pure freckled face lights up the screen. She looks pensive as she considers the question she has been asked. Then she raises her eyes to the camera. "I would like Dick Cheney to come on the show because I have a few things to say to him."

"Wow!" I say.

"I'd tell him that he is a disgrace. I'd tell him to love thy neighbor, that love, not torture or power, is the way of Jesus."

"Let's see if this can fit into next week's episode," I say. "Then we can invite Cheney on the show."

"Rick, we don't want to be too anti-torture. We are torturers, too, right?"

"We're entertainers," corrects Little Ricky. "We are holding a competition examining the marvels and limits of human endurance."

"Exactly, Little Ricky," I say.

Amanda tosses off a nasty glare at her new pal. "Try and hold on to your soul a little while longer. Like maybe a week?"

"The entire reality TV genre is exploitation, Amanda," I say. "Of both the contestants and the audience. That's a given. But maybe the issues we raise will help some people in this country examine how we entertain ourselves or think about torture itself. I know you're shaking your head. But the way I see it, reality TV is like gossip, you can use it as a gauge for yourself."

"Rick," says Amanda, "You are high. Having Sister Rosemarie call out Cheney is nuts. You don't want to politicize this."

"I'm not so sure."

"Well, I am."

I think about our viewers. I think about blurring the story line. "You're probably right," I say.

We never mention the clip again. Maybe I should have. I could have thanked her for stopping me. A little more grace on my part, and Amanda might still be here, checking on me. Rescuing me. Instead, it looks like Marta will have to be my maid in shining apron. She simply has to show up. And when she does, I will put her on staff and retire her from housekeeping. God bless Marta. She's been here through two of my three marriages, the hits, the flop, and now, the terror. She's seen me coked up, suicidai, raging, ecstatic. She was at the bris of my son and the funerals of both my parents. Jesus. I shouldn't just put her on staff, I've gotta put her in my will.

I start to cry. I'm delirious, starving, and I'm praying, praying, for Marta. Whatever I'm paying her—$250 a day?— it's not nearly enough. No benefits, no nothing. I've got to put her in my will. I have to call Jay, my lawyer. I reach for my phone, but of course the phone is in the fucking kitchen.

To add insult to injury, right then the damn phone decides to ring. The ring is getting fainter, which means either the phone is dying or I am. I wonder who is calling. The network, my son Jared in need of money, Veronica at the office? My bowling buddies, Lars and Frank?

Or could it be Marta telling me she's not coming tomorrow?

I can't think of that. Immediately, I feel for the pulse in my wrist. It's pounding.

I force a smile. I let out a laugh. I chant: I'm not gonna die, not gonna die, not gonna die. I'm gonna live and rescue *The King of Pain*. But first I'm gonna do some more reading.

PIERRE THE WAR CRIMINAL

The strangest case in the entire prison—the captive that even the lifers and rapists and serial killers and the sadistic screws felt sorry for—was Pierre the War Criminal.

On the surface, Pierre the War Criminal was guilty as charged. But no jury of his peers would ever convict him. Ask any of the incarcerated.

"Railroaded," said L'Avocat, a disbarred lawyer. "It was self- defense."

"An object lesson in object lessons," said Eric Le Rouge, a ginger-haired thief. "Just the government trying to cover its ass."

"The guy he killed? His uncle was a judge," said con man Albert Greco, spouting a well-known fact.

"That kind of Frenchman always looks guilty of something," said Volpe the Italian. "He was destined to end up here. Just look at him."

As Gallic as his name, Pierre had a long, forlorn face, high-lighted by a prominent nose and sad, tired dark eyes, a hair-line that seemed to start in the middle of his forehead, and a perpetual cigarette dangling from the corner of his mouth, a mouth that was, as you might expect, dutifully thin-lipped.

Mordito the Spanish Assassin said, "In my eyes, it was jus-tifiable homicide."

Let the record show that if questioned further, Mordito would reveal that there was no such thing as "unjustifiable homicide." Nevertheless, the brutal assassin's take on Pierre was accurate. At the center of his case were war and death and survival.

Pierre was an infantryman. His company had been thoroughly decimated, outmanned, and outgunned on the eastern border. On the most horrible days in prison, those bone-chilling winter days when the men huddled together like sheep to keep warm, Pierre remembered all his dead comrades rotting in the trenches and tried to think of himself as lucky.

And Pierre had indeed been briefly, in this regard, a soldier of good fortune. When the enemy had finally moved on, satisfied that enough death and devastation had been meted out at Pierre's part of the front, he found three others who had survived the onslaught of cannon fire, strafing bullets, and mustard gas, and together they discovered a nearby abandoned barn. There wasn't much to the barn. There was no hay, but there was a roof, a pump, a shovel, and a hoe. Afraid of being discovered, the four men began debating what to do. The enemy had overrun the territory. Probably the best option at that moment was to stay put. But where to hide? They looked left, they looked right, they looked up to the rafters, and finally they looked down. Most of the floor was hard earth, but part of the floor at the rear of the barn was covered with wooden slats. They decided to pull up some floorboards and dig. After six months of living in muddy trenches, digging was the natural response to virtually every situation.

The first night they pulled the planks over the ditch and got ready to sleep.

"Jean, wait 'til we fall asleep first, you snoring bastard," said Roland.

"I try to wait," explained the stocky soldier to Roland, Pierre, and Victor, the fourth survivor. "But I can't help it if I breathe through my mouth."

"He snores like some kind of infernal machine," said Roland. "Our captain, God rest his soul, would slap him in the middle of the night to get him to stop."

But the darkness and fatigue put all the men under. And if Jean snored those first few nights, it was news to Roland, Pierre, and Victor.

❧

For one week, things were good. During a full moon, the four survivors returned to the battlefield and found a cache of rations among the bodies. They drank buckets of water from a pump outside the barn. They stole a chicken—just one— from a house not too far from the barn.

On the eighth day, they heard the war again. Airplanes. The report of gunfire and bombs. They imagined that their troops were now pushing back the enemy, regaining lost ground. But they had no way of knowing this for certain.

"Maybe we can help," said Roland.

"Don't be a fool, we'll be caught in the crossfire," said Victor.

"We don't know their positions," observed Pierre.

"I want to try," said Roland.

"Wait," said Victor.

"If we wait too long we'll be pinned. And how will we gather food?"

That made everyone think.

"Tomorrow evening," Pierre said.

"Okay."

But tomorrow turned out to be too late. Timing, as everyone in prison or in a war knows, is everything. And less than an hour after that conversation, just as the light was fading, enemy troops appeared at the edge of the clearing in front of the barn.

"What do we do?"

"I'm going," said Roland.

"You'll get us all killed."

These are impossible moments. These are the mini-wars that all wars generate. Every decision becomes a struggle, a battle to do the right thing.

Everyone was quiet for a moment. Then Roland said: "Hide in the hole if you want. I'll wait until dark and then go."

"Suit yourself," said Victor, pulling up a plank. "If they are truly in retreat, they won't stop here for long."

Pierre, Jean, and Victor rushed into the trench.

Roland slid the floorboards back into place, stomped on them, and hissed, "Good luck to us all."

In the darkness of their hole, they heard the side door of the barn swing open. Thirty seconds later they heard yelling and two gunshots.

Victor turned to Jean. "If they come in here, you can't go to sleep."

"What?"

"They will hear you snoring. Fuck. We should have gone with Roland. Maybe those shots missed."

Pierre gripped his rifle. He knew Victor was right. Because even if Roland had been shot, at least he had taken action. Being slaughtered in a trench, what could be worse than that?

They heard voices. The enemy. They were bunking for the night.

"We'll sleep in shifts," whispered Victor. "One at a time. I will sleep first."

What a night. The boredom and the terror. Years later, when the men would trade personal horror stories, Pierre would think about this night as one of his worst, not because of where it led him—to trial, to prison—but because of the tension. The idea that a single sound—a cough, a fart, a snore—would give them away.

Pierre listened to the enemy above and tried to guess how many men were overhead. He thought about a surprise attack: bursting from the hole and strafing everyone. But he guessed there were as many as twelve men in the barn. Too many to surprise.

Victor was asleep. Pierre started counting. Just as a way of gauging the time until dawn when maybe the enemy would move on. He could hear distant gunfire, and pausing his counting at 1,329, he wondered if the troops above would be forced to leave before sunrise.

He heard a wheeze and jerked his head. He leaned over the sleeping Victor and punched Jean. He tried to aim for Jean's shoulder, but in the darkness he hit Jean in the face.

"Ouch!"

Pierre froze in horror. He counted to 100 while listening as hard as he possibly could. No movement above. He continued counting. At 4,000 he could take it no more. He roused Victor and told Jean to sleep. "If you snore, we'll wake you."

As soon as Jean nodded off, Pierre whispered to Victor, "We have to kill him."

"I know. You have a knife. You do it."

Pierre pulled two matches out of box and broke one of them in half. "We draw."

Victor pulled the long one.

∽

A year later Jean's body was discovered. His uncle the General ordered an inquiry and Pierre's monogrammed knife—a gift from his father—was found in the pit. Investigators located Pierre and Victor, and both men were beaten and questioned and then beaten some more. Victor, faced with accomplice charges, testified, weeping, as conflicted a witness as ever took the stand.

For decades, lawyers and human rights activists have urged Pierre to appeal. There was once a movement to have him decorated for valor, to pay tribute to the fact that he and Victor had busted out of their hideout the next day, killing five enemy troops during their escape, and nine more on their way to rejoin their comrades.

Pierre the War Criminal will not discuss his case anymore. He sends the lawyers and activists away. "I am old," he says to his friends. "My family is gone. What would I do on the outside?"

"Kill the General," says Mordito.

"Sue the government," says L'Avocat.

"Yes," echoes Eric Le Rouge. "Sue them!"

"Don't forget women," says Albert Greco.

"What are they?" says Pierre, lighting a cigarette.

Everyone laughs. But only a little.

SIX

Boy, that story made my blood boil. Fucking bureaucrats! A guy like Pierre should be a hero, not a criminal. I can totally relate. That fucking Walter Fields gave me zero support the other night after CNN. I started boozing because of him. There must have been three phone calls in an hour. Each more frantic than the previous one. He should have been thanking me for defending *The King of Pain*, but instead he was all about me being unstable, irrational, and bad for the show. Okay, so that Apu remark was stupid. But you just issue an apology and move on.

My cell phone has stopped ringing in the kitchen or wherever it is. So at least I don't have to worry about more calls from that prick. Say, if the phone is dead, does the GPS continue to work? Does it still ping some nearby transmitter tower? I wonder about this because if someone decides to look for me—and of course people, or at least journalists, are looking for me—that would be an easy way to find me: triangulate the pings and figure out my location. At least that is what happened in a screenplay I passed on recently. And guess who sent me the script? Walter Fields. His nephew wrote it.

Looking back on it, Walter has been a major pain in the neck ever since I pitched him *The King of Pain*.

It started with the name of the show. From the get-go, I loved *The King of Pain*. I also liked *Agony and Ecstasy*, but

The King of Pain was on the money. It gave you the object of the show right there. But then Walter decided that vampires were hot and maybe we could do better with a gothic castle. So he calls in his research and marketing guys and they brainstorm and test. And *The King of Pain* becomes *Torture Castle*, which isn't bad, except it becomes more about the venue than the concept.

"That's okay for Season One," I tell Walter when he brings me in to see the mock-up ad with gorgeous "contestants" in front of a Transylvanian house of horrors. "But do we really want to make this about location? If these guys are running an ultra-marathon, who cares if they are in Bohemia?"

"We'll think about it. *Survivor* really built location into the show."

"I know that, but I still like *The King of Pain*."

"*King of Pain?*"

"Yeah, what you signed off on, originally. I don't want to be critical, but this mock-up looks like a promo for a *Scooby Doo* movie."

A week later, he calls me. "We've got it. Are you ready?"

"Yes, Walter," I say.

"*King of Pain: Torture Castle.*"

"O-kay."

"Okay? You like it?"

"Much better."

"We think it gives us more flexibility. Then next season we can do *King of Pain: Abu Ghraib*."

"Right," I say.

"This is going to be huge. The 18-35 market is going to go nuts for this."

"I told you that when I pitched it, Walter."

"Right. Of course. Have you found any women contestants?"

"We have women coming out of our eyeballs."

"I'm not talking about your ex-wives, Rick—although they must have been masochists to live with you."

"Actually, we're picking the final 10 soon."

"And you found some women?"

"Walter, take your medication. It's the 21st century. Women can vote and they can audition for reality TV shows."

The shitstorm starts about five minutes after the show is announced at the network's Up Front at Lincoln Center. That's the strange name given to the elaborate dog and pony show networks put on when they announce their fall lineup to the advertising community every spring. Instantly, *The King of Pain* was "controversial," "envelope-pushing," and to some savant "potentially downmarket." Another buyer diagnosed the series as "a cable-ready show on network TV." Nice to know the experts were at the top of their game. The press leeched on to us as the newest flavor of TV—an acrid, vile flavor, but new nonetheless. Plus, my backstory made it even more interesting.

To fan the flames, we screened parts of the first three episodes in July at the Critics Television Association hoedown at the Ritz Carlton in Pasadena, the annual three-week TV publicity binge when the networks trot out their new shows and stars to the critics. The stars all talk about how they "really loved the script." The programmers talk about scheduling, day-parts, and ratings segmentation. And the reporters eat free hotel food non-stop.

The King of Pain pulled 'em away from the hospitality table. Especially when we showed them a brief segment of the episode we'd called "The Hunger." Then the questions started flying and requests for interviews started coming in.

Here's the schedule the contestants faced for the starvathon:

Day One: Big lunch meal.
Day Two: Fruit and liquids.
Day Three: Nothing.
Days Four and Five: Limited fruit and unlimited water.

This was a walk in the park for Sister Rosemarie and Darcy the Dancer. They had fasted with disturbing regularity in their real lives and were used to functioning on fumes. Some of the others, especially the more muscular contestants—the ones who did so well in the first competitions—suffered from big-time hunger. You would have thought that they would stop their morning training, but Sanchez and Annabel Castro both kept at it. Jeremiah Lovell stepped off the astral plane to set them straight: "You guys are burning calories that you can't replace right now. So stop. It's going to make you even hungrier than the rest of us."

With everyone conserving energy, we put them to work fundraising for charity via phone—cold-calling being another form of torture. We chose charity work so that nobody would get mad at us, but of course the charities involved all engaged in plenty of hand-wringing about being on our show. Not that it stopped them from accepting donations from us.

Cold-calling isn't the greatest TV, so we also get 10,000 envelopes, mailers, return envelopes, and brochures for the United Children's Fund and divide the group into five teams of two. Envelope stuffing isn't exactly riveting drama either, but at least you can see the piles grow and listen to the contestants chatter. The two teams that stuff the most envelopes get to sleep in. The other three teams have to repeat the job the next day.

Sister Rosemarie wins this part of the competition with Annabel Castro, while Darcy and Sgt. St. James finish second.

But then Sister Rosemarie shows up the next day to do more. When Sanchez starts tearing up envelopes in frustration, she calms him down. She discovers he likes to sing and so they harmonize on "Guantanamera" together. When Adonis Troy complains of a headache, she gives him a massage. The critics end up gushing about her. She's the best thing to happen to nuns since *The Sound of Music*.

But by day four you can see the life ebbing out of the contestants. They are all visibly thinner. They are irritable. We put them in a classroom for a lecture about nutrition that is followed by a graded quiz. Darcy Minett aces it because as she tells the camera, "Staying skinny was a way of life. I studied it hard. Every dancer does."

Boom! The critics go nuts. The National Association of Anorexia Prevention, FLAX (Fat Ladies Are X-cellent), and legions of health advocacy groups issue statements excoriating the show. The tabloids and TV shows all find a limitless supply of health experts to beat down the show, including my soon-to-be nemesis, Surgeon General Premshaw Cho-udry, who proclaims *The King of Pain* a "national health risk."

With enemies like this, who needs friends? The ratings were strong for our early episodes, but they explode for "The Hunger," which we air over the course of three nights. The third night, when we hold a weigh-in, has everyone howling. Some of the contestants dropped 10 to 20 pounds, and all of them—all the jocks anyway—say it's been worth it. "I haven't been this light since college," gushes Derek Snead, who still weighs in at over 300 pounds. And An-nabel Castro actually thanks the show when she steps off the scale. "God bless you, *King of Pain!* I feel stronger and lighter."

The next day a group of mega-women, every one of them a super-sized walking heart attack, picket the network and threaten to start a boycott of advertisers. But the joke is we get more food ads, because boycott or not, we have the na-tion hooked. And about 50% of the eyeballs belong to wom-en who shop and eat.

Amanda has her first crisis of conscience the next week when reporters desperate for reaction stories dig up tales of copy-cat high school starvathons.

"What have we done?" she moans, clutching a paper with the offending article. "These girls are doing horrible things to themselves."

"Did you confirm Senator O'Brien?" I say, refusing to go there.

"All set. But did you read this? Those stupid girls."

I give up. I grab the bullshit by the horns. "Why don't you go speak to the school?" I offer.

"What do you mean?"

"Represent the show and go and talk to the girls. You'll be an inspiration. Hollywood associate producer, babe, digester of food."

"You think so?"

"I know so. I'll even go with you."

Turns out, it's a terrible idea. Amanda gets massacred. The kids in the audience are fine, but the parents and teachers just rip into her:

"How can you turn starvation into a competitive sport?"

"Don't you have any shame?"

"Do you hate yourself?"

"How can you get up in the morning?"

"Is there anything you won't do for ratings?"

Amanda tried. She told them that half the world was malnourished. That contestants would be shown eating with relish in subsequent episodes. That the show was working with charities to fight hunger, not promote it. But the naysayers would not hear her. When a chant of "Evil! E-vil! E-vil!" starts to drown out Amanda, I stand up and take the mic from her and hold my hand up for silence.

"People, please!" I say. "How about we agree on one thing: Let's say we stop the starvation contest. Never again on *The King of Pain*!"

A roar of agreement goes up.

"Great! And how about next year or maybe next week, we do the opposite? We make them eat and eat and eat— meat, fat, sugar, donuts, and ice cream—for 12 hours one day. Then repeat the next day, and then finally on the third day we hold a special eating competition with a 15-pound turkey, one for each contestant. Do the moral heavyweights among you like that better? Clearly that would be torture, but not for all of you."

The boos start, but I only amp it up:

"I'm Rick Salter, and *The King of Pain* is my show. Shame on you for censoring a great American show and the brave contestants who are trying to push themselves to the limits of endurance. Shame on you all."

I hustle Amanda into our limo, dodging flying empty coke cans and pretzel bags.

"Oh, Rick, thanks!" she says when we get in the car.

"Thanks? I should never have suggested it."

"But you stuck up for me."

"Well, you looked like you needed some help there."

"I did. What is wrong with these people?"

"Let's forget about them."

"That was a great idea, by the way—over-eating as torture."

"Some of those turbo-mamas deserved it just for attacking you. I mean, you are on their side. If you're a bad person, what the hell am I?"

Amanda doesn't answer. But she grabs my hand and squeezes it. Very briefly.

We've got a working outline of the shows we want to do. But after "The Hunger," I'm not sure we have enough firepower for the whole season. We may have set the bar too high. We need more ideas. I assign Little Ricky to research possible themes. He comes back with some insane ones: Iron maidens and torture racks, as if we're going to subject our contestants to that.

"Whipping?" I say, reading the list.

"We just did starvation. How much worse are a few lashes?"

"Maybe in Saudi Arabia. Not on my show."

"The Japanese do weirder stuff."

"Like whipping?"

"Like guys having to spend 24 hours avoiding paid goons who will beat the crap out of them if they catch them."

"I never heard of that."

"That's because they banned it."

"Little Ricky, you are making my points for me. Now look at this: Waterboarding? Are you serious?"

"You asked me to compile a list. It's just brainstorming. And it's not as easy as you think. We've got plenty of stuff blocked out already: endurance, starvation, sleep deprivation. Physical torture is tough because it's graphic."

"Anything else here?" I say, scanning his list.

"The stocks might have been good, except it is sort of boring. Lots of torture is boring. In fact boring is actually synonymous with torture. When a movie is boring, it's 'torture' to watch, right?"

"Thanks for the insight," I say dryly. "The scales are falling from my eyes. How about crawling?"

"What about it," says Ricky.

"I don't know if it's crawling, but we need another kind of journey, like the first competition, but more of a race that is torturous. That hurts. People love races."

"Interesting."

"Go."

"Okay. I'm on it."

"Wait! Forget the crawling. What about something quick and nasty that everyone can identify with?"

"Like going to the dentist?"

"Yeah, but more than that."

We're both silent.

"What about branding?" says Little Ricky.

"I knew there was a reason I hired you! I think that's it. It's quick, it's brutal. You've got to suck it up. Viewers will go nuts."

"So will the contestants."

"They signed contracts. Keep working on this. Let's do it soon."

Can you believe I actually had this conversation? I used to think about this stuff 24/7. I think I'm beginning to understand why Amanda gave me Kaufman's book: I bet she wanted me to think about torture in its real-life context. Not just TV. You know: Torture is someone eating while you are starving. It's being in love and not having it returned. It's unbearable noise and bright lights when you want to sleep. It's paralysis. It's being crushed by your obscenely large home entertainment system, with a nasty burning sensation right around your heart.

The "Hunger" episode is the first where we actually ax contestants, saying goodbye to two contenders. Expulsion is determined by a combination of factors: the judges' scores, viewer responses and the contestants' cumulative performance scores. The first one to go, our Customer Service guy, David Marks, is a no-brainer. He may deal with verbal abuse better than anyone, but he sucked big time at the physical stuff. So much for my hopes for a white-collar hero. The second contestant is more of a surprise. Derek Snead, who survived a lifetime of two-a-day drills in football land, doesn't make the cut either. His knees killed him in our moving competition–he couldn't handle stairs. And that lack of mobility also didn't help during the obstacle course competition. Then his whole relationship to food did him in. Hunger hurt. Let's face it, football linemen are a hybrid of sumo wrestlers and prize oxen. They are raised for size and bulk first (you can't teach size), strength second, agility third. Hey, you could be as agile as a dancer, but if you don't weigh 340 pounds, you're nothing to a coach.

They took it well. No tears. And even some relief.

And so, as I predicted, the women on the show were holding their own and then some. Even the ones who struggled in the first two episodes recovered in "The Hunger." The standings now looked like this:

1. Sanchez
2. Sgt. St. James
3. Sister Rosemarie
4. Darcy Minett
5. Annabel Castro
6. Jeremiah Lovell
7. Kaylene Appleby
8. Adonis Troy

By now our website is constantly on the brink of crashing due to all the traffic. Our outtakes of failed auditions are topping YouTube, and video distributors are begging us to rush release them on a solo DVD. My son calls me from upstate New York, telling me his frat brothers all want jobs on the show.

"How about you?" I ask. "I can definitely hook you up."

"I don't know, Dad," he says. "I was thinking about staying up here this summer. There's this band I want to manage."

"Manage a band?" This is new. I'm a little hurt he doesn't want to join the show, but I'm also intrigued. After 21 years, this is his first sign of showbiz interest.

"That sounds great," I say. "Anything I can do, let me know. Send me some recordings. I'd love to hear these guys."

"Okay, Dad. Keep up the good work. Oh, and one more thing..."

"Yeah?"

"The guys want to know if Kaylene is really going to do a porn film?"

"Where did you hear that?"

"Online."

"Listen, she's in a custody battle for her kids. I seriously doubt she'd do something like that. So, sorry. Tell 'em no way."

Thinking about that conversation now, I feel a little like Aden in the last scene of Goldengrove—a madman, alone. Those he loves the most, unreachable, gone. God, what if Jared were to come and rescue me? How amazing that would be. And how unlikely.

I'm alone. I'm soaked in my own urine because that's what happens eventually when you can't move for three days: the dam bursts. There's a frightening combination of physical relief and pain (I'm dehydrated; my pecker burns

and so do my wounds) and mental torture when your own
piss goes streaming down your thigh. And I'm crippled. But
I'm not as badly off as Aden; I've got some hope left.

   And a book to read.

BAXTER BLOOD

Office hours for Baxter Blood were the worst part of the week. Meetings with his students were fraught with drama; he felt like a priest at a confessional one moment, a dirty old man the next, and an abject failure at the end of most. It all depended on who came to visit and what they wanted to talk about. Some came to discuss their classes and assignments. Some needed tutoring. Many wanted career advice, and this was what Baxter Blood hated. Should they pursue computer programming, or statistics, or go to grad school for higher mathematics? Blood was in no position to give advice. His own career path, if rendered as a graph, would show a steadily descending line to the present. He was bottoming out—the zenith of his nadir, he joked to himself—in terms of personal and professional happiness.

Baxter Blood, who had been awarded assistantships, fellowships, research grants, and tenure, had suspected 20 years ago that he would remain standing—wobbling, really—on the shoulders of giants. He lacked the beautiful mind, the divine circuitry of the chosen ones—Fermat, Ramanujan, Pythagoras, Einstein. Those men floated in another dimension, a place where you were able to leap to associations as if by magic. They were naturals. He was a scholar, an interpreter, a repeater, a water carrier. This was the truth. In the world of mathematical success, the proof is in the proof: discovery, innovation, and publishing; and he had done almost nothing in the last 10 years. He knew from his studies on stasis and inertia that the odds of changing that were very low.

Alice Chen would be coming by in 12 minutes. She had a wonderfully deep, preppy voice that always surprised him. So did the Grecian nose on her oriental face. She defied all his stereotypes, and as always he would have to work hard to pay attention to her questions about the differences between MIT, CIT, and Harvard.

There was light knock on his door, which was open. He looked up and saw a tall woman, maybe 40 years old. She had short, pixie-ish dark hair, and blue eyes and pale skin. Baxter Blood was instantly attracted to her and as instantly self-conscious about his messy office, his scraggy haircut, his tired clothes. He stood up. "May I help you?"

"Hi, I'm Diana Katz. I'm an adjunct in the English Department. Do you have a minute?"

Baxter Blood felt he would have many minutes for this woman. "Have a seat."

"Thank you. I also teach composition at the penitentiary. I wanted to ask you about an inmate there who seems mathematically inclined."

Baxter Blood nodded.

"I hope I'm not wasting your time. But he seems to be able to interpret numbers instantly in interesting ways."

"Like primes and square roots?"

"Yes, but it goes beyond that. He works cross-checking license plates. He wrote an essay about it and how numbers make time go faster."

"Physics?"

Diana Katz laughed. "No. Not a theoretical paper on time, but on passing the time. It's a big issue for prisoners."

"Of course."

Baxter Blood took the paper from Diana Katz. The handwriting was exemplary, perfectly legible, flowing script. As a man who scrawled on blackboards for a living, this was a trait he admired.

I have a very regimented job. I review finished license plates. I check the plate against the numbers and letters on my sheet to make sure they match. It's not the most thrilling job. There's another guy who makes sure none of the plates have profanities on them. Especially personal plates. But I'm not that interested in vanity plates. The numbers on the plates interest me more. I assign digits to letters, to make the numbers longer. So CUD 123 becomes 3 (because C is the third letter in the alphabet) 21 (U is the 21st letter) and D is 4, or 3214123, which is the same backwards as forwards.

When I find an interesting number, I point it out. Of course everyone on the shift laughs at me. But it gives me something to do.

Since I started this job I've been lost in numbers. It's as if all the math I studied has come back to me. Prime numbers, fractions, ratios, pi, percentages. I wish I knew more. Now I study serial numbers on dollar bills, or on the back of a radio, or the bar code number on any item that crosses my path. People here tease me. They call me the Professor or the Accountant. But some people lose themselves in music. Others in soap operas. Others in books. That's what numbers are to me.

Baxter Blood looked up. Alice Chen hovered outside his door.

"Interesting," he said. "Hard to get a sense of his skill, but he certainly has the requisite mathematical nerdiness."

"Oh, but he's sweet. He doesn't care about the mockery."

"Oh, I'm guessing he cares. He's just being a good sport. Would you like me to visit him?"

"Would you? It would be great to get a real opinion."

"Yes," said Baxter Blood. "How's Thursday afternoon?"

Diana Katz drove a beat-up, boxy Volvo. Baxter Blood approved of the vehicle. It was solid, humble in its age. The drive was pleasant. Baxter Blood kept it very professional, asking about her work and education. She always answered in the first person singular—never a "then we moved there" or "then my husband got a job here." She was not a political animal, that much was clear. She was committed to teaching, not scholarship. And she was a little crunchy. "I could never live in the flat Midwest. I need beaches, oceans, hills. I love cities, too. College towns are a little staid, but at least ours has a center. You can walk here."

"Tell me," he said, as they pulled into the parking lot. "Why was Mr. Allen sent up the river?"

"White-collar crime. I think he stole some money."

"Really? From whom? How much?"

"I don't know. I try to work with the inmates in the here and now. If they volunteer things, I'll listen. But I want to feel safe in class. It wouldn't help me to know someone is a wife-beater or a murderer."

They passed through security. Baxter Blood had never been inside a prison before. He felt an invisible force at work, as if the guards, the barbed wire, the watchtowers, the open fields surrounding the prison—as if everything pushed down on him. He wondered if this feeling was caused by his anxiety, or if everyone walking into a prison experienced it. He thought about asking Diana, but then decided his silence might be mistaken for cool.

Diana had arranged to meet Donald Allen in a semi-private room where cameras would watch them.

Donald Allen was a big man. About 35, dark hair and thick features, including a little bit of lantern jaw. He looked strong.

Diana made the introductions then steered Donald, hand-on-shoulder, to a seat at the table. "Dr. Blood wants to ask you some questions."

"Hi, Donald. Let's get started. Ever study mathematics?"

"Basic accounting. I'm not a CPA. But I worked on the books."

"Anyone in the family study mathematics?"

"No."

"Any head injuries?"

"I had a fight in the yard about two years ago. A guy clocked me with a broomstick. We were playing stickball."

"Were you knocked unconscious?"

"I saw stars, I'll tell you that."

"Have you read any math books since high school?"

"No."

"Not even since you started doing license plates?"

"No."

"Okay, let's do some math."

Baxter Blood pulled a stack of index cards from his jacket pocket and started to sift through them.

"Do you know what a prime number is?"

"Any number that can only be divided by itself or 1."

"Do you know what a perfect number is?"

"10?"

Baxter Blood let it pass.

"Differential equations?"

"No."

"Recursive formulas?"

"No."

"The Pythagorean theorem?"

"Oh sure: where c is the hypotenuse."

Blood flashed a card: 10301. "Any thoughts on this number?"

"You can read it forwards and backwards."

"A palindrome, yes. Anything else?"

Allen closed his eyes. "It's a prime, isn't it?"

Another card: 111 x 111.

"12321."

"Look at these equations. Anything interesting about them?"

$$1 + 2 + 3 = 6$$
$$1 + 2 + 4 + 7 + 14 = 28$$

Allen studied the cards. "All the factors can be divided into the sum?"

"Correct. Those are what we call perfect numbers."

"I'll remember that. Interesting."

"They are quite rare."

Baxter Blood went back to his cards, flipping toward the end of the pile. He sensed Diana looking at him, anxious for a sign. Blood resolved to stay poker-faced.

"Here is a formula, do you recognize it?"

an + bn = cn

"Nope."

"This next card contains a theorem. Here's a pencil and paper. I'll give you ten minutes. Tell me what you think it demonstrates, and then we're done."

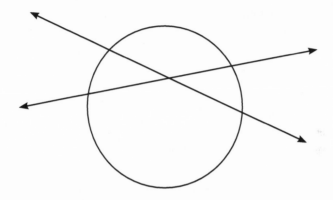

Baxter Blood then excused himself and went to the men's room. He took his time. And when he came back, he took Donald Allen's solution. And shook his hand. "It was a pleasure meeting you, Mr. Allen."

"You too."

"I'll leave you now with this thought: Bertrand Russell once defined mathematics as 'the subject in which we never know what we are talking about, nor whether what we are saying is true.'"

"Ha! That's funny. Thanks."

Baxter Blood's ex-wife, Louise, always joked that mathematicians should have a required class in moral calculus. Blood's silences as he thought through problems had been torture for her. She was not alone. "I'm a math widow," she would tell other faculty wives.

"We all are," was the frequent response.

There was no solace in numbers for her. For Louise, Baxter Blood's habit evolved from endearing passion to insufferable mania. In the end, she told him, she'd had an affair out of equal parts anger and boredom. What was the point of a relationship where one partner disappeared for vast parts of the day? And even when he was physically present, his mind was in—literally—another dimension.

"Academics," she had sneered. "Immersion in a subject doesn't give you the right to ignore the world around you."

Baxter Blood had urged her to find an academic passion. So they would be equals.

"I don't want to. Look, you don't get tenure in a marriage. You have to do the work."

He hadn't been able to do the work.

But he hadn't been able to do the work at work, either. And now, after Diana had dropped him off at campus in time for his statistics class, he wondered if he had been sent a gift. Or a series of gifts. Donald Allen had remarkable computational talents, that much was clear. And he might yet prove to be exceptional, maybe even a math genius. Either way, he represented raw material—raw material to study and to teach. And this connection would keep him in contact with Diana.

She had pressed him in the car. "What did you think?"

"Impressive."

"What does that mean? Did he get the questions right?"

"You were there. Some of them. Most of the basic computational ones."

"So he's gifted."

"Yes. I think so. Probably."

"When will you know?"

"I have to evaluate the answers. Look at the literature. Is he an idiot savant? Does he have Asperger syndrome? Is there a genius lurking there? It's too early to say."

"But he's got something."

"Again, I think so. But he's not about to put a new twist on Fermat's Last Theorem any time soon."

"Oh."

"Don't worry, it only took a few hundred years for someone to crack that one."

"Okay, I understand."

"Genius is very, very rare, Diana."

"I know, but it is such a good story. And he's a sweet guy."

❧

Baxter Blood got home and did what anyone would have done. Anyone except Diana, apparently. He googled Donald Allen. He discovered that "sweet" Mr. Allen had bilked his company's pension fund to pay for a gambling debt. The annual audit had found $2 million missing. Allen's laundering system was evidently as spotty as his handicapping system.

Baxter Blood thought for a moment. He performed some moral calculus, as his ex-wife would have called it:

> *Stealing is wrong.*
> *Stealing from a company pension fund—the fund that*
> *has your coworkers' money in it—is very, very wrong.*
> *Donald Allen was an asshole.*
> *Q.E.D.*

That night Baxter Blood replayed his last exchange with

Diana in an endless loop: "But it is such a good story." Was that her motivation? A story? A book deal? The discovery of a beautiful mind? Blood didn't know much about publishing, but there certainly seemed to be something there.

Then there was her second sentence. "And he's such a nice guy." That muddied the waters. Was she into this...this convict? Sure, he was handsome enough, but... Ah, sure she was into him. Who wouldn't be? The fact was that Blood had googled Diana, too, and Donald clearly had a place near the right ventricle of her bleeding liberal heart. She volunteered at a shelter. She had been in the Peace Corps in Central Africa. She was a do-gooder. Donald was a prime target for her charitable instincts.

Baxter Blood took Donald's final proof out of his pocket. It was pretty damn good. The logic was elaborate and twisted, but in the end he had figured it out:

The internal angles of any two lines that bisect within a circle are equal to half the sum of the arcs they intersect.

This paper was a ticket, but a ticket for what? For more grant money, for an entry into the textbooks of the future, maybe. If Donald proved to be a genius, then for a place in the history of science and mathematics. Well, not a place, but a footnote as the man who found him and brought him to the academy. Baxter Blood wondered if he wanted this E-ZPass to a higher plane of academia. His life was much simpler without it.

As he thought about it more, things became very clear. The poor English teacher with the good looks would trump him. And she might be working on a book! Who would care about

Baxter Blood, a gaunt Dickensian figure with the curdling name? Then there was Allen himself. The criminal redeemed by looks and genius. It was a feel-good fairytale. Could Blood stomach shepherding this duo around the academy, playing the squeaky third wheel in a mutual admiration society? No, was the simple truth. No, he could not.

❧

The next day Diana appeared during office hours. "Any conclusions? How was his proof?"

"I'm afraid I don't see anything there. I mean he has computation skills. And his powers of analysis are savant-like. But he blew a number of questions. And his proof, well, it wasn't what I'd hoped for."

"Really?"

"Yes, sorry. I wish I had better news."

"But he's talented."

"Oh yes. Just don't let him do your books."

"What's that supposed to mean?"

"Mr. Allen stole $2 million from the pension fund at his place of work."

Diana Katz's jaw dropped. It was a lovely, fine-boned jaw.

"Really?" she asked.

"Really."

And in that second, as Diana Katz's blue eyes locked onto his, as her jaw rose and she pursed here lips in a sad, resigned-to-fate smile, Baxter Blood felt a wave of sympathy, even guilt.

"There might be other mathematicians who would have a different verdict," he offered.

Diana shook her head. "How small a company?"

"Small. A mom-and-pop shop, from the report I read. He did the books."

"Some stories are too good to be true, I guess."

"It's still a good story. The license plate genius."

"I'm not so sure," she sighed. "Listen, thanks for your help."

"My pleasure. I'm sorry to deliver bad news."

"No. Thank you. I should have looked into his background a little more."

When he got home that day, Baxter Blood made two lists.

List #1:
What I did was right because
1. Allen should be punished.
2. It is not clear he is a genius.
3. Diana should not rescue a crook.
4. I told Diana my opinion was not definitive.

List #2:
What I did was wrong because
1. I lied. Allen is impressive.
2. Diana deserves a good story.
3. Professors are not gods.

He looked at the lists. He drank some scotch. Then he wrote a confession. He wrote about everything: His affection and admiration for Diana. His jealousy. His deliberately false evaluation of Allen. Then he tore it up.

Months went by. Baxter Blood looked for Diana constantly. Every tall woman spiked his interest and then left him disappointed. He knew she was still teaching—he had checked with the registrar. But he did not dare to seek her out. He wondered if she had sought another evaluation. If someone else had declared Allen a genius. God, if that happened, he would become a laughingstock. Or be denounced for suppressing a mathematical triumph. Thoughts like this had him thinking of quitting. He was in his office looking at websites of Mexican retirement communities the day Diana Katz knocked on his door again. She was smiling.

He stood up immediately, knocking against his desk, spilling his coffee cup.

"Oh shoot," he said, tossing a newspaper over the spill. "Excuse me. Nice to see you."

"Yes. Do you have a minute?"

Baxter Blood felt himself break out in a sweat. He felt fear. "Uh, sure," he said. "Slow day at the office."

"Are you okay? You seem—"

"I'm fine. Well, I'm just glad to see you is all. I felt sort of guilty the last time I saw you. I ruined your story, didn't I?"

"Oh no, turns out you helped my story."

"I did?" Baxter Blood could feel himself turning pale. Anxiety flooded his system. He stopped breathing for a nanosecond while he tried to see where this was going: Allen was a genius? Allen turned out be innocent of his crime? How had he helped the story?

"I thought that instead of writing a true story, I'd turn it into fiction. A math genius with the heart of Bernie Madoff. A teacher who is beguiled by him, and a wise old professor who opens her eyes. Does genius carry less moral responsibility?

I've been writing and writing and writing. And now an editor in New York says he wants to publish it! I sold it because of you!"

"I don't know about that..." said Baxter Blood.

"Oh, but I do!" Diana pulled a bottle of champagne out of her bag, along with two plastic cups.

Baxter Blood was still trying to do the math. Had he done the right thing? A man wallowed in prison. A crush had been shattered. He had just heard himself described as a wise old professor. At least one heart was broken if not more; he had lost hours of sleep and focus; he had suppressed potential— which it was his true mandate as a teacher to discover and nurture. And yet here at the end, a woman, a stranger really, was smiling at him and offering him a drink. He took the clear plastic cup and thought again of his ex-wife and her moral calculus. Was the proof in his hand now? He studied the stream of countless bubbles rising to the top of the cup, then his eyes met Diana's and he said, "Cheers."

SEVEN

Whoa, whoa, whoa. WTF? *That* was a prison story? That's a bit of a stretch. Now I gotta read about math? I'm a little offended, actually. What about the Gulag? Alcatraz? The Panopticon? Where are chain gangs or that crazy penitentiary in Louisiana? What about the low-security prisons filled with white-collar criminals? Or the high-security prisons filled with black ones? Or Robben Island in South Africa? Any of that is going to be a lot more exciting than a fantasy about childless professors in some kind of sexless romance. Makes you wonder if Kaufman's running out of ideas, or if he was just out to lunch on this story. I mean, if I couldn't be a producer, college professor sounds like a pretty good runner-up. All these young people around. Lots of time off. Where's the prison in that? Well, they can't all be hits, right?

But wait a minute. I wonder if this is more pointed. If Amanda thinks I'm Baxter Blood or something? People bring me stories and most of the time I can't help them or I don't want to help them. I'm lonely. I'm old. But hey, I do things. I create things. So I don't think the parallel is fair. I'm gonna kick Amanda's ass, if that's her point.

One thing I do like about the story is the name of the main character. Baxter Blood. That is genius. A name that is possible but also impossible. It's right up there with Ichabod Crane or Rip Van Winkle. Or, come to think of it, Adonis Troy.

If there is one disaster I should have seen coming, it was Adonis Troy.

Some critics are going to say that the disaster wasn't Adonis Troy so much as the branding episode. I'm not so sure, given his tainted past, but I do know one thing: it was the tipping point for Amanda.

Looking back, what sent her over the edge was my asking her to find out if we could somehow isolate and record the sound of searing flesh while the contestants were screaming their heads off.

Her response? "You are totally, totally sick."

"It's theater, honey," I say. "I'm not asking because I'm into it. I'm asking because we are trying to communicate horror and terror."

"Sometimes I think it would be better if we were into it. Then I wouldn't feel like we were manipulating everything just for higher ratings."

"Whatever," I say, because sometimes you get tired of hearing people tell you over and over again just how amoral you are.

"No, not whatever. Do you understand that whenever we're talking about making something more impactful, it's just like a drug dealer figuring out a way to make his stuff stronger and more addictive?"

"If you say so, honey."

"Don't honey me, Rick. You know what? Screw this. I quit."

"Don't quit. Please don't quit. I'm sorry. I get your point. But that's the business we're in: Creating an effect. Drama. Amanda, you are awesome. When this is over, you can run a show for me. Whatever you want."

"No! I can't. These people are killing themselves, and for some fucked-up reason the world thinks it's entertainment."

"Think about it." But I know this is bad because Amanda never swears.

She goes quiet. She shuts her eyes, and for the 1000th time I take a moment to imagine her sleeping beside me, which makes me feel these bubbles of tenderness rising from my heart. Years ago this emotion would have manifested itself in my groin, but not at age 62.

"What symbol are you branding on these people anyway?"

"I can't decide between a peace symbol or U.S.A." I grin.

"Call me when Jay gets you out of your contract with Mephisto."

So Amanda left and I hired a young executive assistant, Veronica, who was born nursing on a BlackBerry and can multi-task like a porn star at a gang-bang. She's also gorgeous and she loves the show. But I miss Amanda.

The branding episode ends up being Adonis Troy's swan song, too. The flamboyant merchant of abuse, who made a bundle starring in bondage, whipping, choking, verbal assault, and vile humiliation videos, couldn't handle a little seared skin.

Turns out his whole career was a scam.

It's no secret that as reality shows grow in popularity, the contestants all go under the microscope of media scrutiny. Given that, it's amazing Adonis Troy's act lasted as long as it did. About three weeks into the series, Amanda was invited to a dinner party with a few gay friends, and they asked her to bring along the audition reel Adonis had submitted to the show. She put it on and they laughed their way through the entire DVD. Then they set her straight, freeze-framing some choice domination scenes. He was a great moaner and screamer, but if you watched frame by frame the point of impact, you can see he's got a rubberized, flesh-looking cover on his skin. So while the guy is a master of humilia-tion, he's not exactly the pain-absorbing sponge he claimed to be. I mean, what's the point of dripping wax on yourself if there's saran wrap on your johnson?

All the contestants protest the branding. In fact they threaten to boycott the whole thing. But once we explain that the contestants can choose their branding—includ-ing "U.S.A."—Sgt. St. James announces he is definitely up for that, and the strike is over. God bless Sgt. St. James. His quick decision saves us from having to serve our contestants with papers. Threatening to sue your TV stars isn't really good for business.

Still, Adonis Troy continues whimpering. "I just don't think this is about endurance," he tells the camera.

Adonis was very much between a rock and a hard place. At the time, I didn't realize quite how hard. Here's the thing: Amanda had just quit and Little Ricky was new and I hadn't found my assistant Veronica yet, so when Adonis told Little Ricky he wanted to talk to me, the Post-It note message got lost in the shuffle. Instead of pushing for a meeting, Adonis retreated into his shell. If you look at the footage from that week, he is vanishing. His endless pat-ter from the earlier episodes is nonexistent, his signature Venus-in-*Flashdance* look of leather and leg-warmers is gone. He's wearing normal clothes. He looks glum and glummer.

Which is understandable, because at this point of the proceedings, Adonis has sunk to the bottom of the rankings. He has zero chance of winning *The King of Pain*, and maybe he realizes this whole appearance on the show is a bad, bad career move, especially for a fraudulent masochist like him.

The day of the branding, our cameras find him nearly catatonic, lying in bed, covers pulled up to his chin. His two roommates try to joke with him but he closes his eyes and mumbles something that might be a prayer. Then he kicks off the covers, rises fully dressed with his shoes on and barks, "Let's do this thing!" In reality TV, it's not always easy to know who is fronting for the camera—trying to get some attention either with bravado or tears—and who is a genuine head case. But Adonis Troy had conned thousand of twisted video buyers, so it's no surprise he conned us. Looking back, we should never have allowed him on the show.

He's jittery all morning. When it's his turn he goes into the branding room—a red-coal fire and an examination table—with the judges. And as our own cowboy, Bob Bunter, makes chit-chat, Adonis Troy walks over to the fire and pulls out the iron and starts waving the damn thing around.

"You bastards," he snarls. "Nobody's gonna brand me."

"What the fuck?" I say, watching from the remote truck.

Fortunately Rittenhouse, the director, has more presence of mind. "Keep rolling guys. If he comes at you, hit him with the fucking camera!"

"Adonis, no one is going to brand you if you don't want

to. We don't keep contestants in prisons," says Dr. Burns. "The door is right there."

"Camera Two, Get the door, please."

"You are free to leave. This is a competition, not a prison."

"Number One, in tight on Adonis's face. Three, stay wide on them. Two, you take Dr. Burns."

"Go on, put the iron down and walk through the door. We've all seen you compete and do a great job. There's nothing wrong with leaving now."

"I'm already at the bottom! Why should I let you brand me if I'm just going home?"

"You don't know that. The rankings are always in flux. But if that's your decision, that's fine. However, please don't threaten us."

"I need more time."

Dr. Burns look at the other judges.

"Let's give him a few minutes."

"15 minutes," I shout. "And somebody call the cops."

"15 minutes," Rittenhouse barks into the mic. "And tell him you're leaving."

"Okay," says Dr Burns. "You have 15 minutes. We'll leave you alone."

"Fuck 15 minutes!" Adonis yells, smashing the iron into the coals. "I'm out of here!"

Naturally we beep that part out later.

He bolts the set, taking refuge in his room and demanding a limo to drive him to Vegas.

"Tell him fine," I say to Little Ricky. "But he owes us an exit interview, or I'll sue him for the rest of his life."

We get the interview. And of course he breaks down about breaking down. You probably saw it on the news or on YouTube or on our show. The watery eyes, the single tear and then the shuddering weep, and finally the eruption of cascading sobs. It was horrible. It was heartbreaking. It was TV gold.

We only broadcast 30 seconds. But believe me when I tell you that he went on forever. About broken dreams, about being a falling star. Jesus.

And then he rolls off, phoning his boyfriend to meet him at the Wynn.

Two weeks later, Adonis Troy is dead.

There's a type of celebrity death that almost seems engineered by the gods of Glitz. Elvis, Sid Vicious, Kurt Cobain, Anna Nicole Smith, Michael Jackson. Creative types or self-promoting geniuses with destructive impulses. Adonis Troy was nowhere near their league. But his demise was just as pathetic. He had the booze, drugs, but worst of all, he immersed himself in self-pity and self-importance in a way that just underscored his B-league celebrity status.

Not to be self-centered, but Adonis Troy's death was just another angle to attack *The King of Pain*. We were "a vehicle for humiliation, which of course is a large part of the torture ethos"—that was a culture critic talking point. And they were right—humiliation is a classic parlor trick of both castle dungeons and corporate boardrooms. It's everywhere. It's a manipulative device, right up there with the carrots of praise, challenge, and reward. None of these windbags ever bothers noticing that the flip side of humiliation is triumph and elation. And that triumph in something as extreme as *The King of Pain* is relative. Just to finish is a win. Me? I would have been out in the first second. In fact, I wouldn't have bothered showing up.

No, what killed Adonis Troy wasn't my show, it was Adonis Troy. He wasn't real—he was a total fake. His name, his videos, his life. And when the slo-mo version of his videos hit the Web, forget it. He instantly became a punchline on late night TV, in the tabloids and all over the web. No wonder he went into a hole. His creation was now a national joke. And, hey, I know something about that, too. But I didn't kill myself over *Goldengrove*.

When Adonis Troy took his final curtain, overdosed in the tub, we issued a statement and paid for his funeral. And we ran a one-minute reel of our time with him. But the train kept a-rolling: the branding episode did very well. The scream-o-meter was a great idea and so was the grimace-cam, which scored facial expressions. I was also proud of using a triple-screen. One side had the branding, the other had a facial close-up, and below the whole thing was the scream-o-meter decibel level display. So the episode had innovation, terror, chaos, and suffering. Everyone you expected to be stoic was. But Kaylene was the big surprise. She didn't even wince.

"I'm the only one here who's given birth, as far as I know," she says. "So I know a little something about pain."

Bingo! This remark turned Kaylene into a polarizing figure. We had a Servant of God in Sister Rosemarie, and now we had an Accidental Feminist in Kaylene. The show kept feeding the nation's op-ed columns and blogs a never-ending supply of subjects and plot lines. Fodder to attack the show or me or the network or the nation itself. And that's fine, because what does it say about a country that plans its nights around a show about torture? When someone asks that question—and it's asked every day—we say it's about the human spirit, not torture. But nobody ever quotes us unless they can hold their noses at the same time.

As you may have gathered by now, I'm no stranger to controversy. Every so often, starting with *Desperately Seeking Goldfarb*, my movies hit a nerve. You remember *Goldfarb*— or maybe you don't: Orthodox Jews hire a salesgirl who is "so blonde she must be a shiksa" and leave their nebbishy son to manage the family jewelry store while they go to the Holy Land. The next day, three large women rob the store. The son is beside himself until the bombshell takes him into clubland to find the drag queens who ripped them off. There are some nice running gags—mostly involving clubkids gushing over Goldfarb's 18th-century clothes and hair as the cutting edge of fashion. And of course, his parents rush back to find their missing son.

According to the witless of the world, this film was anti-Semitic, anti-tradition, anti-drag queen, anti-shiksa, anti-everything. Actually it was pro-comedy. The protests would have been louder and uglier except for one thing: nobody saw the movie. *Goldfarb* did okay on the coasts and in Chicago, but that was it. Worst box office of my career. Even my own relatives boycotted it, complaining that I had embarrassed them at synagogue. Of course that hasn't stopped them from calling me every time they come out west to ask for studio tours.

So now the daggers are out yet again. I am public enemy number one, thanks to my big mouth on Kitty Andrapov's show—and, I finally remember it, that goddamn network statement! That's right, the reason Walter Fields called me after my CNN slip-up was to read me a draft from his army of PR babes and cutthroat lawyers. Motherfuckers. To make matters worse for me, the press will have no one to talk to representing my side of the story. The show PR was handled by the network and I don't have any PR gurus on retainer. Plus Jay, the lawyer who does my contracts, is in India, probably sitting on a white horse waiting to get married. The thing about my Apu remark—not that it's really defensible—is that I got it from Jay, which is short for Sanjay. Sanjay Gupta. He was telling me about his family—"a bunch of quickie-mart owning, computer programming Apus," he had said. "I'm the only one in the entertainment biz."

And I said, "I love those films."

And he said: "*The Simpsons*? Greatest show ever, man."

And I said: "No, *The Apu Trilogy* by Satyajit Ray."

He squinted at me and said: "Never heard of them."

So my some-of-my-best-lawyers-are-Indian spinmeister, who called his own family a bunch of Apus, is eating his weight in pappadams, waiting to be paid millions of rupees to marry a gorgeous Calcutta Brahmin while I, if I survive my current predicament, will swing at high noon in the court of public opinion.

Actually, I'm pretty sure I've already been hung and swung. It is all really starting to come back to me. Walter Fields. The black hole of creativity. The rainmaker. The executioner. He called me at home after my CNN shenanigans with Premshaw Choudry. I was already three sheets to a hurricane, and Walter told me they were writing up a press release condemning my actions. What a prick. But I can't think of this right now or I'll have a heart attack. Amanda will call as soon as she hears the news, I'm sure. Even though she quit. And when I won't pick up, she'll come here. Definitely. Maybe. Or my son. Maybe. If he even reads the papers.

I gotta figure my rescue is close. Nobody will have seen me since the CNN Apu incident. If not Amanda, then one of my pals—Lars or Frank—will track me down. Worst case: When dawn comes tomorrow, I'll have another 24 hours until Marta arrives.

My car. The Jag. That is the key. Did I put it in the garage or leave it out front? Out front would be good, because then people will assume I'm home and come in. If it's in the garage, people will drive by and assume I've gone somewhere. Why do I even have a garage? This is L.A. It's not like it snows. And it's not like I need a place for a lawnmower—the landscapers do all that. Jesus. How appropriate would it be to die in L.A. because somebody doesn't see my car?

I owe a lot to cars. As I've said, I got into the biz as a valet. And *Donny Cycle* was all about cars and bikes. Donny, a biker to his pathetic core, would bleat his Orwellian mantra—two wheels good, four wheels bad—and inevitably get the shit kicked out of him by a car owner. More importantly, I owe my one moment of bliss with Amanda to my Jag.

Yessir, I'm 62 and I got to second base. Well, I was 60 at the time.

She, by the way, was 27.

In baseball, when a hitter hits a long ball and it bounces

over the fence, he is automatically awarded second base. It's called a ground-rule double. I have this idea that when an old guy like me makes out with a 27-year-old and no money or favors are exchanged, it should qualify as a ground-rule sex. No penetration, sure. But it's still sex.

At least that's the way I felt—and still feel—after my red-hot time with Amanda.

We were a little tipsy. I offer to drive her home. I tell her my Jag came with an automatic breathalyzer.

"No way!"

"Way," I lie. "I have a Jag XKE. The breathalyzer is one of the selling points."

"I've never heard of that. It's a terrific idea."

"It's not a standard feature. But Jag dealers are masters of the hand sell. My guy got me one."

"That's kind of clever, I guess."

"Come see it," I say. "I'll pass the test and drive you home."

Of course, my Jag is an antique. A 1962 red, convertible roadster.

"But this is an old car!" laughs Amanda.

"But it was overhauled. By a guy like Q in James Bond."

We get in and I hit a button on the lovely walnut dash-board.

"Damn," I say. "It's not working. The breathalyzer is supposed to pop up."

"You are such a liar! This car is older than I am."

But she's not mad at me: she's laughing. She's wearing a red-and-white checked print dress. She looks like a picnic.

"You're right. It's the first time I've ever lied to you. Forgive me."

She pushes her seat back. Now she's long and flowing in the Jag's tan leather seat.

"You got me here under false pretenses."

"I still want to drive you home. I just need to sober up. Hey! What's that?"

I point at her shoulder strap and then lean over as if to examine it more closely.

When she looks down at the strap, I'm right there.

I guess we make out for about 10 minutes, there in the car on the street, with kids walking by calling out "Get a room!"

"This is so wrong!" she giggles.

Five minutes later, she asks me: "How many times have you been married?"

I plead the Fifth.

"You're a very good kisser," she observes, coming up for air.

"Mmm," I say, nuzzling her neck.

"I like this. This is fun!" she declares.

"Um-mm."

"We work together!" she laughs.

She was drunk.

And me? I'm in heaven. I'm as turned on as the West Coast power grid. I've got my hands running down her arms, caressing her legs. My fingers are drinking in her young, flawless skin. It's smooth, soft, supple, perfect. This is one of the things that get me: skin. Women are beautiful at any age. With luck and effort, their bones and bodies can beat back time. But skin is a completely different story for 99% of us. Skin is a gauge of time.

So when I grab Amanda's hand and lift it to my lips, it is

an intimate, worshipful, adoring moment. But when she lifts my hands to her lips, I watch her and I see a flicker in her eyes as she is confronted with a paw that does not match the perfection of her own. Mine has wrinkles and misshapen digits. And what has begun as a reciprocal moment veers into a nanosecond of withdrawal. And then, with the skill of a master conductor, she brings the make-out session to a quick end: a long kiss, a softly murmured "I have to go," and then one more quick kiss, the period, the closure on the night.

I insist on driving her home, but she's already out of the car and on her cell calling a taxi service.

I crash my car into my front gate on the way home. Nothing too bad. Just the headlights.

In the morning there's an email from her.

Rick, I had a great time. Too great. Please excuse my unprofessional behavior. It won't happen again. Thanks for all your support. Amanda

If I had my BlackBerry within reach now, I could look up that email. I saved it. It's proof I didn't dream the whole thing up. It's been two years now. We've shared dozens of bottles of wine since then, but there has been no repeat of that night. I never mention it, either. But I do complement her. And I cheer her through boyfriends and diets. And I try not to think about the L.A. sun taking its toll on her skin. I still can't believe she left over the branding episode. I wonder if there was something else going on that I'm missing?

Christ, my legs hurt. Amanda, where are you? An old man needs you.

And not in that way.

LONGMAN

Months before martial law was declared, the government had quietly slipped into what might be called a practice mode of authoritarian rule. Newspapers were able to publish freely and opposition parties functioned in their normal floundering way, but sporadically, with no discernible logic, newsprint deliveries would be impounded on trumped up taxation charges; eviction papers on choice locales would be served over allegations of undesirable activity; and politically active citizens had begun to disappear.

Longman was arrested while handing out leaflets for a meeting of the Young Socialist Union. A harmless, devoted idealist, he was a far cry from his name: everything about him was short: his size, his sparsely populated Vandyke, his ill-fitting pants and jacket. But he was very committed, very smart, and driven by his secret feelings for a comrade named Katja. He was booked on suspicion of suspicious activities, which sounds ridiculous but is a deadly serious charge if your country happens to be run by a paranoid regime.

Longman was sent to the city jail. The warden, Smoltec, whose brother-in-law had been arrested in Vinsk for his ties to the Young Capitalist Union, was sympathetic to political prisoners and put them all in the same cell. To put them in with the general population of predators and misfits seemed unconscionable to him. But nothing keeps you safe in prison except for death, and Longman and his idealistic companions quickly found themselves victims of the universal law of "might makes right." Cigarettes were either permanently "borrowed" or stolen. Objections to theft were silenced by punches to the face, kicks in the balls, or near-lethal choke-holds. The political prisoners—Longman the Socialist, Stoyic the Bolshevik, Kroker the Menshevik, Levitt the Anarchist, and Paulus the Democrat—took their victimization well, consoling themselves with the knowledge that their oppressors were shaped by a cruel state, by inequality, by poverty and poor education, and that prison conditions were inhumane and that inhumanity breeds inhumanity.

They would discuss these things over games of chess, over meals, during freezing nights. Longman, to keep from going out of his mind, began to practice writing with his right hand. After a month, the natural lefty was able to entertain onlookers by writing the same poem—Tarshan's "Beauty" or Spychik's "Reflections on Gray"—with both hands going simultaneously.

But boredom was everywhere. News leaked in by letters and with each new arrival. But these were slow, infrequent distractions. Often talk turned to food. How many eggs could a man eat? Longman ventured that he could easily consume two dozen hard-boileds. This led naturally to a debate on the pressing issue of how long it would take for you to shit after eating 24 eggs. Two to three days was the consensus. Other discussions included the best things to eat with bread. The best way to cook a duck. What was the most important vegetable: the onion, which gave flavor to everything, the potato, which was the root of all meals, or the cabbage, which anchored all stews?

Kroker the Menshevik was adamant: "Onions. Without onions, what good is a potato?"

"You can eat a potato without onions, you moron," said Paulus. "And it fills you up a lot more than an onion, which is basically water."

"But in a stew? Or a soup? You need onion. It is a magic ingredient."

"I agree with Kroker," said Leavitt the Anarchist, although no one could trust he was being honest. "Cabbage without onions is like a woman with no breasts."

There also were endless chocolate discussions: Who made the best chocolate? Was dark chocolate an aphrodisiac? Was milk chocolate a French conspiracy? And what would you do if you had a single square of chocolate right now?

Longman hadn't had much experience with chocolate. He was too poor to indulge much in this luxury, so he remained silent on these matters. But he was very much impressed by Stoyic's thoughts on the last question. The Bolshevik had clearly spent some time considering the issue. "If I had one square, I would keep foil around it so as not to waste any on my fingertips. That would be tragic. Then I would pierce it with a needle or toothpick. This way I could handle the square without touching it. Then I would lick it, careful to make sure that my tongue touches nothing, not the side or roof of my mouth, so that I can savor the flavor, the sweetness, the fat, the chocolate. I would sit with a watch and allow myself one lick every five minutes. After an hour, I would take a lick and then press my tongue to the roof of my mouth to spread the flavor. This will make the taste evaporate more quickly, but the pleasure will be greater."

❧

Longman took stock of his situation. He had been incarcerated for three months with no trial. This was not right. He decided to take action. With his new writing skill, he wrote letters to each of the city's two newspapers, simultaneously, announcing his plan. He also wrote to Katja, but decided against sending that letter out of concern it might jeopardize her. Then he informed his cadre, and finally, since he had no access to senior prison or judicial authorities, he approached Jerjicjic, a guard, and told him the news: "I'm going on a hunger strike."

The next day word began to spread that Longman the small political prisoner was on a black hunger strike. People asked what it meant.

"He won't eat or drink anything, not even water. It is brutal."

On the first day of his hunger strike, Longman wrote a follow-up letter to the papers and slept a lot. The letter protested his arrest and prison conditions where men are forced to dream about individual squares of chocolate. On day three he wrote of fatigue and delirium. On day four he wondered how long he could survive.

Fellow prisoners began to come by. They brought him cigarettes and books. One man had him autograph a newspaper that ran a copy of his letter.

Reporters began to make inquiries. They paid off guards for updates. Longman felt weak but good, or if not good, then proud of himself.

On the sixth day he was brought to see the warden, Smoltec.

"Christ, look at you!" Smoltec said. "Bring him tea at once."

"Nothing," rasped Longman. "I'm on a black hunger strike."

"How do you feel?" asked Smoltec.

"Tired. Weak."

"Then eat. You want a steak?"

"Did you bring me here to torture me?"

"You are doing a fine job of that yourself."

Longman sighed.

"I had you brought here to ask you to eat. Please start eating."

"Why?"

"Because I can't have a martyr in my jail. It doesn't work well for me. It doesn't look good."

"That's the point, Warden."

The tea arrived.

"Please have some. Sugar? Milk?"

"No thank you."

Warden Smoltec smiled. "You can't blame me for trying."

Longman shrugged.

"You are not the first hunger striker I have...worked with. When you do start to eat and drink, take only small sips. Your stomach has contracted."

"How long did others go?"

"About seven days."

There was something about Warden Smoltec's tone that seemed pointed. As if he were trying to make something clear. Longman thought it was a warning, but a warning of what?

"My brother is a doctor," Warden Smoltec said. "He says starving yourself is very bad for your body. The organs suffer. The brain suffers. I'm going to ask you to end the strike tonight."

"I want a hearing. I've done nothing wrong. I was handing out flyers."

"I'll make inquiries on your behalf."

"I want a hearing date."

"But if you continue the strike, I will have to withdraw my offer."

"Then I'm no worse off than I am now," said Longman, who was surprised at how easy it was to remain defiant. The truth was he was now curious about himself. About his willpower. There were moments when the hunger abated and he felt truly powerful. He was beating back the most basic urge known to man. It was a strength beyond that of any other man in prison.

"That is your choice, then?" Warden Smoltec frowned and looked grim. "I urge you to reconsider before lights out tonight. Or it will end badly."

Warden Smoltec left the room. Longman felt tired, proud, and confused. The other truth pushing him along was that each day of the strike was another day to impress Katja. Even if she was not that impressed by his orange hair or his slight frame, surely she couldn't miss his inner strength and commitment to the cause.

The next morning Longman was roused at dawn and marched to the prison clinic. There, the guards strapped him to a table, binding his arms and legs with rope. A thick leather strap was tightened across his shoulders and upper chest. Then he was left alone.

"What is this?" Longman shouted. "Torture? Extermination? I was only handing out flyers for a meeting!"

The guards returned and dimmed the lights. Longman screamed louder. "I want to talk to the warden! This is an outrage!" In between screams he heard something clang and men whispering.

"Now!" yelled a guard.

The lights came on. Longman felt himself in a headlock. A hand clamped down on his nose. When he reflexively opened his mouth, a guard came up and jammed a black tube into his mouth and forced it down his throat.

To say Longman was terrified or scared out of his mind would be an understatement. He was choking, his heart pounded as if it would rip through his chest, his body twisted against the restraints so violently that he sliced his skin. Down the tube came some kind of warm mushy liquid. It rushed out, flooding his body, assaulting his stomach, backing up in his throat, all the way into his sinuses. His whole system locked in twisting tides of food, gastric juices, and vomit as the force-feeding continued. Then finally the tube was gone and the men withdrew, leaving Longman there prone, mush and bile dribbling down his face, melding with the cold sweat that rose on his skin. His throat burned, his lungs ached, his stomach raged.

This was assault. Warden Smoltec had ordered it. The fucking warden. Longman, even in the face of his greatest horror, had a moment of empathy. He thought of his two sisters, of anyone physically violated, raped. "God help them," he thought.

Longman was back in his cell an hour later, facing curious eyes.

"Did they beat you?"

"Worse," he rasped, his scraped throat burning, his pride stripped to nothing. "The strike is over."

It took weeks for Longman to emerge from his stupor. He

spoke to no one and remained in his bunk for days. Then one day Stoyic approached him, smiling and holding a letter. "Longman," he said, "cheer up." He broke into a confidential whisper: "Tonight, we will get a show."

Word spread among the inmates that anyone housed along the south wall should look out their tiny barred windows that evening around 10 o'clock.

Longman wondered what kind of show was worth getting so excited about. Would there be an opera staged on the open street? They had all gazed out to the drab grey buildings across the street, where poor tenants hung their laundry out the window, as if to block the even uglier, greyer monolith that was the prison. There were few signs of life.

Stoyic had mentioned specifics to the others: third floor. Four windows from the corner.

Longman and Paulus had peeked earlier in the afternoon and seen a pretty young woman with short hair scrubbing that window. They were at a loss to think what would happen that was making Stoyic so happy and proud.

"She is a wonderful woman, my Petra," Stoyic said, when they told him what they had seen. "Not like the other girls. She understands the cause. The greater good."

That night, the men in the cell—and in cells all along the south wall—settled at their two tiny windows. The guards noticed a flurry of excitement and arranged to have a cell for themselves to watch the mysterious show.

At 10 p.m., a beam of light shone out of Petra's window. Longman wondered if perhaps Petra was going to project a movie or some kind of image.

And then, in front of the beam of light stepped the silhouette of a woman's figure. She wore a short skirt with frills, high-heeled shoes, a top hat, and a bobbed haircut. In her hand was a long cigarette holder. There were gasps in every cell along the south wall. Instantly, without having to be told, all the men knew what was going to happen.

Longman knew, too. And he was torn between this outrageous exploitation of a woman and his own arousal. In front of him, Stoyic dropped his pants. Longman saw his other comrades follow suit. Longman had been shocked by the onanism that went on in prison. And now the thought of his good friends—and himself—joining their ranks filled him with horror.

And yet he could not take his eyes off Petra. She was twirling. She bent over and wiggled her bottom. She showed her profile and marched in place, her lovely bosom bouncing up and down. The men roared and moaned with each pose. Some called out to her. And finally, she began kicking off her shoes, tossing the cigarette aside, pushing her dress lower and lower, flipping her hat away, pulling the dress up over her head until she was a totally naked silhouette, a figure of hips, breasts, nipples, legs. A dancing statue. There were moans, and without realizing it, Longman had joined his comrades, touching himself as he had never done in prison. And when Petra began touching herself, running a hand from her hip to her thigh, it was too much: gasps of pleasure, of release, cascaded through the cruel, frozen old prison.

"Stoyic, we love you!" screamed a voice into the night when it was all over.

❧

Longman began to consider the possibility that he would remain in prison indefinitely. It could be days, it could be years. What would he miss over the years, beside food? Well, he had never had sex. And therefore it went without saying that he did not have a wife or child. Both seemed like the most sacred goals of life to him. Listening to the older prisoners, this is what they bragged about, worried about and, strangely, complained about: their wives, their children. Longman had only his mother, a seamstress who worked and prayed and worked and prayed, and his sisters, who only worked. It was because of his mother that he had sought out the Young Socialist Union. Her body was bent. Her fingers crimped with age, but she shuffled in to work to make the exact same wages she had made twelve years earlier. It was wrong. He had joined, hoping to change conditions for the workingman, but now he had given her nothing but worry.

Longman had been studying law before his incarceration. But while in prison he began to think about other careers. Becoming a chef was at the top of his list. All the talk of food, the discussion of tastes, smells, and dishes, the rhapsodic memories of meals, echoed in his mind. To a young man carrying an aching pit of hunger in his gut, these details just added to his yearning for food. But they also made him feel as if there was a universal language of taste, a series of sensations that he was missing. Food was something he needed to be around. It was vastly more immediate than the law.

What was the law anyway? An agreed-upon set of rules. But if no one is enforcing them, what is the point? Longman imagined that there were rules of law in the kitchen, too. And not just the kosher laws some of his relatives practiced, but laws of preparation or proportion or combination. Or maybe not. Maybe cooking was anarchy—no rules, no laws. Maybe in some cases it was the opposite of law. Not anarchy, but art.

The next week Stachek, Treasurer of the Young Socialist Union, was brought in. Longman was thrilled. Stachek would have news about what was being done on their behalf. And he knew Katja.

"Smashed," said Stachek. "The entire organization. I should have fled. When they started picking up foot soldiers like you, that should have been a sign."

"How is Katja? Why doesn't she write?"

"Ach! Katja. She was a spy, the bitch."

Longman's chest tightened. His stomach lurched. "Katja? Surely she…"

"Marcu caught her at a covert meeting with Magnus of the Royalist Union. He saw Magnus take her hand."

"Her hand?" Longman repeated numbly.

"Then we fed her false information, about a big meeting at St. Lem's Church basement, and the police started hauling in charity workers until the pastor intervened."

"I can't believe it," Longman said.

He immediately wrote Katja a letter demanding an explanation, but he never received her reply, if she sent one, because he was suddenly released from prison. No hearing, no trial, no nothing. And just like that, his ordeal was over.

The country was now in the full lockdown of martial law, and the prisons were swelling with political activists and businessmen whose properties were coveted by the regime. It occurred to Longman that he had been released because a man who handed out flyers was taking up valuable space that would be better reserved for someone with property.

He went to see his mother first, then his sisters. Two days later, he went to Katja's house and waited across the street.

❧

In the early evening a military car drove up. Longman's heart raced. Was this an arrest? Was Stachek's story wrong, as he had hoped? Instantly, dreams of heroism filled his mind. If he arrests her, I will rush him, kill him with his own pistol, and drive away in his car. Or maybe I should slash his tires right now, to prevent him from taking her.

But these were fleeting thoughts. Longman was not only small but also a pacifist, and anyway, when the officer got out of the car, pulled his suit down, spit into his hand and slicked back his hair, Longman's mad rush of hope and bravado was immediately quashed by that one primping movement. This was a social call. Katja had indeed betrayed him.

Longman went home. He told his mother he had to leave the country. She cried. But she said she understood. She was sorry she had so little to give him to take on his journey.

"Don't be silly. I'm sorry I have so little to leave you."

"A mother wants to take care of her children."

"You have."

"There is a cousin. In Rome."

❧

The cousin knew a man who had a friend who owned a restaurant. It all worked out very well for Longman. He met a waitress and married her. They had a son. This was a dream to him. He was surrounded by food every day. Even during the war, he had connections and the skill to turn any ingredient into soup.

When the war was over, he purchased a restaurant. It became a popular spot, with its menu of dishes from the north and the south of the country. Now that he was old, he would go to the market with his son, a grown man who was now the chef of Longman's restaurant. Longman would walk with his son and remember teaching the boy to drink with his eyes, smell with his fingers, taste with his nose, and know the truth with his mouth. Longman still thought this way. He would fondle the vegetables, smell the dirt on the potatoes, and admire the glorious and shiny red mountains of tomatoes. Food was everywhere. The sellers, he knew them all. They forced samples into his hand, and he would take these offerings and place them in a pouch in his apron.

Back at his restaurant, in the big airy kitchen with the huge marble cutting block, three basins, and three ovens, he would empty his haul of freebies and begin to work, washing, drying, and arranging the food. Then he'd grab his big cleaver and begin to chop. Even at his age, with his fingers crimping just as his seamstress mother's hands had, he could still prep with the best of them.

He would always start with the onions. It had been established in prison that onions were the soul of every soup and every stew. And from that first chop for the only dish he would cook that day, when the sweet acid smell hit his nose and the vapors attacked his eyes, he would remember, with onion tears streaming down his face: his mother, his sisters, Stoyic the Bolshevik, Kroker the Menshevik, Levitt the Anarchist, Paulus the Democrat, the naked silhouette of Petra, and even Katja. He would keep chopping and crying, recalling conversations about food he had never tasted, about a life he had never lived. He would pour the onions into a huge soup pot and smile as they started to sizzle in the hot oil. This was his ritual, his homage, his way of giving thanks, and his tragedy: cooking for those he could never feed.

EIGHT

I'm betting Longman is related to Kaufman. I'm not sure why, but it sets my Jewdar pinging: Kaufman. Longman. Longman. Kaufman. Maybe Longman is this guy in the dedication. Whoever he is, he is no stranger to thirst, I'll tell you that. Far worse than my hunger is my thirst. My mouth feels brittle, like a crust is forming everywhere: lips, cheeks, roof, throat. And my tongue periodically breaks it all down, only to have the crust creep up again. After I clean myself up, promote Marta, rehire Amanda and make her head of production and sue the network, I'm going to invest in water. Water, water everywhere. I'm going to donate millions. Thirst is the real torture. We are water, after all. And not drinking water is like making yourself disappear.

Jeez, there really is a lot of deprivation in these stories. Hardly any women, no booze, zero freedom. I guess that's one of the things we did on *The King of Pain*: Take away freedom. Amanda said we were overdoing it. I said we can't be running a Club Med of torture. But maybe she was right. Maybe we overdid it a little. Maybe we deprived people of too much.

To me, deprivation is the most insidious kind of torture, because it functions by your not getting something you need—food, shelter, mental stimulation—until you crack. I guess there are three categories of torture: inflicting physical pain, inflicting mental pain, and deprivation, which can be both physical and mental. And then physical torture can be harnessed into mental torture—so that the threat of physical pain becomes a form of torture. Which is to say that torture is all relative. Branding hurts, no question. The burn lingers, debilitates, becomes infected. But I was always a lot more worried about the sleep deprivation episode we had planned for *The King of Pain*. Because to me, insomnia is a form of madness. There are no antibiotics for sleeplessness. Well, maybe cocaine or speed. They can fight sleeplessness, but they just make you more insane. Of all the competitions, this was the one where I felt like we might actually be torturing the contestants.

I know that sounds overly dramatic. But I'm serious. A lot of the other stuff is all sport—all Guinness Book of Records kind of bullshit. People see how long they can run. How many somersaults they can do in a row. Sure, teenagers and kids on sleepovers like to brag about how they stayed up all night. But nobody wants to go mano-a-mano against sleep. Our species craves sleep. We need it, like we need food and air.

So when we were talking about how far we could go in this episode, we consulted some doctors and shrinks. Most were horrified. Others were "very interested in the idea." But of course even these guys refused to issue statements on our behalf.

Don't get me wrong: I wasn't worried about any potential legal issues. Every contestant had assumed personal responsibility in the event of suffering any mental or physical damage. Honest to God, there's even a VD clause in most reality show contracts, about how if anyone gets dosed from a costar during filming, you can't blame the production company or the network. No, what I'm worried about is me and my conscience. I want someone to assure me I'm not pushing anyone over the edge. I almost feel guilty about Adonis Troy. Almost.

So I send Little Ricky to study the literature. "Or hire someone. We need rules for this thing."

But in the end, during an endless night when I'm sleepless thinking about sleeplessness—that insomnia feedback loop that is so maddening it can make you suicidal—I figure out the rules myself. Right away I get up, write down my thoughts, and then immediately conk out.

The day we announce the challenge—least amount of sleep over seven days, plus points for productivity, and deductions for things like caffeinated drinks—I think hardly anyone really understands how grueling it is going to get. Only Sgt. St. James looks grim. As he tells our cameras, he had a pal at the Waco siege of the Branch Davidians and their nut job leader, David Koresh. "They drove those people crazy with noise, trying to keep 'em awake. It was a barrage that went on for days. My buddy says it drove everyone—the Branch Davidians and law enforcement detail—completely insane."

The others? I believe they thought it was going to be like pulling an all-nighter at college.

Here's what we laid out for the seven days: After 60 hours, the contestants got five hours' grace. Every 12 hours we gave them something different to do. There would be micro-competitions for extra points, like making the most sandwiches for charity, and building the best playground installation for a local daycare.

Towards the end of day two, we catch Sanchez sleeping on the crapper. Kaylene too. Darcy starts throwing food. Jeremiah asks to go running at one in the morning. All the men go out, and for six hours they jog and walk under the stars, nobody saying a word.

It is at dawn that an investigator from OSHA shows up. Little Ricky calls me.

"The feds are here," he says.

As a producer, this is not an easily understood sentence. You don't expect it. Not at 6 a.m. Not ever.

"What?"

"OSHA—the workplace guys. Occupational Safety and Health Administration."

"What do they want from us?"

"To inspect the working conditions. They say they received a complaint."

My lawyer, Jay, is still in the country at this time. I call and have him choppered in. Nap time for the contestants wasn't until 6 p.m. So this investigator was going to see them in the most hideous, sleep-deprived shape possible.

Assuming the worst, I order Little Ricky to take the OSHA rep to breakfast and keep him away from the show until we get there.

"And Little Ricky?" I say.

"Yes, boss?"

"Tell me you started work on that mid-season Greatest Hits package, with the interviews with everyone—contestants and judges?"

"Yeah, we started on it."

"Good, cause if this prick shuts us down, we'll need something to show."

"Right. Good thinking, Mr. Salter."

"That's what I'm here for. And if we don't need it, we can put it on a DVD."

When I show up I'm ready to do three things: call my congressman and make good on 10 years of contributions, sweet-talk this government lackey, or call the press about the whole thing.

Jay arrives looking like three million bucks, of which two million are mine. And he immediately demands to see the formal complaint. Then he asks what defines a work place in a travelling reality show.

"I'm sorry, sir. We're just here to investigate worker abuse."

"Contestants or crew?"

"Both."

"Give me a break," I say. "This is a union show. These guys won't cross the letter T without a union rep. They didn't call you unless the union called you."

"And we have a log of all calls made by the contestants. I'll go check that," says Little Ricky.

"Look," Jay says. "It's a union job and the contestants all signed iron-clad deals that indemnify us."

"Well we got some complaints. I'll need to speak to the contestants. Alone."

"Can I see your ID again?"

He hands it over.

"Little Ricky, call Washington, D.C. and confirm there's an OSHA investigator named Richard Smith here in Nevada."

Richard Smith shrugs.

"Richard Smith," I say. "I think I smell a rat."

The shrug is repeated.

"A big tabloid rat."

He looks straight ahead.

"Let me see your backpack. We have security policies here, even if you're OSHA."

There's a sudden look of alarm on his face.

"You know what the charges are for impersonating a government worker?" I say. "I don't, but I imagine they are significant."

"You got me."

"No kidding." I pick up my cell phone and dial. "I need a crew back here," I say. Then I turn back to Richard Smith. "You tell me who sent you or I'm gonna air this whole thing on the show, and you go to jail."

"*Star News*. Oswald MacEntire."

I call MacEntire right there. That prick's weekly rag went nuts on Adonis Troy, putting him on the cover, calling him a fraud. They ran my picture with the caption "Sadist!" That stuff I can handle. But this is a whole new kind of sleazy. I make it clear to him that he will face conspiracy charges, too, if I decide to file a complaint. And that I will rip his sleazy magazine to shreds on the air. Unless…

And suddenly, *The King of Pain* has an ally of one in the media. I promise MacEntire access in return for a constant stream of positive coverage.

So the sleep episode goes on. Sgt. St. James kicks ass like I knew he would. Only medical interns and residents suffer more sleep abuse than grunts. "Facing snipers really helps keep you awake," he tells us when it's over. "This competition was really hard until the finale. That woke me up."

Ah, the finale of sleeplessness. Perhaps the most profitable product placement in history: Gamer Nation's

Rollercoaster Space Race was the video game we had them play to test their alertness. The segment was a 12-minute multiplayer race filled with laughing, cheering, crashing, burning, and rising again. Gamer Nation paid $4 million to have us use their game—and I even got them to enhance it so our contestants' faces were put on top of the game's normal characters.

Just the sight of Sister Rosemarie screaming with groggy joy was probably worth $10 million to Gamer Nation. How do I know? Because that's what they offered us to put a second game on the show.

"Next year," I tell them.

Video game rookie Sister Rosemarie held her own in our sleepless version of *Rollercoaster Space Race*. Jeremiah, however, fell hard. As a confirmed hippie Luddite, and the oldest guy on the show, he didn't stand a chance. Video killed the long-distance star. And he did not go as gracefully as his Zen masters might have hoped.

"To lose on a video game? That hurts. There's nothing really painful about playing a mindless game, and it doesn't seem right to be penalized for something that's pure technology. Still I'm grateful for this opportunity, and for all the support from the other contestants.

"Who do I think will win? That's tough. Maybe Sister Rosemarie. She has God on her side."

The judges like her too. Two weeks before the final show, the standings are as follows:

1. Sgt. St. James
2. Sanchez

3. Sister Rosemarie
4. Annabel Castro
5. Kaylene
6. Darcy

In my personal standings—which is not exactly the right word for a guy who's been pinned to the floor for an eternity—it's Sunday morning, so just 24 hours to go until Marta will come and free me. At least that's what I'm praying for. The rest of the world seems to have forsaken me. But I can do 24 hours. By my calculation, I've already done 36 at least. And I've watched the pros on my show do it. So I'm feeling a little more confident about my chances. Guess what? It never gets easy. There's no point at which you hit this blissful rhythm, where the repetitions and fatigue become poetry and joy. It's just pain and more pain. And sometimes one pain replaces another. A new ache, a new cramp, a new sore. Oh sure, there are runners who hit a rhythm before they start exhausting their supplies of glucose, carbs, oxygen, and masked steroids. But that doesn't last. Not if they are really pushing. So these 24 hours are gonna suck.

But hey, at least I have *A History of Prisons* and the mystery of what will happen to me at the end. At this point I still don't get it. When I read the book, will I:

- Have a greater understanding of all the kinds of prisons there are?
- Have a better grasp on the kinds of pain that are involved in imprisonment?

- Understand there are prisons all over the world and give more money to Amnesty International and prison reform groups?
- Quickly instruct my accountant to stop inflating deductions so I don't go to prison?

I must be missing something here. There must be hidden meanings Amanda thought would resonate with me. If I have time, I'll reread some of these suckers.

THE GIZLESS DAYS OF THOMAS BINDER

The sentencing is brutal. Total disconnect for six months. No cruise-chat or stripvids. No shows, no games. No pix, no flix, no graphix. No phone, no videx, no music. As the Judge talks to him, Thomas feels deflated, as if the air is seeping out of his body—not just his lungs, but also his brain, his eyes, his arms, his blood cells, everything. Plus, he is worried: At school the kids talk about withdrawal. It can kill you. And if it doesn't kill you, the scrambler chip insertion can burn something fierce and it itches for weeks. Some kids die because they scratch so much. They get infections that go to their brains. Shit like that really happens. Or at least Thomas has heard it does. Or maybe he has read it on a fact-pop on his Giz.

Listening to the Judge yammer on, Thomas wants to hit something. The moment the Judge asks him for his Giz, he wants to pound the device into the man's bulbous face. Instead he drops it into the man's doughy hands, hands that look too fat to dij properly. It is a fact that fat kids can't really dij so well; a kid with chubby fingers can't slide and glide, or click and flick with the same accuracy and speed as a kid with normal fingers.

So: Domestic jail. Virtual Solitary plus Group Therapy. He thinks maybe regular jail would be better. There are other people in prison. You can talk. Without his Giz, and with the scrambler chip insert, he's going to be secluded. He has heard that down in Mexico you can get hooked up with a tricked-out bootleg chip that can't be detected by your penal scrambler chip. Totally illegal. Supposedly these cyber-narcos kill people, remove the victims' active chips, tech 'em up, and then destroy the victims' bodies so nobody will know they are dead. That's because when the Giz Authority finds out someone dies, they immediately disable the deceased's chip so it can't be reused again. And that's why the Mexican overhaul costs a huge chunk of change; you're paying for a hit, a disposal, the tech upgrade and insertion.

Of course, a MexiGiz is out of the question. Even if he had the money, without his Giz and the instant translator app, he can't speak Spanish to make the arrangements. The translator app is so awesome. Without it, he would never have met Makita, who is from the Czech Republic. Not many people really speak Czech, but Thomas did as long as his Giz was around.

Now if Makita videxes him or texts or calls...nothing. He won't learn about it for six months. He should have called her, but he was too embarrassed and depressed by the whole court thing. Damn. Maybe he'll get someone to send her a message.

The guards take him down to the N.Y.C. Criminal Implants Division. Six months on the scrambler chip. Even if he gets a hold of another Giz, the scrambler chip will prevent his permanent chip from hooking up with the Giz. He wonders about the time before chips and Gizzes. The story he heard in Modern History and that his grandpa later confirmed was that nobody was making any money. Music, movies, porn, books, lectures, art, video games, pictures, software—the things that get micro-charged to your monthly account now—were all free. They weren't supposed to be free; his grandpa said that in the old days you used to pay for everything separately—songs, movies, whatever. But once everything went digital, there was so much copying that, over the years, hundreds of billions of dollars were lost. Suddenly, songs or books that might have made $1 million in the pre-digital days only made half that, or less. And movies suffered even more. Some companies decided to stick ads on the files and gave those away. The idea was to make money on the ads or on sponsorships. But then hackers invented adsniffers and adsnuffers and they were able to strip off the ads, and so that revenue stream ran dry as well. The only people who were profiting were the telecom companies that sent the files out, and the companies that built the devices everyone used to play, steal, and store the files that once upon a time made money. Then the government stepped in. Digital regulation. Copyright control. Registration, chips, micro-transactions—and the Giz.

A guard calls his name. He has a big scar on the back of his neck—probably from implantitis, an infection that hit during early chip insertion. It's disgusting, the mottled, red skin, but Thomas can't stop staring at it as he follows the guard into a room.

A technician with a blonde bob framing rosy cheeks offers him a seat. He sneaks a glance while she checks his paperwork. She's got a mild case of buck teeth but that's alright; she's perky and pretty. Then she picks up a scanner and examines the back of Thomas's neck and locates his chip with her finger. It tickles and Thomas's shoulders flinch up toward his ears.

"Relax," she says. "Everybody's ticklish around their chip."

The scanner beeps as she passes it over his chip. "Yes. You are you, Thomas Binder," she confirms, looking at the readout. Then she picks up another device. "Now let me put in this override. You'll just feel a little pinch."

She pulls on her chip gun and he feels a tiny stab.

"There," she says. "You are now officially offline. Stay out of trouble and I'll see you back here in six months."

The first week Thomas is lost. He is a zombie, like the ones in *Frankenzone* who don't feel a thing no matter what you hit 'em with, except that's not totally true because he's really, really pissed off. With nothing to watch, he stares at himself in the mirror. He shaves his head and his scrawny beard; he wishes the rest of his body could change as quickly. Mutate. He does push-ups and sit-ups like he's seen hardened criminals do in prison movies and then looks in the bathroom mirror and sees no change. In a fury, he does more reps. His Group Therapy begins in a week. He wants to be buff by then.

Five months earlier he had crashed his electrozipper and lost his license immediately. The charges were Gizzing while driving, plus intoxication because he had been snorting prosto-mones. He never told anyone, but the prosto made him super horny, and he crashed while Gizzing a stripvid from Makita. Damn. That was a big mistake.

After three days, his mother can't stand his moping around anymore. She outputs some digi-cash from her Giz to the wireless printer and tells him to catch an electrocab and go see his grandfather across town. Thomas doesn't mind. At least it'll be a different kind of boredom, is the way he sees it.

His grandpa's house exudes that smell of old people. He and Makita had discussed this once, so he knows it's not just his grandpa that has this smell. Makita described it as mildew, sweat, and cologne, and Thomas knew exactly what she was talking about.

The door opens on the third ring. His grandpa is cool, but he's moving more slowly these days. They hug.

"How does it feel to be disconnected?" says Grandpa.

"Mom told you? Man! I told her not to tell anyone."

"She didn't tell me. I called you. When you call, there's a message: 'The Giz you are calling has been disabled.'"

"Fuck."

"Language, young man! How long is your sentence?"

"Six goddamn months."

"Thomas, I'm not even going to ask what you did. You can tell me when you are ready. But please. You need to start making smarter choices—language, Gizzing, everything. You're a clever boy."

Suddenly Thomas is really not in the mood to hear a stream of wisdom and criticism from the old guy, even if he means well.

"Grandpa, do you want me to clean the yard?"

"I would love that. Then I have some clothes I need taken to the basement. We'll have lunch after."

Thomas zips through the small back yard, raking leaves and picking up garbage that has blown in from the street. He thinks about taking the Sanitation Department test, but that seems so boring. He can't believe there's a test to throw out the garbage, but there is. Disposal is renewal—that's one of the slogans on the computerized sorter trucks. You have to know your renewables from your disposables. Your aluminum from your tin. And that's just the beginning. You have to know half-life decay. You have to know computer parts—what's reusable, what goes to the landfill. He stuffs the leaves in a bag and hauls it to the curb. Back inside, he grabs the box of clothes on his grandpa's bed and takes it down to the basement, where another bouquet of time hits his nostrils. This is the universal smell of the basement: that cool, musty dampness with a hint of—what exactly? Mothballs? Mold? Time? Thomas has no clue. He wishes he could call Makita about this. She would know. She is into smells and food. And making out. Or at least making out on the Giz.

The basement. He hasn't been down here in a while. This is where he and his brother used to play when they got tired of listening to grown-ups talk, which took about 90 seconds on a good day. There was an ancient Nok Hockey game and a table with checkers and an old version of Monopoly which used fake paper money back then. That was cool. Now the digital version of Monopoly comes with four mini-Gizzes routed together, so kids can calculate fake digicash and see how much they all have.

He puts the box of clothes down and surveys the basement. Something catches his eye on a shelf in the corner. At first he thinks it's an old video game cover—like the single player games he had as a kid a few years back, basic stuff like *Killzone* and *Narcoland*—just before the Giz Act was signed into law. He remembers the exchange program, how everyone had a year to turn their devices and phones in for credits that would be applied to your Giz. He cried when his mom told him he'd have to give up his Play-yah. He loved that Play-yah, the density in his hand, his favorite cartoons and music, and the numbers of everyone he knew all loaded on it. He slept with it. He woke up with it. Now, wondering about this old game, he feels a rush of excitement, the first in days. He reaches toward the cover, which has a big, golden, glowing title: *Easy Come, Easy Go*, and a superhero-sounding name below: John Grind. It's a movie, he thinks, but it's not a mega-def disc. It's too thick. Maybe it's one of those ancient things—a videotape. He grabs it, goes to pop open the cover, but there's no plastic to pop: it just opens and he feels a tiny breeze as pages unfurl and swing. He grabs the other side with his free hand and shuts it.

He feels dumb. As dumb as when the cops busted him. As dumb as when he handed his Giz to that judge. "A book," he mutters, glancing up at the shelf in front of him. The entire thing is filled with books.

Then he gives *Easy Come, Easy Go* another look. John Grind is a pretty cool name. He opens the cover and, on the inside flap, he sees a picture and he laughs. John Grind is a dapper English gent, not the chiseled thug he had expected.

The books on his Giz...he can't remember seeing a picture of the author. Not that he's read much since he finished high school. The way he figures it, reading books on a Giz is like taking a nap during sex. Video games, movies, chat, videx, groupex, maxi-widgets, popflashes, gambling, and gambling on gambling, that was the fun stuff. And his favorite: Cruise-chat—that was sick. A combination of videx, groupex, and chat: Pick a neighborhood and see who's around. That's how he met Makita—he liked to combine cruise-chat with the translator function and go to, say, Sweden, Ethiopia, or Calcutta. Places with good-looking women.

But now: No Giz. It's like he barely exists.

He grabs an empty backpack out of another cardboard box—it has a beagle on it with cute droopy ears and a little yellow bird that rests on the dog's tummy. They look familiar, but he can't remember where the characters are from. He begins to shovel books into the bag.

∽᷈᷈᷈᷈᷈᷈᷈

The group counseling session is exactly what Thomas had imagined. Housed in a drab government building near City Jail—sort of a reminder that if you screw up here, you might end up there—the session is run by a 30-something leader, Ruth, who is attractive in an older woman way: tall, strong features, and a nice body that looks younger than its owner actually is. There's a faded gray carpet and metal folding chairs and crappy overhead lights. And the group members: a fat misfit with tattoos on his neck, a thin misfit with bad acne, a Latina girl who is totally smokin' and, going by her tight, look-at-me clothes, knows it, and a black girl with stylish glasses and a long, streamlined body. It takes a few glances before Thomas understands she's beautiful. Completing the circle is the competition: a swarthy dude who dresses flash, with this crazy outfit that has fabric attached from his sleeves to the body of his shirt, so that if he holds his arms out to his side, he looks like a bat. Thomas has to admit it is pretty cool.

They go around the circle, introducing themselves. Acneman is Paul. He has a raspy voice, as if he gargles with razor blades. The smoking Latina's name is Yolanda. The black girl is Elsa, and she has a nice low voice. The fat guy, Blake, sobs about missing his Giz and this complex multiplayer game he was involved in, and how he was two days away from winning when his sentencing came.

"Yo blubberboy," says the swarthy guy, "What did you do?"

"Dignity, please! That's not how we talk to each other here," says Ruth.

"Sorry. But, please, I hate seeing guys cry."

"I killed my neighbor's cat," confesses Blake.

"I love cats," says Yolanda.

"Me too," Thomas says, even though he doesn't.

"What a jerk!" says Yolanda.

"Dignity!" says Ruth.

"It kept shitting on my front door," continues Blake. "So one day I complained to the owner and the cat comes out of the apartment and starts to go, so I kicked it. But I must have kicked it too hard."

"No kidding," cuts in Elsa.

"Dignity!"

The swarthy hipster guy is named Freddy. Except he tells them it is spelled different at the end—F-R-E-D-D-E-E. He was a stock boy at a designer house. He stole too many clothes, but his real crime was posting two designs before they were manufactured.

"That's serious!" says Blake, clearly glad to call someone else a criminal. "Piracy Violation!"

"They were mad shirts, man. I was a star for two weeks, until the police came. I was showin' to everybody."

"What did those shirts look like?" Yolanda wants to know.

"The collars were these 3-D adjustable things made out of a plastic fabric, like, you could lift up the collar and turn it into a square hood, or make it like a straight up collar, like that Elvis guy, only bigger."

When it's his turn, Thomas talks about boredom. He says he can't believe it, but he wishes he had a job, even though all the jobs he's had so far—dish washing, painting, delivering food—have sucked. But that's the thing with Virtual Solitary: no work, no Giz, and definitely no travel because you have to come to counseling.

"This is your job," says Ruth. "You come here twice a week and think about why you're here and where you'd rather be. Then we can talk about how you might get there."

That night he cracks open two Tintin books, which are a bit like the graphix on his Giz, except the panels don't talk and the characters don't move inside the panels, and there are no story-line options. But it's still pretty cool. There's a guy who talks really funny and gets drunk a lot. And two idiotic identical detectives. And Tintin reminds him of a regular kid. It's easy to be a hero when you have superpowers, he thinks, but much cooler when all you have is smarts and toughness. Then he reads Dr. Seuss' *The Cat in the Hat*. Then he reads *Animal Farm*, which is just so awesome. It's the first time Thomas can ever remember wishing a book would be longer.

During the fifth group session, Thomas reaches into his bag when it's his turn to speak and hands out books. *Little House on the Prairie*, *Animal Farm*, *The Corrections*, *Harry Potter and the Sorcerer's Stone*, and *The Calculus Affair* starring Tintin. He tells them about his grandfather's house and how he has read a bunch of books.

"So?" says Freddee, flipping through *The Corrections*. "This shit is ancient. No music function, no reorg options, no alternate story lines, no optional character voicings. You act like we never saw a book before. Damn!"

"True," says Thomas, "But at the last meeting everyone said they were bored. Or at least when I said I was bored, you all nodded. I started reading some of these books, and they are not boring. Some of them are funny, some of them are really interesting. I didn't read the *Little House* one, but my grandpa said everyone used to love that book so much they made it into a TV show."

"Thank you, Thomas," says Ruth. Thomas is pretty sure she looks pleased.

In fact, Ruth kicks off the next meeting by asking if anyone read the books. Everyone has, except for Yolanda, who says she left hers at her boyfriend's house and they had a fight so that was that.

"I hope I get the book back," she says. "But I might not."

Thomas and Freddee exchange glances at that piece of information.

At the end of the session, Blake calls after him. Thomas is a little annoyed because he doesn't want Yolanda or Elsa to think this guy is his friend.

"What is it?" It's hard to be nice to a fat kid with a tattoo on his neck.

The kid hands him back *Animal Farm*. "Do you have any more books?"

Thomas reaches into his bag. He was going to start something called *A Confederacy of Dunces*, which is supposed to be "Hilarious!" But he gives it to the kid. He'll read *High Fidelity* instead, which the cover assures him is "Brilliantly funny!"

Thomas likes exploring books. The cover hinting at the story, leaving clues. Sometimes loud and powerful, sometimes understated. It can really set the tone. Then there's the book sleeve copy, introducing the story, building up expectations, telling you what is so good about this thing that you are holding in your hands. Then you make your way inside. Some books have author bios on the first page, but usually only paperbacks by older writers that have tons of books. Otherwise the bios come at the end. Thomas likes them at the front because, really, the author is like the star, or maybe the director, of the book. They make it go, and you want to know a little bit about the storyteller. What did they do before they wrote the book you're about to read? Is the story autobiographical? Are they an expert in something? Some authors seem totally normal from the bios, while others seem like gods who just make up story after story. He found one French mystery writer on his grandpa's shelves who wrote over 200 books. Thomas is pretty sure he hasn't read 200 books in his life.

But there's only so much reading a guy can do. Now, around eight every night, after dinner with his mom—if she's off from the hospital, that is—he goes out walking. He feels like an explorer, discovering the city, learning it, unfolding it, reading it. His circle widens with every day, and he journeys into the various Offtowns that have sprouted in the city's uninhabitable spots—the outer boroughs, by dumps, riverfronts where the tide can suddenly swamp the shores. He visits various Coffee/Pots—the bars that serve pot-based drinks like Bhango! and THCola, or JavaKava, which comes from some islands way out in the Pacific and gets you amped in a mellow way.

Walking in the Offtown across the river one evening, he

sees a man standing over an array of books laid out on the sidewalk. Thomas goes over to take a look.

"Hey there," the guy says. "Are you a man of letters?"

"Not really," says Thomas. "Lost my Giz and started reading."

"Ah, you mean you started living."

"You have a Giz?"

"I don't want one. It didn't knock my socks off."

Thomas looks down at the books. "Do you think you lose something on the Giz? When you're reading, compared to books?"

"The Giz is a magical object, but it takes the magic out of the book. It makes a book weightless, it strips off its heft, the time and effort that went into making it. I'm not even talking about the cover art. I'm just talking about the printed page. Books on the Giz aren't really objects, the Giz is the object. I mean, in a real book just turning a page is a communion, a physical bonding."

"But if you've never seen a book and just grown up with a Giz, how can you be missing something?"

"What do you think?"

"I don't know. I like that books are private, that they are old. It's cool. But reading is reading."

"Did you ever write something? Did you ever print it out from your Giz? A poem? A letter? Anything? Try it. Then give it to someone. Sure, you can put it on a web site. That feels good. You can send the link around. But it needs a Giz or a computer to display it. It needs a server to serve it. It needs a search engine to find it. It needs a browser to read it. Now, with paper—all you need is light to read it. And it can last hundreds of years. That's magic."

Thomas looks at the bookseller and nods as if he agrees. He looks down at the books and suddenly remembers what he wants to read.

"Do you have a book called *1984*?"

"For you? Two dollars. Double the price for everybody else."

Thomas laughs. He reaches for his wallet—

NINE

"VVVVVWWWWRRRRRRRRR!"

"What the fuck?" I say, because I really was into this story and am annoyed at the interruption.

"VVVVVWWWWRRRRRRRRR!"

Hang on—this sounds like a lawnmower. A lawnmower on my lawn. The landscaping guys! I can't believe it. It makes no sense at first. I've given Marta specific orders never to have the landscapers here on the weekend. Never, never, never. Who wants the noise or intrusion? So why are they here? I can only come up with one answer: it's Marta's revenge. She's mad at me about the time off request. This is her fuck you to me. She'll tell me she forgot.

"Hey there!" I call out. "Hey! Help!"

The only answer is the whirling lawnmower.

"HEY, LANDSCAPING GUYS! HELP!"

It's no use. The lawnmower is too loud. The guys must be too far away. I'm frantic. I cup my hands around my mouth and shout again. "HELP ME! I'll pay you each a week's extra salary. I'll pay you each a month's salary!"

Nothing. I grab my DVD disc and start trying to angle a reflection out toward the back door. "Come on," I urge them. "Help me out of here..."

I'm grinding my teeth. I'm wiggling against the fucking shelves, fighting the fucking thing, trying to squeeze my legs out from under it. But it's no use.

Then suddenly there comes a crash, followed by a tinkle of glass. I can hear the pool deck door open.

"Oh my god, you heard me! Thank god you're here!"

There is silence, except of course for the VVVVVWW-WWRRRRRRR of the mower.

"Oh shit!" comes a voice. "Yo, Mass! There's somebody in the fucking house."

The mower stops.

"Hey!" I call, "I don't care you're here on the weekend. I'm glad you're here, in fact. You saved my life."

I hear a fainter voice: "Ain't nobody here, Stevie. I cased it 24/7 yesterday. Nothing moved."

"Yo! You! In the house! Say something."

"Hello and welcome!" I call out, trying to sound as up-beat as possible. "Please come in and help me."

"See?"

"Fuck."

"Come on in," I say. "I don't care about the broken window. Accidents happen. Come on in and lend me a hand."

I can hear the guys talking. I can't make out what they're saying, but I know from the furious tone that they are having an argument.

"Guys, guys!" I say. "I've really got myself in a jam. Come on in."

They stop talking.

"Guys, gentlemen, dudes! I need your help."

And then, finally, a head peers into the room. I can see a crew cut and an eyeball. It's a white guy. I'm guessing mid-20s. The head and the eye look tense and confused.

"Hi," I say. "I'm a little stuck here."

"Oh, shit!" The head focuses on me, and then the guy bursts into a smile. "Hey! We're cool. Check this guy out."

The body attached to the head now steps into the room. Before me stands a lanky kid. He's wearing a shirt that says Landscapers 'R Us. Behind him comes a squarely built black guy. Same age, same shirt, more muscles.

And suddenly it dawns on me that something is wrong.

"Did Toma Landscaping have a name change?" I ask.

"What?" says the white guy.

"He means the shirts," says the black guy. "No, sir. We're freelancers and we've just given you a freebie lawn massage in exchange for your future business."

"You got it. Where do I sign?"

"Thing is, our business is stealing things."

"Go right ahead, you can start with the three flat screens in this wall unit."

"No way," says the white guy. "Those screens are probably cracked. A hot broken TV ain't worth shit."

"Damn," says the black guy. "We could've backed a truck up for this stuff. But it's all junk now."

"How about you lift this off me and I buy each of you a unit of your own?"

They look at each other. White guy nods his head towards the kitchen. They go in and whisper.

I listen again to rising and falling voices, punctuated by "Oh, shit! Look at this." And I can feel my stress levels rising.

"Look, you clowns!" I call out. "I'm sorry to say this, but you screwed up. You picked a house with no women, so no jewelry. Plus, you've picked a house that isn't empty. So how about turning two negatives into a positive?"

There is a pause, and then white guy leaps out of the kitchen. "Who you calling a clown, motherfucker?"

"Sorry, I—"

"You are definitely sorry. We ain't clowns. We are smart, smart businessmen. One little trip to the kitchen and we found a sweet flatscreen and a ton of solid silverware, but I bet that ain't nothing compared to this."

He holds up my car keys. The Jag. The amazing thing is that at this point I don't even care.

"And I bet this painting over here is worth some money, too. Whatcha think, Mass?"

"Don't call me by my motherfucking name."

"Sorry."

"What I think is there is more upstairs. Let's go and get it."

And that's just what they do. They harvest my electronics and they hoot and holler at my decor, my photos, and my pathetic lack of bling. Then they truck the goods into the kitchen to exit by the side door.

"How much you gonna net on this?" I ask. "What have you got? Three TVs, some silverware, a laptop and a computer? Is that it? Guys, I'm sorry I called you clowns, but you have to understand that I'm under a bit of pressure here. How about I give you five grand each if you help me out of here? And you get to keep all that stuff. You can even keep the car!"

"We can't do that, man!"

"Why not?"

"You might call the cops."

"We should do it," says the white guy.

"Nah, we can't risk it, Stevie."

"Dude, no names!"

I think about something. "Hey, how did you know the alarm wasn't set?"

"We got a partner. With connections."

"So you got to cut him in. Even less money for you. Come on, I'll give you six grand each."

"You hear that, Mass?" says Stevie.

"No names, you asshole. Look, you're forgetting one thing. The car is gonna get us ten grand in Mexico. Now let's go."

I wonder whether I should enlighten these clowns as to the actual value of my car, but I just can't see anything good coming from it. So instead I say: "Give me some water! Please. Call the cops. Leave me with my phone. I'll wait 30 minutes to call for help."

"Sorry, man, ain't happening."

"Guys! Don't do this. I'm gonna die here. I'm dying. How can you possibly live with the knowledge you let a man die?"

"By not going to jail. That's how."

"So you leave me in my jail?"

"Stop talking to grandpa. Damn."

Mass and Stevie, Mass and Stevie, Mass and Stevie, I hammer their names and faces into my memory. I couldn't give a damn about the TVs. Everything on the computers is backed up at the office. The car? Who cares? It's not as if I'm ever going to make out in it with Amanda again. No, it's what they've done to me that makes me want blood. They've abandoned a man in need of medical assistance. There ought to be a fucking law against that.

Mass and Stevie close the door behind them to a nonstop stream of pleas and curses from me. My blood sugar is so low, my heart rate so high, it's the perfect combo for a fit of rage and a heart attack. "You selfish, shit-for-brains fuckwits! I hope you mow over your own dicks. Slowly! You douchebag scumbags! You scat-loving vomit-brained greed-sucking assholes! I hope you impale yourselves with hedge clippers. What kind of hellhole did you crawl out of? What kind of sad, sad world do we live in where scum like you is allowed to grow?"

I stop to catch my breath, and over my huffing I hear the revving of two engines—their truck and my Jag—as they drive away. I have developed a whole new set of aches: My throat is rawer than ever; in my fury I contorted and jerked against the shelves and now, as I try to relax, I feel the dents and chaffs and bruises. I wipe my brow and my tears. I'm sweating, I'm hot. I close my eyes. I pray for the end. I pray for sleep. Motherfuckers.

I wake up itching. My crotch is on fire. My pubes are burning and I can't scratch the itch. I reach down and actually scratch the wooden shelf that's blocking me from reaching my dick. I'm scratching by proxy.

Then I have this thought: We could have done an itching contest on the show. The fewest scratches, the longest time between a harmless but super-itchy infection and a shower.

"Oh boy, Rick," I say aloud. "You are now officially off your rocker."

But I'm not. There's a four-alarm blaze in my crotch. I guess that's what happens when you piss yourself and can't change. The moisture breeds. As torture goes, jock itch isn't lethal. But in my hermetically sealed life, it's about the only discomfort I have ever known. Headaches, jock itch, heartburn, and heartbreak: these are the pains in my life. And a wounded ego. And failure, although that is the same as heartbreak.

I mean really, other than fasting on Yom Kippur a couple of times and working through lunch, what do I know of hunger? Or fatigue? Or isolation? I know about misinformation and lies because I work in Hollywood. But that's it. So on some level, maybe this is all good for me, even the skin-searing rash rising in my nether region. Christ. I shift from side to side, a micro-centimeter, to try to adjust my johnson. I pick up the book again.

Mass and Stevie, Mass and Stevie, Mass and Stevie.

THE GIZLESS DAYS OF THOMAS BINDER (cont.)

—and pays the man. Then he takes the paperback in his right hand and uses his left thumb to flip through the book, zipping through the yellowing pages and sending a damp, mildewed breeze to his face. It's a good smell. "Thanks," he says.

❧

"Elsa, do you want to talk about why you're here?"

Everyone has told their story. Everyone but Elsa.

"I was charged with physical assault."

"Oh, shit!" says Freddee.

"Do you want to tell us what happened?" prods Ruth.

"It was Giz-gossip, I guess. Some girls in school were talking trash, posting about me. Me! I'm a virgin!"

"What a waste, girl!" says Freddee.

"Dignity!" yells Yolanda.

"I don't care," says Elsa. "I don't even do nasty online stuff."

"But that's all safe," says Blake. "You can't catch anything on the Giz. Right, Thomas?"

Freddee chimes in, "Pornoboy!"

"No comment," says Thomas, who can't believe he told

the group about the stripvid Makita sent him on the day he was busted.

"So you had a cat fight," says Blake.

"Meow!" says Paul.

Thomas wants to point out that a fight is a fight. But he only says, "Shut up, guys."

Elsa just looks into her hands. Thomas likes that she has long fingers and doesn't wear the scary, giant press-on nails that Yolanda has.

"Elsa, do you want to continue?" asks Ruth.

"If you jerks think a broken cheekbone is a little girlie cat fight, come give me a try."

"Whoa, you did that?" says Freddee, and it sounds more like a statement of admiration than a question.

Elsa is looking into her hands again. Thomas thinks she is beautiful. You can see that she is long and strong. Everything about her is perfect: her narrow waist, her perfectly curved butt in tight jeans, her long legs. Her hair—or maybe it's a wig, Thomas can never tell with black girls—is cut in a bob that accentuates her cheekbones.

"What do you guys think violence is?" asks Ruth.

"Hitting," says Blake.

"Breaking shit," says Yolanda.

"Hurting someone or something," says Thomas. "Could be words, could be force."

"Yelling and screaming at someone," says Blake.

"Yeah, like right in their face," says Yolanda.

Ruth nods. "What can you do to survive a violent situation?"

"Remove yourself from the situation," says Thomas.

"Pray," says Yolanda.

"Count to ten," says Paul.

"But if somebody hits you, you have to defend yourself," insists Elsa.

❧

"Why did they stop making books?" Thomas asks his grandfather during his next visit.

"They didn't stop. Books are available. You can probably read every book on my shelves on a Giz."

"Yeah, but it's not really the same. I can't tell you what the cover looks like on a Giz. There are no notes about the kind of typeface. Or blurbs about other books."

"You've got a point."

"All the kids in my group want more books."

His grandfather shakes his head. "You've never been to a library, have you?"

"My Giz has a library."

"No, I mean a real library. A place filled with real, physical books, books you can borrow or read right there."

"Where's that?"

"They all closed."

Thomas wonders where these libraries used to be. He says: "So why did they stop selling books, real books?"

"They stopped selling everything. CDs, DVDs, movies, games, porno mags, magazines, art posters, greeting cards, postcards. Because everything was available for free. Everything was flying around in digital versions."

"Oh, like the Internet and on email."

"Yes. And these things called peer-to-peer applications. A movie would come out, and the moment it was digitized, it could be shared with people all over the world. Studios threatened to stop making movies, book publishers went broke, music companies died a thousand deaths. For years pirates put out illegal copies—China would just print up books, CDs, and DVDs and sell 'em super cheap. 'Devaluing the commodity,' people called it. So the world began to stop caring about physical copies. Didn't think they were worth it. Plus, it was a green thing, too."

"What do you mean?"

"If you can get a book without killing a tree, or without getting in your car to drive ten miles to buy it, or without the publisher shipping it, then you are helping the environment. That was the reasoning, anyway, although they sure filled a lot of landfills with all those devices that led up to the Giz. With digital, you couldn't print too many and then have to burn them or shred the extras, which happened all the time. All that stuff on your Giz—it's just numbers. It's not even air. It's less than air."

⌒⌒⌒

A few sessions later Elsa asks if there are more books. Could he bring in extras for her?

Ruth volunteers to bring some in, too. "You know," she adds, "You can get books on your Giz when you get them back. Do you think you might use it for that?"

"I don't know," says Elsa. "Real books are nice. Plus, no one can see what you are doing."

Ruth looks puzzled. "Is that an issue?"

"Hell, yes," says Yolanda. "We may get our Gizzes back, but they'll be monitored. We're still on parole."

"They watch who we call, what we play, or what apps we use."

"No hotchat," says Blake.

Everyone laughs.

"Dignity!" mocks Freddee.

"No *Hitman* or *Cleanzer*, or *Ultimate Death Battle*," says Paul. "Even after we clear parole, everyone's Giz use is scanned, or at least it's all traceable to us since we all get billed."

"Unless you get a MexGiz that's been re-ripped."

"I'm gonna look for old books when I can," Thomas says. "They're more private. Plus, every book looks different, the covers, the pages."

After the session, Thomas follows Elsa out the door, determined to make some contact.

"Hey," he says. "Where are you heading?"

"Home. You?"

"The same. But I might go to an Offtown by the river. I found a guy who sells books."

"Really? Does he have a lot?"

Thomas nods. "I could show you sometime."

Elsa smiles. "Okay. I'm up for that."

"Cool," says Thomas, who feels nervous. Talking to girls was so much easier on cruise-chat. "Listen, you want to go now? Or head to the Square?"

"Yeah, let's go there. There's always music."

It's true. The Square, a downtown park, has always had musicians. Even his grandpa remembers hearing performances there back in the '70s. And people still show up: punks, skaters, haters, electros, pirates. Kids who sit there and mix on their laptops and pads, and then remix their neighbor's mixes. They are the most popular, cutting, pasting, and manipulating every hit under the sun. But Thomas finds himself drawn to instrumentalists—horn players, singers with guitars—magicians, and comedians.

"Who are all these people?" Elsa wants to know.

"What do you mean?"

"Everyone I know goes to school or works or Gizzes."

"We don't work."

"We're in rehab, basically, Thomas."

"Therapy."

"Whatever. Prison," she says.

"It used to feel like prison, but I kind of like it now."

"You can get used to prisons."

"Well it feels like the sentence backfired."

Elsa nods. They listen to a man playing the violin. The notes fly by, and it sounds like something old and American to Thomas. Like stuff his grandfather listens to. It must be great to actually play an instrument instead of playing at playing an instrument like all the games on his Giz—Maestro-blast, Guitar Hellion, Voxizer.

They go to a nearby Coffee/Pot. Elsa has never had a pot drink, so Thomas buys a Bhango! for her and a THCola for himself.

"What's the difference?"

"Bhango is the older drink," Thomas says. "It's an age-old pot derivative and it's from Africa and India. THCola is more synthetic. It's a little stronger."

Elsa makes a face. "It's not the best-tasting thing in the world."

"Give it time."

"Are you a druggie?"

"Why do you say that?"

"'Cause of your sentence. You were on Prosto!" Elsa laughs and gives him a teasing look. "I can't believe you were driving and—"

"Hey, come on! That stuff makes you horny. Those other guys in the group, they would have crashed and died if they saw what Makita sent me."

"Who's she? Your girlfriend?"

"I don't have a girlfriend. She's someone who lives far away. In the Czech Republic."

"And she sends you stripvids." Elsa crinkles her face as she says it. Then she laughs. "I feel funny."

"Funny good, right?"

"Yeah. Stop staring."

"I'm not staring. I'm admiring."

"Ha. Get in line."

"Ouch. Don't I rate a little?"

"Maybe. But we're all Bhango-ed up. And anyway you're a druggie."

"And you're a thug."

"You know what you said about liking our group?" she says. "There's a name for that. Or sort of a name: Stockholm Syndrome. It's when you get kidnapped and wind up sympathizing with your captors."

"I don't sympathize! It's just nice to meet, you know...you."

"Take me to an Offtown."

"Classic. Change the subject. You are a master at not talking. How long did we meet until you told your story?"

"I don't know. Who cares?"

Thomas rolls his eyes. He is getting nowhere. "Let's go," he says.

His mom is there when he gets home. He's confused by Elsa, who held his hand and his arm as they walked through the

Offtown. They came by a circle of women knitting clothes by a burning garbage can. Elsa had never seen knitting before. "Sometimes discovering all this stuff, reading books, talking—it makes me feel stupid."

"Yeah," says Thomas.

"But I feel proud, too. Smarter sometimes, but also dumb and sheltered."

"School and Giz and avoid the sun—that's not much of a prescription for exploring. The other night I heard a guy down here ranting about how the sun warnings were just another ploy to hook you into your Giz."

"I don't know about that."

"Me either. My father died of skin cancer. He was a lifeguard at the beach for years when he was our age."

She had squeezed his hand hard at that, and rubbed his shoulder. But when he stepped closer to touch her face, she pulled away.

Now his mom says: "How's the nightwatcher?"

"Good. We went to hear music in the Village. Then we walked over to the Offtown by the river. "

"We?"

Thomas feels a glow spread across his face. Most of his "personal" life has existed on the Giz and he's never discussed it with his mom. "My friend Elsa. She's in the group. She got a raw deal."

"And you?"

"I deserved it. But I'm glad it happened."

"I'm glad it happened, too."

"Even though I was totally humiliated."

"Me too."

"Mom, how much info does a Giz bill give you?"

"Just a usage amount and a total charge."

"Oh."

"But there's a site where you can see the itemized charges."

Thomas just nods. So she knows everything. Elsa was right: the more you learn, the stupider you feel.

⁓

Elsa lives near the river, in one of those big old buildings that have thick walls. He remembers stories that Gizzes are a little slower here because of the walls. He has no idea if it's true. He rings her buzzer and her clear low voice comes through the intercom: "I'm coming down."

Good. Thomas doesn't want to meet her family. Yet.

They walk uptown, through the Park. "Where are we going?" Elsa asks.

"It's a surprise."

Uptown they take a right and walk through the gates of the University.

"And you took me here because?"

"You'll see. Or I hope you'll see. Just follow me. And do what I do. It will be cool."

They walk into a building. There's a guard at a desk. Thomas grabs Elsa's hand and bolts up a stairway.

"Hey! You kids, I need some ID!"

They ignore the guard and keep running. Once they've reached the landing, they run down a corridor and turn into another stairwell. This time they go down two flights, to the basement, and Thomas turns right. They are walking fast now. Thomas turns around to see if anyone is behind them.

"Where the hell are we going, Thomas? Couldn't we just go have some Bhango!?"

"If this works, it's going to be better than Bhango! My grandpa researched it for me. He found the plans. Quick, in here."

He pulls her into a classroom and shuts off the lights.

"This isn't exactly how I imagined a first date," she says.

She's a little pissed off, but not too much, Thomas thinks. "Let's just wait here for a minute. See if they've figured it out. I couldn't tell if they have cameras down here."

"If I get busted, I'm going to kill you."

"Guess where we are?"

"Is this a science lab? Is there a laser beam, so I can blow you up?" She shakes her head. "I must be an idiot, following you in here. Compared to the rest of the group, you seemed sensible."

"Sensible? The other day I was a 'druggie.'"

"Okay. So you're smart, and maybe a little cute."

Thomas fights off a smile. "Just give me five minutes. If we can't get in, we'll go get some food and go to a Sensaround."

"Vice versa. Never eat before going on the Sensaround." She looks at her watch. "You have exactly five minutes."

"Man," says Thomas, "my grandfather was so right."

"About what?"

"He told me that half the women in the world love surprises as long as they know what's going to happen and the other half hate surprises unless they know what's going to happen."

"Comedy gold. I'm still here."

"Yeah, but if you and I had discussed it beforehand, this would be something we'd do together. I think that was what he was trying to tell me."

"Try it next time. You have four minutes, 30 seconds."

They walk down the empty corridor. A worn signs says: "Library."

Thomas tries the door. It's locked.

"Damn," says Thomas, looking around.

He uses a water fountain as a boost, rises, and pushes up against the ceiling tile. Then he chins himself up and peers into the crawl space.

"Elsa," he says, "give me a couple of minutes."

"You have three left."

Thomas gasps as he pulls himself upward. All those bore-dom-inspired workouts are finally paying off. He drags his body into the crawl space. Little beams of light glow from below.

"Wait for me," he calls.

"We'll see about that."

He crawls from one metal crossbeam to the next, grimy dust and hanging wires everywhere. He prays the wires are dead. Electrocution can really ruin a date.

A few yards in and he can feel the beams change, a heavier metal, darker, steel. He's moved between buildings. The Library. He goes over more rafters then lifts up a tile, revealing a wooden, flat, finished surface. He tries the next panel and there's wood covering only half of it; the other half is open space. Then it dawns on him: it's not a wooden ceiling below. He lifts the next tile, peers into the gap, and sees a bookshelf. He swings down, using the shelf as a ladder to descend, and drops to the floor.

Now, to the door. He's got to get Elsa in. He pushes the bar and the door swings open.

"Welcome to a house of books," Thomas says.

"Oh," Elsa says, and Thomas can tell she's impressed,

even though she's trying not to show it. Together, she and Thomas take it in: the room before them is the size of a classroom, and books are everywhere, the walls are lined floor to ceiling, and old wooden shelves divide the room into four aisles.

She walks through the room in a daze. Thomas follows, his eyes shifting back and forth to watch Elsa and take in the library unfolding before them.

"What is this? Where are we?" Elsa's eyes are big and shining.

"We're in the basement of the university library. It's a whole building full of books."

They walk into another dark and dusty room, the glow of exit lights leading them on. They come to a wide staircase and walk up.

There is a worn and faded wooden kiosk with ancient computers. It sits by a huge, boarded-up double door. He walks over, grabs a yellowing piece of paper and unfolds it.

"What's that?"

"A map, I think. Look."

Elsa comes close. He can feel her breath on his cheek. It is hard to stay focused on the map.

"Look, they have rooms for everything: A Latin room, an Asian room—"

"This must have been the entrance," Thomas interrupts her. "And, I guess, the exit. My grandpa says there was a desk where you could check out books. Borrow them. The circulation desk, he called it."

"If this is the entrance, let's start at the beginning," says Elsa, walking to the boarded up door and turning around. "Wow."

Through the arched hallway, a cavernous room opens up.

"It's like a chapel. I mean, like Notre Dame. Like in Paris or something," Elsa says.

They walk toward the cavernous room. Thomas holds her hand. He wonders if she even notices—the room before them is pretty tough competition for her attention—but she turns and looks at him and gives his hand a squeeze. Then they step into the room, and it's dazzling: the ceilings are 40 feet high at least. The afternoon light comes in through enormous windows. The floors are made of black and beige stone and have elaborate geometric patterns on them.

"So is this surprise worth it?"

"Not bad."

"Come on." Thomas steers her forward, into the gigantic room the map says is called The Grand Hall.

Miles of bookshelves line the room. Elsa goes left, into a corridor of books. Thomas follows. He reads the spines, not sure what he is looking at, names and titles, and strange letters and numbers taped on the outside of each volume. It is too much. There must be thousands of titles here. Maybe millions. More books than anyone could ever read in a lifetime. He sees that the aisle is labeled "Reference."

"Oh my god," Elsa's voice echoes through the huge room. "Look at all these books!"

They stroll down an aisle, admiring the thick, authoritative volumes. Books with embossed titles whose heavy, hard covers seem almost like armor, designed to look mighty and to protect what is inside. It's a parade: dictionaries, and not just standard ones, but also rhyming ones, slang ones, foreign ones, fat and fatter ones, and multi-volumes, including some that rival encyclopedias. They walk by directories, indices, census reports, atlases, thesauri, almanacs, handbooks, manuals, and reports.

Thomas spots something called *Encyclopedia Americana, Volume E* and pulls it out. He flops it open on a big table. "E is for Elsa."

"Stop," Elsa calls.

"Look, this is everything E...elastic, electricity, elephant, anybody famous named Elsa? Not as a last name except...a lion!"

"You mean a lioness. A teacher told me about her. I found a movie on my Giz, it was pretty cool."

They are leaning over the book together. Thomas is on high alert. Their shoulders touch. He can feel her breath on his ear. He calibrates just how much he can lean into her without her pulling back. Then finally, instead of looking at the book, he looks at her. She raises her eyes at him, her big, coy eyes and then it happens, this simple thing that Thomas has never done despite two years of cruise-chat, despite viewing every conceivable coupling on his Giz over the last four years. They kiss. It's soft, warm, wet, and electric. It's like laughter and dreaming and Bhango! to the tenth power. But way, way better. Their weight shifts. Their tongues mesh, he pulls her toward him and her hand touches his face, which is something that never happened before either. His heart is racing and that's not all. He shifts his hips, hoping she won't notice his arousal. But she drops one hand and starts rubbing him. His eyes open in shock. And then they open further.

Footsteps echo on the marble floor.

"Oh shit," whispers Elsa, as they pull apart.

"Okay, I don't want any trouble!" calls a scratchy, older

voice. "I'm coming over, so get your clothes on or put your drugs away."

"Drugs? Clothes?" says Elsa. "You got the wrong girl."

"It's okay, sir," calls Thomas. "We're not like that."

A security guard, grey hair, tall, and powerful-looking in spite of a prominent belly, steps out from behind a stack. He shines a flashlight on them.

"We had a report about two kids. Sure didn't think I'd find you here. Kids usually hit next door looking for chemicals and burners."

"Not us."

"This is breaking and entering. Trespassing. You could lose your Giz for something like this."

"Ha," laughs Elsa. "That's what got us here."

The guard looks at them. He's not smiling. But he's not scowling, either. "What do you mean—that got you here?"

"We both got de-Gizzed in court. But we get them back next month," says Elsa.

"We started reading books 'cause we had nothing to do," says Thomas. "And we liked it. So when my grandfather told me about this place, I knew I had to bring Elsa here. She's innocent, really. She had no idea where I was bringing her."

"Amazing, isn't it?" The guard stands tall and looks at the grand vaulted ceilings. "And nobody ever sees it. Once in a while the Board of Directors comes by, wondering what to do. Convert it to dorms? Turn it into a hotel? Or get this: Sell the collection!"

The guard throws his head up and roars as if he's just told a great joke. "Can you imagine? Sell the collection, the priceless collection? As if that could be done."

"Why not?"

"The short of it is: there's a fine line between priceless and worthless, and it's been crossed, my boy."

"When?" asks Elsa. "And why?"

"These books? Everyone has 'em. Or can have 'em. For FREE! Oh, you'll get charged a penny or two on your Giz bill for each one you read. Or you can grab 'em free from some websites. Not the hard versions, but digital. So these books—some of which are the only original editions in the world—are now everywhere. Collectors would have paid big money once. But now? No one cares."

"Devalued," says Thomas, thinking of what his grandfather has told him.

"Smart man!"

"My name is Elsa and this is Thomas. We like books. Real ones."

"Me too. I'm Matt Cotter. Sorry if I got carried away."

"No problem," says Thomas. "It was interesting."

"Thanks. Not a lot of company on this shift."

"Are you going to arrest us, Mr. Cotter?" asks Elsa.

"Only if you don't come back."

A smile spreads across Thomas's face. He is holding Elsa's hand. He lifts his eyes upward. The campus lights are on, streaming in from outside, catching the ancient, swirling dust of the building. He follows the beams as they hit the stacks. In the strange light, he thinks the room looks like that cathedral Elsa mentioned, a holy place, anyway. The books seem to glow up there.

"We'd like that very much, Mr. Cotter," he says.

◦◦◦◦◦

Thomas and Elsa go to the Criminal Implants Division together. The day before had been their last Group session. They exchanged food and hugs and Giz numbers, and Thomas handed out the last round of books: Sci-fi for the geeks, a book of cute cat photos for Yolanda, and a copy of *1984* for Freddee, who immediately mocked the first sentence, squeaking: "It was a bright cold day in April, and the clocks were striking thirteen."

"Freddee," Ruth said, "It's our last class. Don't make me say it."

"Dignity!" they all chanted one last time.

Ruth laughed and told them how proud she was of the group. Then she handed out Graduation Certificates.

"This is more than just a pat on the back, you guys. This is proof you worked hard and can now get your Gizzes back. Of course, they also have your records on file downtown, but it's nice to have a piece of paper."

"Paper! Like an old schoolbook, right, Pornoboy?"

"Knock it off, Freddee. That's dead and gone."

"Sorry, Thomas."

Now in the courthouse he hears his name again: "Thomas, Thomas Binder!" calls the lab technician. It's the same blonde who put in his scrambler chip.

Thomas stands and nods at Elsa. "Can you switch her chip, too? We came down together."

"Sure."

The technician checks their names and lets her scanner confirm their identity.

"You guys excited?" the tech asks.

"Not as much as I thought I would be," says Elsa.

"Really? Most people are going nuts when they get their Giz back."

"We had a pretty good time being Gizless."

"Well, the beginning was hard," admits Thomas.

"Glad to hear it. I guess people—the ones that don't get all depressed—lose weight during their sentences. They exercise more since they have nothing to do."

Her scanner beeps and she reads it. "You're all set. Go to the pick-up window and get your Gizzes back."

Thomas has been dreading this moment. Life has been pretty simple lately. The Giz may change everything.

"What are you going to do first?" asks Elsa. "IMs, email, videxes, chat-vites? I bet there are new apps we know nothing about."

They are at the window. Elsa gets hers first. Thomas watches her smile as she holds it in her hand, enjoying its familiar weight. Then it's Thomas's turn. The clerk hands him his device. Thomas remembers the thrill, and the automatic reflex of reaching for it, an almost involuntary action, like breathing. He wonders if he still has all the dij moves he used to. Probably lost his chops. The Giz feels good. He can't deny it. He looks at Elsa. She's dijjing.

"Hey Elsa."

"Yeah?" She doesn't look up.

Which bums Thomas out. He doesn't want things to change between them. But the Giz—it's already happening. The Giz can take you anywhere and will take you nowhere.

"Elsa, what are you doing?"

"Wait," she says, finishing dijjing. Then she looks up, "Turn on your Giz and find out." Thomas notes the amused smirk on her face.

He boots up the little machine and watches the connection

bars burst forth. Then the apps load and the On message flashes. He swipes over to Directory and sees Elsa's name at the top of recent activity. He clicks. A message opens, subject line: 4 things.

1. Gizzing makes it harder to hold hands.
2. Boyfriends are not allowed to cruise-chat.
3. Let's go see Mr. Cotter in the Library.
4. But first, kiss me.

TEN

Wow! "The Giz," that's one hell of an after-school TV special. Smart, sensitive, romantic. Advertisers would want all the druggy shit taken out, though. They always do. I remember from my teen-film days. When it would play on TV, some networks always wanted us to edit out kids smoking. Give me a break. That's what kids do. But "The Giz," bam! That's a great story. It's sort of *Breakfast Club* meets *Dead Poets Society* meets *A Clockwork Orange*. Plus the world will really understand this addiction to devices. I swear, cell phones and smartphones just inspire this masturbatory reflex—gotta go play with myself. I'm sure some of my current discomfort—which is considerable—is really BlackBerry withdrawal. I'm not kidding. No email. No browsing. No BrickBreaker. It can drive you crazy.

Wait. Do they even make after-school specials anymore? I don't think so. Now everyone has after-school. My son had it: soccer, soccer, and soccer. Then piano and baseball. Then Robotics, which cost me a friggin' fortune, just so he and his friends could build a remote-control mini cherry picker that could do the same thing a three-year-old can: grab an object and move it somewhere. Whatever happened to playing in a schoolyard and then going home and watching TV? Ah, shit, that's probably what Mass and Stevie did growing up, that and play *Grand Theft Auto*. Those pricks.

Jeez, my knees hurt.

My lower back is in need of amputation.

My pecker is gonna need a skin graft.

And that burning sensation right around my heart is now itching like crazy.

All my muscles are just seizing up. My lumbar region is fucking with me. It's agony. I don't have a clock, but it seems like I can't sleep more than a few minutes without some throb or stab pulling me back to consciousness. I try to look on the bright side: The one good thing about pain is that while you can remember it, you can't recreate it; you can't truly think it into recurring. You can rate it in retrospect—a toothache vs. banging your funny bone—but it doesn't work the way words or music do. You can hear things in your head, voices, music, over and over. You can close your eyes and visualize a place. But pain, the experience of it, either is or isn't. You are in pain, or you aren't.

Memory can haunt you. But memories don't really activate the neurons and fire up the senses. At worst a memory can trigger a reaction—a panic attack, guys reflexively crossing their legs at a grisly dick joke, a wave of nausea over a sickening story. But, frankly, all this is cold comfort when your head is pounding from dehydration, your stomach is an abyss of raging hunger, and every time you try to move an inch—literally, a fucking inch!—there is a burning or stabbing sensation around the area you are moving, and shooting pains that travel everywhere else

Pain is boring. Unless you're watching others experience it. Which is why The King of Pain became such a hit. You can see pain and internalize it. Something you can't really imagine is made real before you.

The unimaginable also happened when you consider the four contestants that are left for our April sweeps. Two have been contenders since they first stepped into focus. But the other two, Kaylene and Sister Rosemarie are miracles. As we had hoped—no, prayed—Sister Rosemarie is still beating the odds after winning the hunger competition and finishing in the top half of every other battle, including a second in Branding—a very understated In God We Trust seared into her forearm. Plus, she is always kind, sweet, encouraging, and even proud to be suffering for the greater glory. Whenever our judges ask her about the pain, she only talks about feeling God's love.

I could use some of that now. But never mind.

Our big dilemma going into the end of the season is whether we may actually be pushing the envelope too far. It's hard for me to get a read on what exactly it is that we are doing. I really wish Amanda was around, but at least I still have my director Rittenhouse and Little Ricky, who is a surprisingly good sounding board, probably because he doesn't say much. But even between the three of us, it's difficult to really know how the major whammy we've cooked up is going to play.

The upcoming major mega-mind freak of a whammy is emotional torture.

The quartet has been living in a bubble in boot camp for weeks now. They are exhausted and miserable. They've been starved, burned, humiliated, embarrassed, frozen, and deprived of sleep. And now we are about to put them under heavy emotional stress by deliberately feeding them extremely upsetting misinformation about somebody close to them. I am on the fence: there's no question that what we're going to do has tremendous dramatic potential, but

I worry that if it backfires—if the contestants freak out, or if the press and the audience reacts poorly—we'll finally go down in the flames of public opinion.

OK, I'm not that worried. I was uptight about the sleep deprivation, and that turned out fine. I'm used to living on the edge.

I take a deep breath. "Gentlemen, let's do it now," I say. "Give them the bad news."

"Won't their bullshit detectors go off if we hit them all at once?" asks Little Ricky.

"Interesting point," I say. "But I've already thought that through. Let's tell them all at the same time. Then, after they go nuts, let's announce that only one of the scenarios is true."

"You are an evil genius," says Rittenhouse.

"Thank you."

"But," suggests Rittenhouse, "let's do it when they are relaxed. Let's do up the mess hall, turn it into a plush restaurant, give 'em champagne, and then whack 'em."

"You are the evil genius, Rittenhouse."

"What's the budget?" Little Ricky asks.

"Do it up, Mr. Associate Producer. 40 grand if you need it. This episode is all in the editing, right Rittenhouse?"

"Always, boss."

"Of course this is going to be live TV, Little Ricky. But there's still editing, just live editing."

"Got it, Mr. Salter. But one more thing: Did you just promote me?"

"Maybe," I shrug.

"Evil," laughs Rittenhouse.

The real evil thing about mental torture is—but wait, where are my storytelling skills? Let's go back to the setup: We wine and dine 'em big time. Tuxes, flowers, champagne; the mess hall is transformed into a red velvet boudoir. The judges recall their favorite moments over an opulent banquet of ribeye steaks, tofu burgers, sushi, Sacher torte, and carob power bars. Whatever our contestants' overstressed hearts desire. Season highlights are replayed on a huge flatscreen.

Our four finalists are the aforementioned Sister Rosemarie, the amazing Sanchez, Sgt. St. James, and Kaylene Appleby, who narrowly beat out Annabel Castro in the noise attack episode that came after the sleep deprivation show. I wasn't surprised: with two kids and a car stereo-obsessed ex-husband, I knew she would outlast Castro. The big surprise in that event was again Sister Rosemarie, who had lived among the quiet and hallowed nunnery walls. Or so I thought. Turns out she worked in a boarding school for deaf kids. And deaf kids love to feel vibrations. They dance to insanely loud, bass-buzzing music, slam doors, smack tables, and generally express themselves like you'd expect a teenager who can't talk would. No wonder she finished fourth, instead of crumbling after 48 hours of pneumatic drills, heavy metal growling, atonal screeching, and those awful loops of people screaming and sobbing from Jonestown. She probably could have won the damn thing, but one of her strategies was to pray. And so the praying cut into her timed tasks: everyone had to haul 100 50-pound boxes across a field, dig a trench, and alphabetize 1,000 sheets of paper. I'm telling you, there's nothing like a truly pointless task to really get to people. You could take a break, get away from the noise, but we'd deduct points.

Sgt. St. James endured the noise the same way he had endured everything else—with no emotion whatsoever—and won the competition.

"That guy is a cold pisser," Rittenhouse says, "I don't know what his Achilles' heel is."

It's true: Sgt. St. James does seem to have superior powers. His stoic performance week in and week out has increased army enlistment by 5% a week since we went on the air, according to a story in the *Times*. He's a one-man P.R. division. I should have charged a placement fee to the Armed Forces. Come to think of it, next season we should have a little bidding war between Army, Air Force, and Navy to see where the next contestant should come from. The noise was nothing to this guy. He deals with the sound of automatic weapons, heavy machinery, ordnance, choppers, and C-120 planes—his job is a 24/7 ROAR. So the noise competition was just a walk in the park for him.

But mental and emotional torture is going to be a different story. And the dinner party is just perfect: a beautiful trap. The contestants look great. Kaylene Appleby wears a black dress that puts the "lunge" in plunge. Sgt. St. James sports a metallic purple tux. Sister Rosemarie finds a high-collared dress that makes her look like a pilgrim, and Sanchez looks sharp in an Italian suit. They have wine and camaraderie. It is one big group hug, without the nastiness and defiance and belligerence of Annabel Castro, who was 100% right when she bitterly complained that she was doomed in a popularity contest against a nun and a blonde single mom, just before being voted out.

The final four shared words of praise for each other, and everyone commented on how surprised they were by

Kaylene and Sister Rosemarie. Even the linguistically chal-
lenged, monosyllabic Sanchez, who doubtless didn't say
much in Spanish either, put it out there, wiping his eyes
and delivering his own version of the Gettysburg Address:
"Since I lost my compadres in the desert, I have never hung
with no one as cool as you."

And then, when everyone was in a touchy-feely mood,
the smooth, always slightly empathic Dr. Burns stabbed
them in the back.

"Before we move on to a truly mouth-watering dessert,
I'm afraid I have to change the mood," he begins. "Over the
course of the show you have been isolated, receiving only
letters and emails we approved. This was an arrangement
you all agreed to before the competition started. And I know
it has been especially hard to be out of telephone contact
with your loved ones. As a result of this communications
embargo, we have kept some troubling and in some cases
horrifying news from each of you. Until now."

The camera cuts to each contestant's face as this grim news
is digested. Deep synth stabs rumble in the background.

"The news we are about to deliver may change not only
this competition, but more importantly your lives and the
lives of those closest to you."

Eyes are narrowing. Facial muscles grow taut. All smiles
have evaporated.

"Kaylene," says Dr. Burns, a wash of eerie synthesizer
punctuating the tension. "Your ex-husband has filed papers
challenging you for the custody of your children. Meanwhile, your oldest daughter, Micah, caught fire while roast-
ing marshmallows at your mother's house. She is okay, but
suffered first degree burns to her right arm."

"My BABY! You didn't tell me about my baby!" She turns directly to the camera: "Micah, are you okay? This is Mommy. I'm going to call you right now. Who has a phone? Cameradude, give me your phone right now."

"Kaylene," interjects Dr. Burns, "Please. Micah is not in any danger, although she'll need a skin graft."

"And nobody thought to fu-BEEP-ing tell me?"

"We did discuss it. And had it been life-threatening, of course we would have. But ER doctors assured—"

"What if they were wrong?"

"Kaylene," whispers Sister Rosemarie, who is up from her seat and at Kaylene's side. She puts her mouth to the distressed woman's ear. And eventually, Kaylene calms down and nods.

"Thank you, Sister Rosemarie," she says as soon as their little conference is over. "Obviously, Dr. Burns, I am very shocked and disturbed and I will request a leave of absence as soon as this episode is over."

"Thank you, Kaylene," continues the unflappable Dr. Burns. "Now Mr. Sanchez"—"3rd Place" flashes on the screen—"I regret to inform you that your mother has been diagnosed with bone cancer. We have flown her to Mexico City for treatment at the city's top hospital."

"Why you didn't fly her here?"

"She has no passport. This is the quickest way to get her treatment."

Sanchez nods. "Thank you for telling."

He looks stunned at first and then somehow embarrassed or ashamed. His head droops, he wipes his eyes and then looks at his hands. "I would like to call her also."

"We realize these are extraordinary events for all of you,"

interjects Mayhew. "At the end of these announcements you will have the opportunity to make some requests. Please bear with us."

"Now, Sister Rosemarie," Dr. Burns continues, as more ominous music flares and Sister Rosemarie appears on screen, the words "2nd Place" flashing in front of her. "Your nunnery has had a fire in the bakery. Two sisters have been hospitalized and Mother Superior has had a heart attack and is also in the hospital."

Sister Rosemarie bows her head, her lips move in silent prayer. The music plays on, now to a grim martial beat. She lifts her head.

"Dr. Burns, I must return to convent at once."

"Please, Sister Rosemarie, give us a few more minutes of your time and then all your choices will be clearer."

Sister Rosemarie nods, her brown eyes wide with concern.

"Sister Rosemarie, the fire happened two months ago, just after you joined our show. It has crippled the finances of the nunnery, which has existed, as you well know, on a wing and prayer."

Close-up: Sister Rosemarie's rapt, tear-stained face. The camera pulls out to see her fingers tracing the silver cross around her neck.

"The order shut its soup kitchen and is one week away from filing for bankruptcy protection. I'm sorry to have to share this terrible news with you."

Sister Rosemarie's silently moving lips pick up speed. She begins rocking back and forth, eyes closed, deep in prayer, tears streaming down her cheeks. From my perspective right now, those tears might as well have been blood. This footage, more than anything else, marked the point when the tide started turning against me and the show. But once again I'm getting ahead of myself.

The beat suddenly changes to an even more martial drum and fife loop, just in time for Sgt. St. James—#1 in the standings—to get his briefing from Mary Lamb.

"And now, Sgt. St. James, you too have some stressful news. Your grandmother, the woman who raised you, was hospitalized last week with kidney failure. Meanwhile, we regret to inform you that in Afghanistan, three members of your Special Forces unit died in a rescue mission. We are very, very sorry."

Sgt. St. James bows his head for a moment and then assumes his ramrod-at-attention stance. "Where is my grandmother and who are the fallen, Madame?" he asks.

"I'm sorry," Dr. Burns cuts in. "We seem to have lost track of time. We'll have to address all your questions tomorrow. I realize this will be torture for all of you. But then that's what this show is all about, isn't it? See you all back here tomorrow at eight. Good night."

So we gave them a night to dwell on this terrible information, each contestant separated from the other. This was the truly mean part, because, as I have said before, the powerful thing about torture, besides the actual pain, is the anticipation of pain. And the scenarios we had presented were brutal. Probably too brutal. In retrospect, breaking the show into two segments was a terrible idea—it gave the audience too much time to empathize. The next day every friggin' talk show, every editorial writer, every blog, was on my jock. I was being portrayed as the master torturer: one of the tabloids photoshopped me holding a cat-o'-nine-tails, standing beside an Iron Maiden. The ratings, however, were out of this world. We eclipsed everyone—the networks, cable, movie theaters. Even restaurant attendance dropped.

And it only got better the next night.

"Kaylene, Sanchez, Sister Rosemarie, and Sgt. St. James," droned Dr. Burns, sounding like a suicidal undertaker, "We owe you an apology. We lied to three of you last night. Only one of the horror stories we told you is true. This means there is a three-in-four chance your loved ones are safe. Naturally, you still may wish to make contact with the outside world, and you can do so..."

The music surges.

"... but calling will impact your score and your rankings. And visiting will have an even greater cost. You'll lose 100 points per call and 300 points per visit. For you, Sgt. St. James, a visit would hand Sister Rosemarie the lead and bounce you to third place. Sister Rosemarie, your call would give second place to Sanchez. For Sanchez, a visit to his dying mother would bounce Kaylene into third place. And for Kaylene, a visit might put first place totally out of reach."

"You bastards!" yells Kaylene." If I don't call, my husband will use this against me in his battle for custody!"

"We're very sorry," says Dr. Burns. "We can imagine how much pain this must be causing you. And we all know how hard you've worked in this competition."

"Kaylene," says Sanchez sympathetically, "For all of us the odds are in our favor."

"Odds don't mean s-BEEP-t if your number comes up," Kaylene spits.

Sister Rosemarie raises her hand. "Excuse me, judges, but could I have a word with my colleagues?"

Dr. Burns looks momentarily shocked; panic creeps over his face for a nanosecond. This is live TV, the greatest TV there is, in my opinion, the only time there's a possibility of spontaneity or chaos. That's why I watch awards shows: In the hopes of seeing a speech, a gesture, or something that feels real. I hit the talk button and tell Burns through his earpiece: "No way. Tell her no collusion."

"I'm sorry," Dr. Burns relays. "But the rules laid out beforehand state clearly that collusion among contestants is expressly prohibited."

"May I go first, then," says Sister Rosemarie.

"We were going to start with the leader."

"Ladies first, sir," says Sgt. St. James.

"Kaylene, Sanchez? Any objections?"

They shake their heads.

"Thank you," says Sister Rosemarie. "I would like to make a call and hope that my colleagues will also call so that we will all keep our current place in the standings."

"Holy shit!" I say, punching the talk button to Dr. Burns and looking at Rittenhouse. "Cut to a commercial!"

When we come back on the air, Burns has his instructions. As planned, he hands Sister Rosemarie a Red Phone and a warning. "Here is your phone call. But my fellow judges and I will meet after the show to determine if you have bent the rules with your previous speech."

"It was not collusion. I merely pointed out the obvious."

"We'll be the judges of that. You certainly did push to go first. Make your call, please. I believe you are calling a friend at the nunnery?"

"Yes, Sister Theresa. She is the business manager so she has a cell phone."

As we well knew, everything was fine at the mission, although Sister Theresa made sure to say the mission was always short on cash and welcomed any and all donations. Once she had finished her call, Sister Rosemarie wiped away tears of joy and turned to the others. "My prayers are with you."

Kaylene steps up. "I have to call my kids," she says. When her daughter answers, the tough-as-nails blonde starts sobbing. "Honey," she says, "it's Mommy. Are you okay?"

"They are lying to you, Mom! I'm fine. We were all yelling at the TV. Can we sue them for lying?"

"Oh thank God!" Kaylene starts sobbing and blubbering.

"We love you, Mommy," says the girl. "We're so proud of you!"

"I love you, too, honey. All of you! I can't wait to see and hold my little angels."

Sanchez steps up. "I must call my mother," he says. This was a tough TV moment for us: Should we translate the conversation or allow the camera to talk? I went with just the visuals. More suspenseful. Since I don't speak Spanish, I can't tell you what Sanchez said, other than Mami, mio dios, no, no, and te amo. But the intense close-up, the trembling lips, the cracking voice, and the watering eyes said it all. His mother was dying.

With the last adios, he puts down the phone and gets the most sincere group hug in the history of reality TV. When the four break apart, the military man approaches the phone.

"Sgt. St. James," says Burns, "you already know that your grandmother is fine and your compatriots are alive. If you don't make the call, you will gain 100 points on each of your rivals with only two competitions left. That lead will eliminate Kaylene and will mean it'll take a minor miracle for Sanchez to win. What are you going to do?"

Now at this point, anyone following the show knows that Sanchez grabbed the lone water bottle on a table during the final stage of the opening endurance race, elbowing the exhausted Sgt. St. James for it, and then cruelly tossing it after one sip. The Sergeant, in his one humiliating moment of the competition, cramped up and barely made it the last 200 yards to finish the race. So the big man looks long and hard at Sanchez, who gives him a tough guy's do-what-you-gotta-do shrug. Sgt. St. James nods to himself and says, "I want to say hi to my granny."

The contestants went nuts. Live bloggers and chat groups cheered, the 10 and 11 o'clock news programs led with our show. The Nielsen meters spiked to the highest point of the season, trouncing the Branding episode and Hunger week. My son called me to tell me the show "totally rocked." Walter Fields left a message saying that if his fourth wife should ever get pregnant, he would name their kid after me. Marta, my saint, had even left me champagne on ice with a rose and a cupcake with a smiley face. And even though I didn't hear from Amanda, I went to bed a happy man.

I let my guard down that night. I had temporarily forgotten that the light is always brightest before someone yells cut.

SNOW ISLAND

When Sadhu Shakti arrived at Snow Island, the notorious Indian maximum-security prison that now exists only as a dark, bloody stain in the history books of penal justice, everyone in the frozen fortress was instantly curious. What was a holy man doing in such a god-forsaken spot?

"He's a charlatan, sir," the assistant warden explained to his boss. "And an embezzler, con artist, seducer, tax dodger," he said, reading from the file.

"No murder or Eve-teasing?" joked the warden, laughing about his inmates' predilection for homicide and molestation.

"Allegations only. No convictions, sir."

"Amazing."

Sadhu Shakti settled in his cell, spread out a blanket on the floor and sat motionless for hours, his legs folded before him, his arms resting on his thighs; only his wild stringy hair rustled in the drafty cell. Kumar Rahman, the Kashmiri dacoit who was serving ten years for robbing an entire bus of tourists outside Srinagar, tried to talk to him.

"Not now," said Sadhu Shakti. "First I must pray."

After a week of silence and model behavior, Sadhu Shakti's meditation was broken by a big brutal guard who was nicknamed Lathi, in honor of the Indian police's favorite weapon—a six-foot pole used to club, prod, and, if you were really unlucky, penetrate. Banging his namesake on the cell bar,

Lathi said, "Gandu—I mean, Sadhu—you have a package." Then he tossed it into the cell and waited while Sadhu Shakti unwrapped the parcel.

"Ha," Lathi roared, "Dead flowers, incense, Ganesh picture! Here on Snow Island, you need Shiva! You need power to survive."

Sadhu Shakti quietly went about setting up a little altar, ignoring Lathi.

"You don't fool me, Sadhu!" Lathi bellowed. "You are a con man! The only followers you left behind are poor beggars now."

"Hey, Lathi," called a voice down the corridor, "leave him alone, you bahen chud."

Others chimed in along the hallway, a spontaneous chorus of insults.

Lathi laughed at the men, slamming his club against the prison bars as he walked away.

The next day, after their torturous walk in the icy yard—15 minutes of calisthenics and then 15 minutes of shuffling around freezing—Sadhu Shakti and his roommate Kumar returned to find Lathi in their cell holding up a shiv. He was smiling.

"Kumar, what is this, yar? A present for the holy man?"

"You know what this is, Lathi," said Kumar. "It's a plant."

"He pulled it out of his ass while we were gone!" mocked somebody in the cell across the hall.

"Bullshit, bullshit, bullshit," began a chorus on the cell block.

Lathi blew his whistle three times, and an octet of officers rushed to his side. They entered several cells and walloped the most vocal prisoners while Lathi handcuffed Kumar.

"I look forward to your return, Kumarji," said Sadhu Shakti, "I will write the warden about this."

❧

Sadhu Shakti was standing on his head when Lathi returned the following afternoon.

"Look," taunted Lathi, "I get you a single room and this is what you do?"

"Tell me, Mister Guard, what do you do when you are not working?" asked Sadhu Shakti.

"What do we do? We eat, drink, watch filmi. We have a projector, Sadhu."

"It's the one they use for our Sunday cinema!" called a voice from across the corridor. "They hoard it—bahen-chuds!"

Lathi clenched his nightstick.

"Ignore them, sahib. And where do you live? In the mountains?"

"The Guards' compound. We have rooms, common kitchens, ping pong."

"Ooh! Ping pong! That's how he got his balls!"

"Shut up, gandu, or I'll play ping pong with your head."

"Please," said Sadhu Shakti. "It sounds very nice. Is there a town nearby?"

Lathi narrowed his eyes, wondering if he was being pumped for information.

"There is nothing nearby. Snow Island was built by one of Shah Jahan's evil sons over six summers. Many men died."

"No family, Guard-sahib?"

"Still looking," Lathi said, lowering his booming voice.

"Yes, me too."

"Ha!" laughed Lathi. "This is no place to find a bride, unless you are a gandu."

"Lathi, my friend, we are in the same place."

The huge guard stepped toward Sadhu Shakti, a friendly smile spreading across his face. Sahdu Shakti smiled in return and was rewarded with a vicious smack across the face that sent him sprawling toward his string bed.

Lathi headed for the cell door. "Same place but not same place, Sadhu," he said. "I can leave anytime."

He shut the cell door and ambled down the corridor.

◆

Over the next few weeks, Sadhu Shakti talked to the prison guards at every opportunity. He was humble and solicitous. He asked about their health, their birth dates, their bowels, and their families. He wondered if any of them had seen Kumar in the hole, never failing to shake his head and mumble how odd it was that the shiv had been suddenly found by Lathi, and that it was a strange brand of justice to automatically take one man's word over another's.

One evening, he struck up another conversation with Lathi: "Lathiji, I arrived at night, my head wrapped in a bag. Can you tell me more about the surrounding area—these thugees here think the wildest things: Shangri-La is nearby, or the Chinese army is ten miles away."

"It's just what you think, yar. We are on an island in the middle of a frozen lake that is in the middle of the Himalayas. The lake is frozen half the year. There is snow all over the place. The roads shut in the winter. And the only way to civilization is an airstrip on the north shore—if the warden orders prisoners to clear it of snow. "

"I would love to see snow. I'm from the south. Pity there are no views."

"Yes, Sahdu, no view for the prisoners. You see, yar, we are not in the same place," laughed Lathi.

"But we are, ji. We are."

When Kumar returned from solitary, there was a party—or what passes for a party—in the yard. Except for a bruised cheek and a gaunt look, he seemed fine. The men clapped and sang some popular filmi songs. And then broke into a boisterous chant:

> *Who had a quiet night?*
> *Kumar, Kumar*
> *Wondering if the rats will bite?*
> *Kumar, Kumar*
> *And celebrating man's great right*
> *Kumar, Kumar*
> *to masturbate alone!*

The younger dacoits and thugs did flips and walked on their hands. Sadhu Shakti, 55 if he was a day, did a cartwheel, landed in front of Kumar, and hugged him. A guard appeared and gave the men a five- minute warning. Shakti greeted him warmly. "Sahib, do guards have many celebrations, too?"

"Not since the warden banned alcohol."

"My goodness," said Shakti, "You are prisoners, too."

"What happens in the coldest months, yar?"

Sadhu Shakti was talking with the Chef. "Where does the food come from when the roads are closed?"

"Storage. We have rooms full of bins of rice, flour, potatoes, and lentils. You should see the rats downstairs. Guards go down there every day, shooting them. That is our target practice."

Not long after this exchange, disaster struck: a vigilant guard took a shot at a rat, missed, and pierced a water pipe. The food stocks were flooded and bags of flour and sugar and salt were soaked and ruined. It was early November and the roads were already closed.

A crew of prisoners was assigned to mop up and dispose of the spoiled food. They marched some of it to the furnace and some of it to the frozen dump. This was an unsightly mound of garbage dumped on the ice behind the prison. In the spring, the ice would melt and the garbage would simply drop into the water. When they returned to the stock room for a last run, Sita Gupta, a Bengali jewelry thief, saw some guards hauling untainted rice toward the guards' quarters. He sought out Sadhu Shakti, who by now had a reputation as a wise man and as someone who had a reasonable relationship with the guards.

When Sita had told him what he'd seen, Sadhu Shakti looked very concerned. "You are right to bring this story to me, Sitaji. They are hoarding for themselves and that means there will be rationing for us. I tell them we are all in this together, but they do not listen."

At lunch, his fears were justified by a paltry scoop of rice and disgracefully watery dhal. And one week later, it was announced that the prisoners would eat only twice a day until spring.

"Defensive measure, yar," explained the head cook. "To ensure survival."

An inmate who worked in the kitchen came to Sadhu Shakti and said, "We are under orders to give smaller portions."

Sadhu Shakti shook his head. "Thank you, ji," he said. "I have formulated a plan to help us get more food."

The next day, Sadhu Shakti approached the assistant warden.

"Assistantji," he said. "In these times of hardship, I would like to have a demonstration to show off the powers of the mind. To remind everyone that the mind is stronger than the body."

"What is needed, Sadhu?"

"Not much. A piece of string. Hot coals. A place to gather—the mess hall, perhaps—and your permission of course. Oh, and a bed of nails to remind everyone how comfortable they really are."

"I like it! Inspirational and entertaining. I shall consult the warden."

So it was arranged that one week hence the dining hall would be transformed into a temporary theater, with a coal pit and a bed of nails to be constructed by the guards themselves.

The day of the performance arrived. It was decided, at Shakti's suggestion, that he perform two shows: "More people, more distractions," reasoned Sadhu Shakti. "With smaller crowds, the lessons of mind and discipline will reach more of them."

The assistant warden hesitated. "I don't know. Security—"

"Handcuff the most dangerous. Bring extra guards. They will benefit too."

"First show or last?"

"First. Then we can relax."

⌘

The warden introduced Sadhu Shakti, calling him a "model inmate" and praising him for "volunteering in this most brutal and hungry winter to demonstrate the power of the mind to rule over the body and the emotions."

The men roared. For many it was the first theatrical entertainment they had seen outside of Bollywood movies and mongoose-against-cobra shows.

Sadhu Shakti stood barefoot before them. He clasped his hands together and bowed in a humble greeting.

"Thank you, gentlemen. All my life I have strived to control my internal being, to feel less pain, to be strong. Today I hope to demonstrate my skill. First some basics, which doubtlessly will leave you unmoved, but will allow me to get in the right frame of mind. Please be patient."

He assumed a number of yoga positions, eventually standing on his head, motionless for one full minute. Then he lowered himself down, and, sitting cross-legged, produced a piece of string and inserted one end in his right nostril and then pulled it out of his left nostril. With a string end in each hand, he pulled back and forth while a few men laughed and others groaned.

Sadhu Shakti discarded the string and grabbed a megaphone. "I invite any man to come up and assist me. Ah, you, with the pockmarks, come up. Take this stethoscope and put it on. Very good. Now listen to my heart. Still beating?"

The man nodded. The men laughed.

"But he's deaf!" called one prankster.

Sadhu Shakti took the earpieces of the stethoscope and taped them to the mouthpiece of the megaphone. He gave the contraption to his assistant and put the stethoscope sensor to his chest. His scratchy heartbeat fed the room. Sadhu took a deep breath and closed his eyes.

The beating stopped.

Sadhu Shakti opened his eyes. He saw the men staring at him in horror.

The beating started up again. The men clapped and cheered.

"I am sorry, my brothers, this has been a most boring start. Just the discipline of yoga, which can be learned by any man," said Sadhu Shakti. "But just now we have something worth watching." With that he picked up a white sheet and, with a flourish, revealed a vicious-looking contraption—a plywood board embedded with five-inch nails pointing upward. Sadhu Shakti stripped off his kurta, revealing his thin, muscular body. He turned his back to the audience. "You see?" he joked. "Smooth like the lips of Lakshimi Lakh!" The men roared at the mention of everyone's favorite Bollywood temptress.

"There are a lot of tough men here. Big shots. I-do-solitary-on-my-head-for-vacation. But that is balderdash. Who wants a real rest on my bed? Guards? Anyone?"

There were no takers.

"OK. Allow me."

Placing his hands on the bars that lined the sides of the bed, the holy man lifted himself, his legs straight out so his body was in an L position, and lowered himself onto the nails.

Weight distribution was the key to this trick, so he lowered his back slowly, one vertebra at a time. "Not much different from the beds in our cells," he said.

Two guards came by and lifted a 50-pound barbell into his hands and he did five reps.

When he got off the bed of nails, a small rivulet of blood trickled from his left side.

Sadhu Shakti grabbed a loose nail off the bed. "I feel good," he announced. "But I have a slight pain in my head." With this, he placed the nail near the tip of his nose and then inserted it into his nostril.

The men howled.

"Don't sneeze, yar!" shouted a voice from the audience. "You'll kill someone."

Sadhu Shakti withdrew the nail and shook his head. "Ah, much better."

He nodded to the guards by the kitchen, and soon four prisoners carried out enormous steaming pots and dumped their contents inside a 20-foot-long rectangle of bricks, filling it with red-hot coals.

"I will only do this once, friends. Or maybe twice. The mind, like the body, gets weaker and needs rest. But I hope you have learned a lesson today. You can control things: What you feel, what you do, how you respond to painful situations. You have control."

Then he stood silent and gazed at the coals, breathing softly. The pause had two purposes. The first was that it created drama. But the more important thing was that the longer the coals burned, the more ash was created. Ash was one of the buffers that would allow him to do this trick, providing a thin layer of protection against the embers. He approached the coals, raised his foot as if to step into the pit, but suddenly shook his head and turned back.

"It's been three years since I did this. I don't want to burn," he said, fear—all of it completely fake—in his voice.

He closed his eyes again, took a deep breath and stepped forward.

He walked quickly and steadily, his feet flat in order not to stir the coals and release more heat. Four times he crossed the pit and when he stepped out, he spoke: "If you don't believe what you've seen was real, I invite you to inspect the coals."

This was the crucial moment, and it worked perfectly and horribly. The biggest and most brutal prisoners rose up and went to the stage. Some guards joined too, pulling rank and cutting to the front of the coal pit. As the guards bent down, a group of dacoits quickly lifted the bed of nails and brought it crashing down on the men, impaling them and pushing them into the coals.

The sound of men burning cannot be captured on paper.

As the dacoits lifted the bed of nails up, Lathi, seeing his comrades burning, lurched toward them. Three steps into his journey Kumar stabbed him between the shoulder blades with a shiv. The warden and the assistant warden were beaten to death. Other guards were attacked with chairs, burning coals, and makeshift brass knuckles. Some guards beat a retreat toward the exit, but they didn't' stand a chance.

Sadhu Shakti stood back and waited. He watched the dacoits approach the exit, crouching behind the bed of nails. Singh-Singh took a bullet in the shoulder and went down but the others kept going, bullets bouncing off their contraption. As they got closer, one rifleman turned to open the doors.

Kumar yelled "Jeldi jeldi!" and the bed of nails was launched at the guards.

In less than five minutes the prisoners had seized control of the mess hall and the kitchen. Now armed with rifles, they killed two dozen guards and prison administrators. The rest of Snow Island fell soon after. At first many guards were executed. Some quickly, others at a more painful and leisurely pace, depending on the whims of their captors. But then, Sadhu Shakti, realizing that there was still work to be done, sent orders to keep as many of them alive as possible.

The prisoners were triumphant. They ate like kings for a week. They had the remaining guards burn their dead brethren out by the lake. They took turns being jailers, locking their former guards in cells and leaving them without food.

"What will happen, wise man?" Sadhu Shakti was asked.

The Sadhu was grim. He said: "The wicked have killed the wicked. We have only winter to protect us. Soon it will dawn on the authorities what has happened. Perhaps they already know. Perhaps an SOS was sent from the administration offices. We have no way of knowing."

"In the spring they will come for us," called a voice.

"Yes. They will come from the south," agreed Sadhu Shakti.

"We are in deep shit."

"I am thinking."

❧

One week later Sadhu Shakti instructed the men to put aside reserves of food. Then, during the day, he had them build igloos. No one had ever made an igloo, but some of the men had heard of such a thing, and through trial and error, they succeeded in fashioning bricks of ice and constructing freestanding structures. In February, as the days began to get longer, he had men break apart office furniture to make sleds with narrow runners. He sent four sled teams out: one to the north, one to the east, one to the west and one to the southeast. The teams were to travel up over the hills that surrounded Snow Island as far as possible and build igloos and return. The next day, the teams went out again and laid in supplies of food, blankets, and clothing. After a few days' rest, the teams went out again, this time to build an igloo several miles beyond their first igloo.

By now it was clear that the plan was to set the stage for a mass escape. The prisoners, the vast majority of whom had grown up in the steamy south of Madras and Kerala and Bombay, or the blistering deserts of Rajasthan, were not fans of an icy escape. But they realized they had no alternative.

"The army will come, yar, and blow us to bits."

"My god, we will spend the rest of our lives in solitary after what we've done."

Someone suggested that they lock themselves back up and accuse the guards of a mutiny. But no one really believed that would work.

In April, Sadhu Shakti announced he was going on a two-day inspection of the escape route to see if his plan was even remotely likely to succeed. "Killing guards is one thing. But having you freeze to death—I can't have that on my conscience."

Together with Kumar and three other men, he pulled a sled of food and clothing toward the southeast passage. On the first day they got to the second igloo. On the second day, they marched for many miles and built another igloo, then marched back. On the third day, they transported the food and clothing from the second igloo to the third igloo. They were now about 10 frigid miles from Snow Island. Sadhu Shakti figured—correctly, it turned out—that on the fourth day, a group of prisoners would come looking for them but would not have the supplies to catch up.

After another two days, the supplies had dwindled to only a sleighful, so the men were able to travel without doubling back to retrieve supplies. It took them ten days to reach the outskirts of Simla, where Sadhu Shakti gave each man 2,000 rupees—stolen from the warden's cash box—and everybody went his own way.

Back at Snow Island, the men waited. It was hard to know exactly when to make a break. Ten days after the Sadhu's departure, they decided to send another team to the east. They were caught in a blizzard and froze to death. A second team of 20 men went out and was taken out by an avalanche caused by melting snow. The rest of the men—most of whom had had nothing to do with the uprising—stayed put. When the army arrived in May, they were living in relative harmony with the surviving guards and were transferred to other prisons.

Kumar was arrested two years later in New Delhi, caught red-handed while he was burglarizing the Raja Suite in the Ashok Hotel.

In the late '70s, in an act that was both an Indian Air Force training session and a show of force to Pakistan and China, Snow Island was bombed and completely obliterated. It remains a heap of frozen rubble to this day.

The whereabouts of Sadhu Shakti remain unknown.

ELEVEN

Snow Island. I love that. I love con men. *The Sting, The Hustler, Trouble in Paradise, Paper Moon*. And I love the theater of escape. You know the ultimate movie for that, right? Sing it with me: The hills are alive / with the sound of music! That's right, the Von Trapp singers stuck it to the Nazis right under their horrible little mustaches. As for other fancy flight flicks, there's *The Great Escape* and *Escape from Alcatraz* and *Papillon*. I also seem to remember a great escape in *The Count of Monte Cristo*, but I saw that a lifetime ago.

One important thing about "Snow Island": it's the final story in *A History of Prisons*. I'm not sure that's the finale I would have chosen. I'm kinda bummed that you don't know where good old Sadhu Shakti has gone. But maybe that's the point. That escapees can vanish, especially smart survivors like that old scamster. That not everyone has to linger like that poor French bastard, or get fed to the crocodiles, or teach math. Me? I'm still lingering. And I'm still wondering about Amanda's cryptic quote. I've gotten to the end and what am I?

Finished?

Ah, but it's been light for a while. And it's not the blazing white light of death, but that crystalline light of smog-free L.A. on a Monday morning. Any minute now—

Holy shit! I hear it. A lock turning! The door creaking?

The most beautiful sound in the world. "Marta?" I croak, sounding worse than Brando in *Apocalypse Now.*

I hear some faint swearing in Spanish. A vague memory of rampaging through the house, of being drunk with anger and scotch and destroying and throwing everything in my path, becomes a little less vague.

"Marta!"

She's coming closer. I think I can hear something about a loco fucking gringo and then:

"Mr. Rick! Mio dios!"

"Marta," I rasp. "Call the cops and get me some water. No, wait. Scratch that. Don't call the cops. Call your sons. I'll pay them."

"Mierda, it stinks in here, Mr. Rick."

"Go, water, sons, please."

She comes back with water and I gulp it down. "More," I beg. "I've been here for days. Three days at least."

"Wow," she says, her brown eyes looking at me hard. "That's bad. And I had something important to ask you, too, Mr. Rick."

"Anything. Just call your sons and please get me some more water. And my medicine, plus some cortisone cream from my bathroom. I got nuclear-meltdown jock itch here."

"Mr. Rick, I need you to marry me," she says, taking the glass and walking off.

I must be delirious, because I'm hearing things. "Marta, slap me. Wake me up."

"I'm serious. I got to marry someone."

"Listen, Marta, when you get me out of here, I'll sign this whole goddamn house over to you. I've been lying here thinking about how to reward you. I was gonna put you on staff with the production company. But if you want the house—"

"Mr. Rick, shut your face." She hands me more water, and a grimace flashes on her face. "Damn, it smells worse than death in here. Listen to me, Mr. Rick: I have to marry someone or I get deported. The agents came to my house looking for me. I'm gonna have to hide out. This is my country."

"But no one is going to believe it if I marry you, Marta." I can't believe I'm having this discussion with my house-keeper.

"Why not? You don't think I'm sexy? And you are old. In my country everyone understands."

"Okay, okay. Marta, will you marry me and call my god-damn future stepsons already so they can rescue their future papa?"

"I wanna big wedding, too. I planned a lot of parties for you."

"You got it. We can rent the friggin' Staples Center if you want."

"Malibu."

"Call your sons!"

She bends over and kisses me on the cheek. "You smell bad, papi!" She, on the other hand, smells great. Her cheeks are rouged, but not too much. Her hair is the same—jet black and cut in the bangs—as it was when I started having maid fantasies about her 20 years ago. Now the realist in me intrudes. I give our union 18 months and separate rooms. Actually, I don't want separate bedrooms, and I hope I'll want more than 18 months with Marta. She's fun. Just listening to her yammer on the phone right now is fun.

What do I know about Marta? She loves music. She has two sons. Their father walked out on her years ago. She has grandchildren. She hated my ex #2 but liked ex #3. She loves my son and he loves her. She loves Christmas and feels sorry for Jews because we don't have it. She likes chocolate chip cookies without the chocolate chips. She threatened to kill me once when I made eyes at her niece, inviting me into the kitchen and telling me the story of the muy bad carrot, which she illustrated with savage re-enactments involving a meat cleaver. When ex #2 left, she called her sons to drag me to bed when she found me comatose by the pool. She should have been a producer; she makes things happen. She found Ivan the roofer when a big leak drenched our living room. She ran every party I hosted between #2 and #3. She hired the caterers, ordered the flowers and the valets. Christ, after all this time we know more about each other than your average 18-months-and-done Hollywood couple. So marrying her doesn't seem such a crazy idea after all. Never mind that she's kind of made it a precondition of rescuing me.

In my fatigue and insanity I start to cry. My life has been saved by competent women. Marta. Amanda. Sally, who made *Evergreen* happen but quit midway through *Goldengrove*. I don't deserve them. I am sobbing now. I am the most hated man in America—I've been called an exploiter, racist, loudmouth, torturer—and yet all these women have been good to me. Sally still sends me updates on her kids, whose names and birthdays I never remember. And Amanda, even when she can't stand me, when my show forces her to quit, sends me the book that ends up practically saving my life. I would have died of boredom without those fucking prison stories.

"Don't come in here!" That's me, suddenly frantic and self-conscious as I hear Marta approach.

"Mr. Rick! Are you okay?"

"Fine, Marta. Just a little crazy right now."

"That's okay."

"You saved my life, Marta. If you hadn't showed up, I could have died."

"Well, everyone is looking for you. There are 47 messages on the phone."

"I wanted to answer every damn one of them. Even the telemarketers."

"Can I come in, papi?"

"No, not until your sons get here and I get cleaned up. I'm the most disgusting man in America right now. Me. Your fiancé."

Marta laughs. I like her laugh. She tries to cover her mouth with her hand, but her laughter, high pitched and lovely, escapes.

"Could you get me something to eat, Marta, please? Some toast. A sandwich?"

"Sure. And Mr. Rick?"

"Yes, Marta?"

"After we get married, I quit."

"You're gonna fart through silk, babe."

She laughs again.

All weekend, since I woke up pinned to the ground, there's been the haunted, grim shadow of the angel of death hovering over me. Thoughts of my own mortality have been bubbling away in the back of my mind, kept at bay only by Kaufman's *A History of Prisons*—which has been both a great escapist distraction and a huge inspiration for me to keep going and get the fuck out of this jam—and by my tremendous propensity for denial. About to be dragged under, I'll insist I'm waving, not drowning. Self-doubt is your biggest enemy in Hollywood. The notion that you might not be able to fix something—a bad story line, a shitty performance, crappy dialogue—is almost never discussed once a project is greenlit. Throw money and talent at a problem and, Christ, you can at least recoup on cable and DVD rights. All of which is to say that the stories I've been telling myself, my oral history here, has been one big pep talk, an ode to a survivor, a symphonic whistle in the dark.

When Marta's boys—the slender Hector and the robust Mikey, both in their early 20s, with matching stupid mullet haircuts—show up, that shadow—that creeping thought that I might die—finally seems to be fading away.

"Thank you, gentlemen," I croak. "You have saved my life."

"Mierda," they swear in unison, barely looking at me. No doubt they are taken aback by the wall unit and my unappealing scent.

They start unplugging wires. Lifting the fucking unit back up with all the hardware is a lost cause, all the players and screens are spilling out of it, but they're still all linked together. If they can unplug enough of them, they can lift the unit and leave the big pieces on the floor.

On the count of quatro they haul my prison off of me. The release is hard to describe. I let out a gasp and a moan.

My body, at once numb and aching, goes nuts. I piss myself again. I feel my circulation rev up. There is blood rushing into my legs. My heart is beating wildly.

"Mierda! Sangre!"

I start to shiver and my teeth start to chatter like some kind of possessed South American percussion instrument. And I'm freezing. It's like the first known case of hypothermia in L.A.

"Blankets! Please! I need blankets. I'm freezing!"

"Hold on Mr. Rick—I mean, 'honey!'" says Marta.

"Shit, man," says Hector, "there's a lot of dried blood here. And some wet stuff."

"Yo, Ma," says Mikey, "he's dying. Call 911."

"No!" I cry. "Do not call 911!"

"But you're bleeding, man!"

"And I'm freezing to death. Marta, I need some blankets!"

I cross my arms over my chest, which is still unbelievably sore, hug myself, and roll stiffly over to my side. I am shaking uncontrollably.

"Mami! Mr. Rick is freaking."

"Mio Dios!" Marta rushes back to the room. "Mr. Rick, somebody stole your TVs and computer!"

"I n-n-n-need a f-f-f-fucking blanket!"

"Here you are, papi. It's the comforter."

"Thank you." I shiver as she unfurls it on top of me. "Please, turn down the A/C. And I need my heart pills. And more water."

"Ai! Look, you got blood on the comforter."

"Yeah, I'm bleeding. I'm sure when these guys lifted up the wall unit, some of my scabs broke."

"It's a lot of blood, man," says Mikey.

"Papi, I don't want to marry a dead man or a cripple," Marta wails, "Let me call 911."

"Marry?" says Hector.

"No, not 911!" I insist.

"If you don't want 911, who I'm gonna call?"

"Call Dr. Lambert. Let me speak to him, please."

Being a Hollywood doctor, Lambert just listens to what I tell him and immediately understands my situation. "I'll send two medics in our flower truck."

A flower truck! What a pro!

"Give me 45 minutes. They're on another job. An hour max."

I hang up, and as I put the phone at my side, my hand feels something wet. I lean over and I see this giant pool of red around my hip.

The shadow is back. It's lowering, covering me like a shroud.

I pass out.

Marta swears my eyes rolled back in my head, my tongue popped out of my mouth, and I looked like a dead man. My future sons-in-law took this opportunity to slap my face a few times, while screaming for their mother to call 911.

But Marta, true to form, told them no way.

Eventually, I open my eyes.

"Oh, shit, he's alive!"

I close them again.

"You okay, papi?" asks Marta.

"Yes, I think so."

"What happened?"

"That's a lot of blood. I didn't realize I was so messed up."

"Let me get you some more water. Who stole our stuff?"

"Two clowns named Mass and Stevie. I think they stole my Jag, too."

"No!" Marta rattles off some Spanish to Hector, and he heads to the garage via the kitchen.

I feel my shivers abating. My body temperature is going up. "It's gone," calls Hector to us. "The car is gone."

"Jeez, we gotta call the cops," says Marta. "You love that car."

"No cops. Not yet. I'll report it later. It was just a toy. It's insured. I'm sure it's in Mexico by now."

Marta raises her eyebrows and gives me a look as if she thinks I'm insulting her home country, but before she can lay into me, Mikey comes out of the kitchen carrying a knife and plastic bag. "What's this about a wedding?" he says.

Mikey is built like a small refrigerator. His question and his weapon are hard to fathom and there's moment of silence before his mom starts a rapid-fire exchange of "abba-dabba-dabba" Spanish with her sons.

When both boys—I guess that's what I should start calling them—send a nod of satisfaction in my general direction, I breathe easier. Apparently, Mikey is not going to stab me for marrying his mother.

"Your mother is a wonderful woman," I say when they look at me again, this time shaking their heads. I'm not sure what the shakes mean. Amusement? Sorrow? Exasperation? I'm going with amusement.

Mikey brings the knife toward me.

My heart jumps a bit, and there's really no room for it to jump right now. But then he grabs the bottom of my pant leg and starts cutting away.

Marta shouts, and Hector leaves the room and returns with towels and lays them on my stomach. "To cover yourself," he says.

"Thank you," I smile at him. Then I add: "Son."

We start with my lower, grosser regions. But it's taking my shirt off that freaks out Marta.

And me.

"Aye, Rick, when did you get that?"

"What?"

"Look, Papi! On your chest."

There's some green lettering just below my nipple. The burning, itching sore spot? It's a fucking tattoo.

"Jesus!" I say, reflexively rubbing at the lettering. "It's upside-down to me. What does it say?"

Marta comes close. "'The King of Pain,'" she says. Then she looks at me, her eyes narrowing with concern. "You don't remember?"

I shake my head. "Nothing."

I'm feeling marginally better when I convince Marta's boys to slide me against my gigantic white leather sectional couch so I can lean against something. My legs reverberate in agony, but we make it and are all relieved when this 8 foot journey is over.

"Thanks guys," I say.

"Mr. Rick," says Hector. "If you don't mind my asking, how did that thing fall on you?"

"Just call me Rick, okay, Hector? You're a little old for this Mr. Rick bullshit. Now, about your question, I've got no fucking idea. I've been trying to figure it out for two days. Last I remember, I was screaming on the phone at this network prick and getting sloshed and it was getting late at night...and..." I stop. A new murky detail has popped into my mind. It's not a detail I like.

"He remember something now," says Marta.

I squint, as if that will help me see into the past. "I have a feeling—maybe— that I might have called someone."

"I bet you called the Asian massage girls!" says Marta. "I know you, papi."

"Maybe. I'm not too clear. But I have a tattoo on my chest. And I have no fucking idea of how it got there. I'm Jewish, for chrissakes. We don't do tattoos."

"It looks nice," offers Marta.

"Thank you." I love my future wife.

"Were you, like, watching something or playing a video game? And do those girls come with, like, pimps?" she suggests.

"They are masseuses, not prostitutes," I explain, their exact job title being a grey area, if you know what I mean. "So Yumi and Yoko always come alone. I mean, together. But no chaperone. As for the games, they're for Jared. I don't have time for that crap."

Hector looks around the room. "Man, you got this huge system. You musta been doing something." He checks out the DVD player.

"I doubt anything is plugged in anymore," I say.

Mikey says something to his mother in Spanish

and then goes into the kitchen and returns with an extension cord, finds a working plug, and the DVD player lights up.

"It's set on repeat," he announces, hitting the eject button. He holds up the disc so I can see what's scrawled on it: *The King of Pain*.

"Repeat? I've never seen that disc in my life," I say, but now there's a feeling of dread in my stomach.

"You have any other TV screens around?"

"There's an old laptop in the pantry," says Marta. "I didn't wanna throw it out, you know? Let me get it."

"Can I have some more water, please?"

When she returns, we huddle before the biggest home entertainment system in the free world and fix our eyes on the tiny laptop screen. Mikey slots in the disc and it starts to play.

TWELVE

It's dark. The camera swings up and focuses on my front door. A voice says: "Ring the bell."

I know that voice, but I can't place it. Then there's a voice I can place: mine. "Hey! Yumi? Yoko? Man, that was qui— Holy shit, what are you guys doing here?"

The camera swings over to me. I'm doing the bob and weave, smiling. I hold up my sloshing scotch glass. "Cheers. Are you guys in for the reunion show? I thought I told Little Ricky to tell you we'd start next week."

I'm answered by silence.

"Darcy, Annabel, and Jeremiah! I figured the only time I'd see you together would be down in hell!"

More silence. The wind whistles into the camera mic.

"That was a joke. Come on in and—whoa, Derek! I didn't see you over there, and with a video camera! I didn't realize you were artistically inclined. Hey, who is this gentleman with you?"

The camera pans to a thin hipster with a ponytail and a goatee. He's carrying a bag of some sort. My question goes unanswered and the camera pans back to me. I study their faces, trying to decipher the situation, which is hard because I'm obviously drunk as a skidrow skunk. I choose to muster some bravado; the next thing I say is: "Well, this conversation is just too damn good for me. I'm going to talk to my bottle of single malt."

I turn my back on them and we wobble, handheld cam style, into the house.

The camera follows me into the kitchen. I'm pouring more scotch. "Anyone want to join me? No? Say, is this against the show rules, you guys being together without show supervision? I think that's part of the Anti-Collusion clause. But I guess that might go out the window once you've been voted off. Interesting. Say, is my mic on? Come on, people! Can't I get a laugh for that?"

I look at my drink and grimace. "I need some ice here. Whenever anyone asked my uncle if he wanted water in his drink he'd say, 'The ice is water.' I always remembered that."

I list toward the fridge. I'm clearly toasted. You can see a look of disgust on Annabel Castro's face as I pass by. Or is it hatred?

The doorbell rings again.

"Hey, maybe that's Yumi and Yoko! God I love them. Their English is a lot worse than yours, but I have to tell you that they are much better conversationalists. And they have better manners, too."

"Sit down!" snarls Derek off camera.

"Oh, no. This is my house, I have to see to the guests."

Darcy puts a hand on my shoulder to stop me. "Sit down, Rick. I'll get the door."

"You guys, you all seem angry! What's the matter? You want a raise? 1,600 bucks a week is pretty good. Way better than cable reality shows."

"Sorry we're late." It's another voice I recognize but can't place.

The camera swings away from me for a brief second and catches a glimpse of St. James and his rival Sanchez walking into the kitchen, which seems kind of small for all the people that have gathered in it.

"What are you guys doing here? I thought you went to see your family! Sanchez, how's your mom?"

"Shut the fuck up," says Sgt. St. James.

Jeremiah steps up to the table and pours more scotch in my glass. "I'm doing you a favor," he says. "Drink this."

"I'm already bombed."

"It'll help."

"Help with what? What the fuck is going on? I want some answers or…"—I pat my pockets looking for my cell phone, which I can't find—"or I'm gonna call the cops!"

"You crossed the line, Rick," says Darcy.

"Big time," says Sgt. St. James.

"Even I have a hard time forgiving you."

A look of astonishment slowly spreads across my face.

"Jesus Christ, am I glad to see you, Sister Rosemarie! Welcome to my home."

"Rick, show some respect. She's a nun," says Annabel.

I'm bombed. I ignore her. The words are coming slower, directed toward Sister Rosemarie. "I wish…I knew you were coming. I… I would have had Marta call the caterers…"

"That's not necessary, Rick," says Sister Rosemarie. "What we need now is to have a little talk. A talk maybe we should have had before we all signed up."

"Rick, do you know why we're here? We're here because you crossed the line," says Jeremiah.

"How did I cross the line? It's a fucking TV show. A competition. You all agreed to compete."

"You crossed the line with the branding, Rick," says Jeremiah.

"You screwed us all," says Darcy. "I have In God We Trust seared into my calf."

"Well, nobody died."

"Adonis died, Rick."

"He OD'd because…because he was an idiot."

"The show sent him on his way."

"He should have never auditioned. And that goes for all of you. You…sissies! If you can't take the heat…"

"That's it," says Annabel. "I've had enough of your bullshit." She grabs the booze and pours it down the sink.

"We're not sissies. We're suckers. Look."

Someone slams an article in front of me. I pick it up and try to read it, but I'm too drunk to focus.

"It's an article from the *Wall Street Journal*. With Walter Fields of the network talking about how *The King of Pain* is a billion dollar franchise. And that's in just one year."

"Walter Fields is an asshole."

"A billion dollars! And you paid us less than a quarter of a million to make the show."

"I understand that sucks. But you fucking guys signed fucking contracts. I didn't screw anybody. If it bombed, the network would be out some big change."

"You also crossed the line with Kaylene," says Sgt. St. James. "And with Sister Rosemarie. You screwed with their hearts and minds. Their souls."

"Mr. Salter, how long my mother was sick before you tole me?" asks Sanchez.

"I don't fucking know. A week? Two weeks max. We got her the best care we could. And we did the show. As far as I remember, there's no 'If my mamma gets sick' exit clause in the contract. We had our rights. And we took care of her. And then we took care of you and gave you a week off."

"If she had died while I was on the show, I would have killed you."

"Yeah, well, killing me is definitely not in the contract."

The doorbell rings. Again.

"Thank god," I say. "That must be Yumi and Yoko. You guys can use the pool, whatever, but I have an appointment."

"Sit down, you drunken fool," says Jeremiah.

I look down at the table. I start mumbling to myself.

The camera captures the sound of the kitchen door opening and then swings over to film Annabel Castro leading the two Asian girls in. "As you can see, we're having a little party, but Mr. Rick isn't feeling so good."

"We no do orgy," says Yumi with her signature giggle. "Just massagee."

"You know what?" suggests Darcy. "Why don't you take off Mr. Rick's shirt and give him a quick shoulder rub?"

"Now you're talkin'!" I say.

My eyes are closed. While the girls come to unbutton my shirt, my head is rolling around on my shoulders in the aimless manner of a balloon on a string. I probably don't even hear it when Jeremiah says: "Let's get set up in the living room. And these ladies can go after they get Rick ready."

The camera goes blank for a second, and when the picture returns, there's a close up of my mouth.

It's open wide.

I'm screaming my head off. And every "STOP YOU MOTHERFUCKERS" distorts the tiny speakers on the laptop.

The camera pulls out and you can see I'm crying and moving my head around violently as I scream.

"STOP THIS RIGHT NOW! WHAT THE FUCK DO YOU WANT FROM ME? RAPE! RAPE! RAPE! YOU GUYS WANT MONEY? I'LL FUCKING PAY YOU, YOU FUCKING WHINING SISSY CRYBABY PIECES OF SHIT!"

"Somebody gag him!"

"With what?"

"HELP! HELP ME, SOMEBODY!"

"His shirt. Just stuff it in!"

The camera pulls out a bit. The stranger is hovering over me, straddling me, in fact. He's got a safety razor in his hand and lowers it.

"Lemmegoyufkr!" I moan through the gag.

"Okay, hand me the transfer. Thanks. Now hold him tight and gimme the sponge. Great."

"MRRFRKR!"

"Okay, Rick, the less you struggle, the quicker this is over. Gimme the tray."

The camera zooms over the guy's shoulder and on to my red, tear-drenched face. All of a sudden my eyes open and bulge.

"SCMFKRSMBWWMKRR!"

The camera goes black again. When it comes back, the mystery man is rising off of me. "Here," he says. "Take a look. It's official."

Zoom in on a freshly etched tattoo on my fucking chest.

"Okay, get him up and let's go to the pool," says Sgt. St. James.

Annabel and Jeremiah prop me up and take me out toward the deck. I look like a rag doll that is nothing but rags.

"Sanchez, get the board and the rope from the car."

When I hear this I start flailing like crazy. I elbow Annabel in the face.

"You son of a bitch," she says, spinning around, pulling my arm around my back and forcing me to my knees.

"THERE IS NO FUCKING WAY YOU GUYS ARE GOING TO WATERBOARD ME, YOU DOUBLE DEALING PRIMA FUCKING DONNAS. YOU THINK WATERBOARDING DIDN'T COME UP WHEN WE DISCUSSED THE SHOW? Please! I'll do whatever I can. Anything. Just name it."

"Fuck this." It's Sgt. St. James. He comes over and lifts me up, cradling me like I'm an oversized baby. He strides to the edge of the pool and drops me in.

I come up out of the water. More flailing. "No," I sputter. "You guys have made your point. I'm fucking on the verge of a heart attack here."

Sgt. St. James leans over the edge of the pool. "You're finally learning your lesson," he says. "Get out of the pool."

"Oh my god, thank you. Thank you."

"Hey, let's stick to the plan," says Darcy, "and get out of here."

"I'm freezing," I say through chattering teeth.

"Too bad. Here's your shirt. Go inside. We're almost done."

The screen goes black.

"Damn!" says Mikey, with a touch too much enthusiasm. "That was like *The Blair Witch Project!*"

"Can you believe that? Those bastards fucking attacked

me in my own home!" If I wasn't feeling sick to my stomach from what I've just seen, I'd be apoplectic with rage.

"You should call the police," says Marta.

"Are you kidding? If the police get hold of this, it'll be on the Web faster than you can say YouTube."

"You don't remember any of this?"

"I drank half a bottle of scotch. Then I was tortured. I blanked. And I still don't know how the fuck I got pinned under the wall unit."

At that moment, there's the faint rumble of a car driving up.

"Finally! I can get to Dr. Lambert."

Marta goes to the kitchen to look out the window. "Rick!" she calls excitedly in a loud stage whisper. "It's Amanda!"

My heart lurches: I haven't seen her since the branding episode.

When she walks in, she looks fabulous. A standard issue, well-groomed L.A. super babe—sexy sleeveless dress showing off flabless arms, great haircut, Ray-Bans, and only a dusting of makeup because the hue of her skin has been perfectly calibrated on a pool deck—only better. Wouldn't you know it? And on the day I am hooking up permanently and forever with Marta.

Little Ricky is there, too, slumping in the background.

"Amanda!" I say. "Wow! You look great. What brings you here?"

"Oh my god! Are you alright? What are you doing lying there like a zombie? And what's that gash on your head? Are you okay?" She looks around the room and does a double take. "What the hell happened here? Were you attacked?"

"Yeah. By an angry mob—the friggin' contestants from the show, if you can believe it—and then, apparently, by my wall unit."

"It fell on him!" says Hector. "The whole thing collapsed on him. He was trapped all weekend."

"Amanda, this is Hector, Marta's son. He rescued me with his brother. Otherwise I'd still be trapped. Why are you here?"

"Nice to meet you, Hector," she says and then turns to me. "I was worried about you. You didn't answer the phone. You always take my calls. And then this morning I got a mysterious phone call from Sister Rosemarie. And then a reporter–"

"Sister Rosemarie? Turns out she's a hell's angel. She didn't even say a word on my behalf."

Amanda squints at me. It's a look of incomprehension. Then she says: "Well, she told me to check up on you. And to tell you two things."

"I can hardly wait."

"She said to tell you that through suffering comes grace."

"Ha! I'll try and remember that. She wasn't exactly the picture of grace the other night. No sticking up for the underdog there."

Amanda looks thoroughly confused now. "I'll explain later," I say. "What was the other thing she said?"

"She said to thank you—the misinformation episode brought in over a million dollars in pledges to the Mission."

"Well then I guess her suffering did bring grace. I wonder what I get out of my date in hell? Although it is nice to finally see you. I need you more than ever."

"I have something to tell you as well, Rick, and then I want to hear exactly what happened here last night."

"Whoa! Hold it right there. You are too late, Amanda, I'm off the market. Marta and I are the hottest thing since the invention of internet porn."

Amanda looks at Marta.

Marta smiles. "Si. We're getting married."

"That's great. Because I was going to tell you I'm here to help, Rick. But I have strings attached."

It's my turn to squint. I don't get it. "I've told you many times: Do whatever you want to do, I'll back you."

"No, I mean the wooing. It has got to stop."

"What? The flirting? My heart beats only for Marta now."

"Oh, you can flirt, papi. It's funny. You can't help it."

"Thank you, honey."

"I mean it," says Amanda.

"What's the big deal?"

"I have a boyfriend. A real one."

"A boyfriend. Wow! He should get down on his knees and thank god."

"See? That's what has to stop."

"Okay, I get it. Anyone I know?"

At which point Little Ricky pipes up: "Me, sir."

"You?" I say, and immediately regret the incredulity in my voice. "I mean, you! Wow! You are a lucky man." I nod. I'm having a moment of clarity in the midst of all this insanity. They're rare in L.A., these moments, but I've had them before: Returning from the editing room to find my wives gone; signing papers at a lawyer's office; waiting for the box office numbers to come in on a Sunday. And now I can see that I am really going to marry Marta. That these two kids are a good match. And that I actually feel paternal towards them.

I reach out to shake Little Ricky's hand, wondering if Amanda has any idea that it was Little Ricky who came up with the idea for the branding episode.

"Thank you, sir," he says.

"You're fired."

"Rick!" howls Amanda.

"Just kidding. In fact, I will need you both. I'm going to be busy learning to crawl."

"And going on vacation, papi."

"That's right, Marta. Wherever you want."

"Sir?" It's Little Ricky.

"Yeah? What's been happening, Ricky? All I remember is fucking Walter Fields threatening me and talking about press releases. Then I got bombed, tortured, and trapped. What happened?"

"The network claims you are no longer with the show. They released a statement Saturday morning after your CNN clips were all over the place."

"Oh yeah?" I say, the fog lifting a bit more, and I seem to remember something about Walter Fields threatening to invoke a clause in my contract that said the network could control the show if I exhibited "fiscal or behavioral irresponsibility." "Well if I'm not running the show, who is?"

"They canceled it. They said all four finalists would split the grand prize."

"No shit?"

"They got $100K each."

The house phone starts ringing.

Marta answers, then hands me the cordless. "It's Jay."

I grab the phone. "Jay, you bastard! They shit-canned the show and are making me the fall guy. They can't do this."

"I heard. You are big news over here. You almost fucked up my wedding. They were blogging Apu 24/7 here. I had to promise the in-laws not to work with you ever again."

"But I got that Apu crap from you in the first place. You used it about your own family!"

"Relax, Rick. I told them I would drop you, but I didn't say when. And anyway, you will sway them when you make a huge donation to the Indo-American Fellowship Society."

"Hey, I'm showless. Don't hit me up for cash. I might never work again."

"Are you kidding? We're gonna sue, sue, sue. They can't just cancel a hit show and deprive you of your earnings. Sleazy network bastards."

"When are you coming back?"

"We honeymoon in Bhutan next week, but you can handle a lot of this yourself. First you need a flack."

"Oh boy."

"How about Trudy Goodshoes?"

"No way."

"Helene Musk?"

"The worst."

"Elaine Tropez."

"OK," I sigh. "I'll put her on six months retainer."

"And you want to make that donation, right?"

"Ten grand."

"A hundred."

"Twenty-five."

"Rick, you screwed up, is what I'm hearing. You need a write-off anyway."

"Fifty. And that's my final word."

"Nice, sahibji! Discuss it with Elaine—announce it on TV, on *Ellen* or something, to get maximum karma. Maybe with that nun."

"Well, she might do me a favor. I'm not sure."

"Then when I get back we will sue them for wrongful termination and defamation. They got nothing to stand on. You never damaged the show. You were defending it. Between me and the nun, you'll get forgiveness and restitution." I hear a female voice in the background, then Jay comes back on: "Sorry Rick, got to go. Matrimonial duties beckon."

The line goes dead, and I hand the phone back to Marta. I feel a strange mixture of exhaustion and elation. This may be the most fucked up hour of my entire life, but it's also one of the most exhilarating. I'm alive.

The medics have arrived while I've been yapping to Jay. They start to strap me to the stabilizing board, but before they carry me out to Dr. Lambert's ingenious flower truck ambulance, there's another thing I really need to know. I grab *A History of Prisons* and show it to Amanda. "I have to thank you for this book," I say. "There's great stuff in here. But what the hell did you mean by the inscription? I've been lying here for the last 48 hours thinking about it."

She takes the book and opens it. "Oh, that! Gee, let's see… 'Dear Rick, Read this book. The stories are meant for you. And at the end you'll really be…you know!'" A mischievous smile spreads across her face. "You know what, I think I'll give you a little more time to figure it out for yourself."

"What?" I cry. "Amanda, you can't do that to an old man. I need to know!" But she just gives me another smile. I don't know what else to say, so I tell her: "Ah screw it. Please go get the rights. Let's make 'The Giz.' Great teen romance."

Amanda looks at me and nods. She seems a little bit sad, but also amused, even though I'll be damned if I know why.

And then, as the medics prepare to stretcher me off, Marta hands me my BlackBerry, booted up with a spare battery from my office. 100 phone messages. 200 emails. I scroll back to Friday night. I see my final drunken exchange with Walter Fields, where he tells me he is booting me for the instability clause. And here is my reply:

"Fuk u, u prick. I'd rather just pay off the finalists and end the show, than see you milk it and ruin it. U fuking eunch. U R going to spend your golden years in court. That's a promise."

As I'm reading this, Marta comes out of the bathroom, holding my toothbrush and a bunch of rope. "Look what I found in the bathroom, papi," she says. "Did they tie you up or something?"

And finally I bust through the wall of alcohol and terror that has been wrapped around my memory.

I see myself. I'm out of the pool. I'm dripping wet. The pool water and the scotch are doing a dance in my stomach. Things are spinning. I retch into a flowerpot. Then I'm sitting down. The out-of-it, nauseous, tortured drunk, nodding off while the contestants are spinning around me, talking, making plans. And then Darcy the dancer is telling me I'm going to be all right, that I just have to watch a movie. She and

Derek are tying a rope around me, binding me to the chair. I'm moaning and whining. And asking whywhywhywhywhy because now the alcohol is really zipping through my veins. Sanchez and Derek lift the chair and leave me in front of the wall unit watching a movie of me screaming and cursing. I must have nodded off for a while, and when I come to again, I've got to piss so bad it's like Niagara Falls is lodged in my bladder. But I'm tied up. And this fucking video—the video I've just watched with Marta and her sons—is blaring at me. I struggle with the ropes. Bondage is not Darcy's area of expertise, or maybe she took pity on me, because I manage to undo the rope, or most of it. And when I stand up, I'm in a fucking blind red rage, but I really have to piss. So I grab the chair, smash it down and then race to the john, with some of the rope still threaded around my leg. When I'm done, I guess I must have shaken off the rope, because the next thing I remember is rushing back into the living room where my screams are blasting at me from the TV speaker, hammering me. It's like I'm trapped in my own snuff movie. I can't find the fucking clicker, the remote, to make this go away. I'm in a fury to make this stop. All of it. Me, the moaning, the pathetic cursing, the begging, TV, the show, those fucking contestants, Hollywood, Nielsen ratings, CNN, dollars, residuals, agents, suits: fuck them all. But I can't find the damn remote. So I leap, still drunk as a skunk, at the TV. I use the low shelf as a boost and make it to the top of that damn 72-inch hi-def screen. What was I thinking? What was my plan? I've got no idea. Probably to find an off switch somewhere. So now I'm stuck there on the TV, my feet dangling a yard or so above the ground. Then the whole thing starts to tilt, and I sense I'm in actual danger. I scramble over to the right as I feel the TV start to come down, but I don't make it far enough over. Instantly, the hardware that's hooked up to the falling TV starts sliding after it. And when I plant my weight onto a shelf, the massive unit busts loose from the wall. Gravity takes over and the whole monstrosity goes down. Thank god for the lower, wider shelves at the bottom of the unit. As it tilts further and further, those wider shelves hit the ground first, slowing the momentum of the top half. Without them, I'd have been crushed to death. Of course the shelves, once everything settled, also created the angle that helped pin me, but I think it's a fair trade. Pain and torture vs. death.

The medics carry me as if I were a child. They follow Marta out the side door, out of sight from the front gate. The rest of my entourage, Amanda, Little Ricky, Hector, and Mikey, follow us. My wife-to-be holds up a bag.

"I put pajamas and your charger for your phone in here. And a toothbrush and your pills, Rick."

"Marta, if I can treat you half as well as you treat me, it will be a miracle. You realize that? I have a bad track record."

"I know. You make some bad choices. You need a vacation. A big one."

"Where?"

"Around the world, papi. When I have a passport, I want to go around the world with the last stop Mexico."

"You realize I snore."

She laughs. Her mouth goes wide with full, straight white teeth, framed by those lovely, generous lips.

"I hear you every morning." She lowers her head, strokes

my hair, and kisses my forehead. These are miracles. These are the sparks of life. An hour ago I was numb, dying. Now I'm flying effortlessly, soaring on a wooden board toward the future. Suddenly I think about the Translator in *A History of Prisons*, when he gets out of solitary. And I really get it. I know. I feel it in my bones.

They hike me up into the flower truck. "Marta!" I call out, "Amanda!" positive they'll understand. "Life on the island is wide open!"

THANKS...

To Daniel Blackman, Chris McConnell, Scott Moyers, Chuck and Sue Montgomery, Jamie Pallot, and Jenny Taylor for feedback and encouragement.

To Rebecca, Noah, and Susan Kaufman for a lifetime of support.

To Amanda McPherson and Leigh Huffine for the design and vision. And Paula Sosin for key input.

To Tim O'Connell for pushing the story further.

To Markus Hoffmann for being as good an agent, editor, and trumpet player as any writer could hope for.

To Theo and Hilary for being truly great escapes.

To Susan for absolutely everything.

ABOUT THE AUTHOR

Seth Kaufman has been a reporter for the *NY Post's* Page Six and Editorial Director of TV Guide.com. His work has appeared in the *New York Times*, *N.Y. Observer*, *N.Y. Daily News*, and elsewhere. He plays guitar in The Fancy Shapes. He lives in Brooklyn, NY, with his wife and two children.

24456259R00174